"Bowen's winning third R___ Spyness whodunit . . . will please fans of romantic, hu___rous historicals . . . Bowen, who's won both Agatha and Anthony awards, puts a fresh slant on it."

—*Publishers Weekly*

"As in previous entries in the series, Georgiana makes a superb sleuth, but much of the fun comes in the contrast between impoverished Georgie and the royal life of which—financial circumstances n___ ___ ___ ___ Also intriguing is the ___ ___ interest."

"A satisfying Roy___

"Bowen captures England's complicated era when an economic depression was between the world wars. The author's use of real people, such as Simpson, for whom the Prince of Wales would eventually give up the crown, enhances *Royal Flush* . . . *Royal Flush* is a solid story full of scandal, intrigue and a glimpse into an era that changed history." —*The Buffalo News*

"As usual, Georgie's high spirits and the author's frothy prose are utterly captivating." —*The Denver Post*

"Fans of Georgette Heyer will enjoy the nice mix of romance and mystery in Georgiana's third adventure from the period between the wars." —*Kirkus Reviews*

"This third entry in Bowen's charming, delightfully fresh series earns high marks in painting a nostalgic picture of 1932 England, enriched by a look into the royal family's everyday life. Fans of historical cozies who like Kerry Greenwood's Phryne Fisher series will snap this up." —*Library Journal*

continued . . .

A Royal Pain

Her Royal Spyness

Royal Flush

Rhys Bowen

BERKLEY PRIME CRIME, NEW YORK

THE BERKLEY PUBLISHING GROUP
Published by the Penguin Group
Penguin Group (USA) Inc.
375 Hudson Street, New York, New York 10014, USA
Penguin Group (Canada), 90 Eglinton Avenue East, Suite 700, Toronto, Ontario M4P 2Y3, Canada
(a division of Pearson Penguin Canada Inc.)
Penguin Books Ltd., 80 Strand, London WC2R 0RL, England
Penguin Group Ireland, 25 St. Stephen's Green, Dublin 2, Ireland (a division of Penguin Books Ltd.)
Penguin Group (Australia), 250 Camberwell Road, Camberwell, Victoria 3124, Australia
(a division of Pearson Australia Group Pty. Ltd.)
Penguin Books India Pvt. Ltd., 11 Community Centre, Panchsheel Park, New Delhi—110 017, India
Penguin Group (NZ), 67 Apollo Drive, Rosedale, North Shore 0632, New Zealand
(a division of Pearson New Zealand Ltd.)
Penguin Books (South Africa) (Pty.) Ltd., 24 Sturdee Avenue, Rosebank, Johannesburg 2196,
South Africa

Penguin Books Ltd., Registered Offices: 80 Strand, London WC2R 0RL, England

This is a work of fiction. Names, characters, places, and incidents either are the product of the author's
imagination or are used fictitiously, and any resemblance to actual persons, living or dead, business
establishments, events, or locales is entirely coincidental. The publisher does not have any control over
and does not assume any responsibility for author or third-party websites or their content.

ROYAL FLUSH

A Berkley Prime Crime Book / published by arrangement with the author

PRINTING HISTORY
Berkley Prime Crime hardcover edition / July 2009
Berkley Prime Crime mass-market edition / September 2010

Copyright © 2009 by Janet Quin-Harkin.
The Edgar® name is a registered service mark of the Mystery Writers of America, Inc.
Cover illustration by John Mattos.
Cover design by Rita Frangie.
Interior text design by Tiffany Estreicher.

ISBN: 978-0-425-23639-0

BERKLEY® PRIME CRIME
Berkley Prime Crime Books are published by The Berkley Publishing Group,
a division of Penguin Group (USA) Inc.,
375 Hudson Street, New York, New York 10014.
BERKLEY® PRIME CRIME and the PRIME CRIME logo are trademarks of Penguin Group (USA) Inc.

PRINTED IN THE UNITED STATES OF AMERICA

10 9 8 7 6 5 4 3 2

This book is dedicated to Merion Webster Sauer and her son, Lee, who have been temporarily elevated to the peerage.

My grateful thanks as always to John and Jane for their wonderful insights and critiques, and to Jackie Cantor and Meg Ruley for making my writing life so easy, pleasant and fun.

Author's Note

Although real people walk across these pages, this book is purely fictional. Balmoral is portrayed just as it is, but if you try to find Castle Rannoch on the map, it only exists in my imagination. And I'm afraid I've taken liberties with the road from Balmoral to Castle Rannoch. There really is no serviceable direct route, but I've had one made through the mountains for the purposes of this book.

Chapter 1

Rannoch House
Belgrave Square
London W.1.
August 12, 1932

It is my opinion that there is no place on earth more uncomfortable than London during a heat wave. I should probably qualify this by confessing that I have never gone up
the Congo River into the Heart of Darkness with Conrad,
nor have I crossed the Sahara by camel. But at least people
venturing to those parts are prepared to be uncomfortable.
London is so seldom even vaguely warm that we are always
caught completely unprepared. The tube turns into a good
imitation of the infamous Black Hole of Calcutta and the
smell of unwashed armpits, strap-hanging inches from one's
face, is overwhelming.

You may be wondering whether members of the royal
family frequently ride on the underground. The answer, of
course, is no. My austere relatives King George V and Queen
Mary would have only the vaguest idea of what the tube train
was. Of course, I am only thirty-fourth in line to the throne,
and I am probably the only member of my family who was at

that moment penniless and trying to survive on her own, in London, without servants. So let me introduce myself before we continue. My full name is Lady Victoria Georgiana Charlotte Eugenie of Glen Garry and Rannoch. My grandmother was the least attractive of Queen Victoria's many daughters, judging by those early photographs I've seen of her. But then those old photographs did tend to make most people look grouchy, didn't they? Anyway, no proposals from kaisers or kings were forthcoming for her, so she was hitched to a Scottish duke and lived at Castle Rannoch, in remotest Scotland, until she died of fresh air and boredom.

My brother, Binky, is the current duke. He's also pretty much penniless, our father having lost the last of the family fortune in the great crash of '29, before shooting himself on the moors and saddling Binky with horrendous death duties. At least Binky's got the estate with the home farm and the huntin', shootin' and fishin', as the landed gentry are wont to say, so he's not exactly starving. I've been living on baked beans, toast and tea. I was raised with no skills other than passable French, knowing how to walk with a book on my head and where to seat a bishop at a dinner table. Hardly enough to tempt a prospective employer, if getting an ordinary job were not frowned upon for someone in my position. I tried it once—the cosmetics counter at Harrods. I lasted all of four hours.

And of course England is in the midst of a most awful depression. You only have to look on any street corner at those tragic men standing with signs saying *Will accept any kind of work* to know that things are pretty grim for most people. Not for most of my social class, however. For most of them life goes on unchanged, with yachts on the Med and extravagant parties. They probably don't even know the country is in a bad way.

So now you know why there is no Bentley and chauffeur parked outside Rannoch House, our family's London home on Belgrave Square, and why I can't even afford to take a taxicab too often. I do usually try to avoid the tube, however. For a country-bred girl like myself the descent into that black hole has always been a cause for alarm—and more so since I was almost pushed under a train by a man who was trying to kill me.

But on this occasion I had no choice. Central London was so unbearably stifling that I decided to go and visit my grandfather, who lives on the fringes of London in Essex, and the District Line was the way to travel. Oh, and I suppose I should clarify that I'm not speaking about my grandfather the Scottish duke, whose ghost is still reputed to play the bagpipes on the battlements of our ancestral home, Castle Rannoch in Perthshire, Scotland. I'm speaking of my non-royal grandfather, who lives just outside London in a modest semidetached with gnomes in the front garden. You see, my mother was an actress and the daughter of a Cockney policeman. She was also a notorious bolter. She left my father when I was only two and has subsequently worked her way from an Argentinian polo player, to a Monte Carlo rally driver and a Texan oil millionaire. Her romantic exploits have truly spanned the globe, unlike her daughter who has yet to have a romantic exploit.

After she bolted I was raised at Castle Rannoch. As you can imagine, I was kept well away from my mother's side of the family when I was growing up. So I have only just got to know my grandfather and frankly I adore him. He is the only person in the world with whom I can be myself. It's like having a real family for once!

To my intense disappointment my grandfather was not at home. Neither was the widow next door with whom he had developed a close friendship. If Granddad had been on the phone, I could have saved myself the trip. But the idea of telephone communication hadn't exactly reached darkest Essex yet. I was standing in Granddad's front garden, under the disapproving stare of those gnomes, not sure what to do next, when an elderly man walked past with an elderly dog on a leash. He looked at me then shook his head.

"He ain't there, love. He's gone." (He pronounced it "gawn.")

"Gone? Where?" I asked in alarm as visions of hospitals or worse swam into my head. Granddad's health had not been too brilliant recently.

"Down Clacton."

I had no idea what a Clacton was or how one went down it. "Down Clacton?" I repeated hopefully.

He nodded. "Yeah. Workingmen's club outing. In the charabanc. Her next door went with him." And he gave me a knowing wink. I let out a sigh of relief. An outing. In a coach. Probably to the seaside. So even my grandfather was managing to escape the heat. I had no choice but to take the train back to the city. All my friends had deserted London for their country estates, their yachts or the Continent, and here I was, feeling hot and increasingly despondent in a carriage full of sweaty bodies.

"What am I doing here?" I asked myself. I had no skills, no hope of employment and no idea where to turn next. Nobody with any sense and money stayed in London during the month of August. And as for Darcy, the wild son of an Irish peer whom I thought was my current boyfriend . . . I hadn't heard from him since he disappeared yet again, ostensibly to go home to Ireland to recover from his gunshot wound. This might be true, or it might not. With Darcy one never knew.

Of course I could go home to Scotland, I told myself, as the air in the tube train became stifling. The memory of the cold wind sweeping down the loch and the equally cold drafts sweeping down the corridors of Castle Rannoch was sorely tempting as I rode the escalator up from St. James's tube station, dabbing ineffectively at the beads of sweat trickling down my face. And yes, I know ladies don't sweat, but something was running down my face in great rivulets.

I was almost ready to rush home to Belgrave Square, pack a suitcase and catch the next train to Edinburgh, when I reminded myself why I had left home in the first place. The answer was Fig, my sister-in-law, the current duchess—mean-spirited, judgmental and utterly awful. Fig had made it very clear that I was a burden to them, no longer wanted at Castle Rannoch, and that she begrudged my eating their food. So when it came to enduring the heat and loneliness in London or enduring Fig, the heat won out.

Only two more weeks, I told myself as I walked home through Hyde Park. In two weeks' time I was invited to Scotland, not to my ancestral home, but to Balmoral. The king and queen had already gone up to their Scottish castle, just a few miles from our own, in time for the Glorious Twelfth, the day when the grouse shooting season officially begins. They would remain there, shooting and stalking anything with fur or feathers, for the next month and expected their various relatives to come and stay for at least part of this time. Most people tried to avoid this: they found the bagpipes at dawn, the wind moaning down the chimney, the Highland dances and the tartan wallpaper hard to endure. I was used to all this. It was just like Castle Rannoch.

Cheered by the prospect of good, fresh Highland air in the not-too-distant future, I picked my way past the bodies in Green Park. It looked like the aftermath of a particularly nasty battle—with half-naked corpses strewn everywhere. They were, in fact, London office workers making the most of the weather, sunbathing with their shirts off. A frightful sight—the bodies striped white and red depending on which parts of them had been exposed to the sun. I was halfway across the park when the bodies started to move. I noticed the sun had disappeared and at the very moment I looked up there was an ominous rumble of thunder.

The sky darkened quickly as storm clouds gathered. The sunbathers were hastily putting on their shirts and making for shelter. I began to hurry too. Not fast enough, however. Without warning the heavens opened and rain came down in a solid sheet. Girls ran screaming to the shelter of trees, which was probably not wise, given the approaching sounds of thunder. Hail bounced from the footpaths. There was no point in my seeking shelter. I was already soaked to the skin and home was only minutes away. So I ran, my hair plastered to my face, my summer frock clinging suggestively to my body, until I staggered up the steps of Rannoch House.

If I had felt depressed before, I was now well and truly in the dumps. What else could possibly go wrong? I had come to London full of hope and excitement, and nothing seemed to be working out. Then I caught sight of myself in the hall stand mirror and recoiled in horror. "Just look at you!" I said aloud. "You look like a drowned rat. If the queen could see you now." Then I started to laugh. I laughed all the way upstairs to the bathroom, where I took a long soak in the tub. By the time I had dried myself off I was feeling quite normal again. And I wasn't going to spend another dreary evening alone in Rannoch House with only the radio for company. Someone apart from me must be in London. And of course I immediately thought of Belinda. She was one of those people who never stayed in one place for long. When last seen she was flitting off to a villa in Italy but there was just a chance she might have tired of Italians and come home.

I sought out the least rumpled of my summer dresses (having had no maid to iron my clothes for a while now and very little idea how to iron them myself), hid my wet hair under a demure cloche hat and set off for Belinda's mews cottage, in nearby Knightsbridge. Unlike me, Belinda had come into an inheritance when she turned twenty-one. This had enabled her to buy a dinky little mews establishment and keep a maid. Also her living costs were practically nil, given the amount of time she spent in other people's homes, not to mention their beds.

The thunderstorm had passed over, leaving the evening air slightly cooler but still muggy. I picked my way past puddles and avoided the taxicabs that splashed through standing water on the street. I was at the entrance to the mews when I heard a loud roaring sound behind me. I was conscious of a sleek dark shape hurtling toward me and only just had time to fling myself aside as a motor bicycle came at me. It shot through the enormous puddle that had collected at the mews entrance, sending a great sheet of muddy water all over me.

"I say!" I tried to shout over the roar of the engine as it continued into the mews without slowing. I took off in pursuit, absolutely boiling with rage now, not pausing to consider whether the bike riders might be bank robbers or burglars fleeing from the police. The motorbike skidded to a halt farther down the mews and two men dressed in leather jackets, leather helmets and goggles were starting to dismount.

"What the devil do you think you were doing?" I demanded as I approached them, my anger still blinding me to the fact that I was alone in a backstreet with two distinctly antisocial characters. "Just look at what you did. I'm soaked."

"Yes, you do appear to have become a trifle wet," the first rider said, and to my extreme annoyance, he started to laugh.

"It's not funny!" I snapped. "You have ruined a perfectly good dress, and as for my hat . . ."

The person who had been riding pillion dismounted and was in the process of unbuckling a helmet. "Of course it's not funny, Paolo." The voice was female, and she pulled off her helmet and goggles with a flourish, shaking out a sleek head of dark bobbed hair.

"Belinda!" I exclaimed.

Chapter 2

Belinda Warburton-Stoke's mews cottage
Knightsbridge
London W.1.
August 12, 1932

Belinda's eyes opened wide with recognition. "Georgie! Oh, my goodness, you poor thing. Just look at you. Paolo, you've nearly drowned my best friend."

The other motorcycle rider had now removed his own helmet and was revealed to be an absolutely gorgeous man of the Latin type, with dark, flashing eyes and luxuriant black hair. "So sorry," he said. "I did not see you. The shadows, you know. And we were going rather fast." He spoke with a pronounced foreign accent, overlaid with an English education at some stage.

"Paolo just loves anything fast," Belinda said, gazing at him adoringly. The thought crossed my mind that she probably fit this criterion. Fast and loose, that was Belinda all right.

"We've just come from Brooklands," she went on. "Paolo's been practicing his motor racing. And he flies an aeroplane too. He's promised to take me up."

"You must introduce me, Belinda," Paolo said, "and then you must take your friend inside, give her a drink to calm her nerves and clean her up a little."

"Of course, darling," Belinda said. "Georgie, this is Paolo."

Paolo turned those incredible dark eyes on me. "Georgie? This is a name for a boy, no?"

"It's short for Georgiana," I said.

"Oh, very well, I suppose I had better introduce you formally," Belinda said. "May I present Count Paolo di Marola e Martini. Paolo, this is my dearest friend, Lady Georgiana of Glen Garry and Rannoch."

Paolo turned that devastating gaze onto me again. "You are Binky's sister?" he asked.

"I am. How do you know Binky?"

"We were at school together for one dreadful year," Paolo said. "My father wanted to turn me into a Civilized English Gentleman. He did not succeed. I loathed it. All those cold baths and hearty rugby games. Luckily I was asked to leave because I pinched the bottoms of the maids."

"Yes. That sounds like you," Belinda said. She opened her front door and ushered us in. "Florrie," she called, "I need a bath run straight away." She turned to look at me. "I'd ask you to sit down but frankly you'd make an awful mess of my sofa. But you can mix her a drink, Paolo. A good strong one."

"I'm afraid I have to be on my way, *cara mia*," Paolo said. "I will leave you two girls to your gossip. But tonight we will go dancing, *sì*? Or I take you to Crockford's for a little gambling, and then to a nightclub if you like."

"I'd adore it," Belinda said, "but unfortunately I'm busy this evening."

"Nonsense," Paolo said. "Telephone whoever it is and say

your long-lost cousin just came into town, or your sister has had a baby, or you've come down with chicken pox."

"I must admit it's very tempting," Belinda said. "But I really can't back out now. The poor dear would be devastated."

"Another man?" Paolo demanded, eyes flashing.

"Keep your hair on," Belinda said.

"My hair? What has this to do with my hair?"

Belinda chuckled. "It's an expression, darling. It means don't get upset over nothing."

"These English expressions are very silly," Paolo said. "Why should I not get upset if you have a date with another man?"

"Don't be silly. Of course I don't have a date with another man," Belinda said. "I'm doing my brother a favor and entertaining an old American who wants to buy one of his racehorses."

"And you could not cancel that for me?" Paolo moved dangerously close to her and ran his fingertips across her cheek. I could see her weakening.

"No, I couldn't let my brother down," Belinda said.

"I shall be devastated," Paolo moaned. "Absolutely brokenhearted. I shall think that you don't truly love me."

Why did men never say things like this to me, I wondered.

"You know, I've just had a brilliant idea." Belinda swiveled around to look at me. "Georgie could go instead of me, couldn't you, darling?"

"Oh yes," I said bitterly. "I'm certainly dressed for entertaining visiting Americans."

"It's not until eight thirty, darling," Belinda said, "and you can have a bath here and wear whatever you like from my wardrobe. My maid will help you dress, won't you, Florrie?" She turned to the maid, who was hovering at the foot of the stairs.

Nobody waited for the maid to reply.

"Splendid," Paolo said, clapping his hands. "Then I bid you ladies *arrivederci* and I will call for you at nine, *cara mia*."

"Not on your motorcycle, Paolo," Belinda said. "I refuse to perch on the pillion in my evening togs."

"Dogs? You wish to bring dogs?"

"Togs, darling. Another word for clothes."

"English is such a silly language," Paolo said again. He bowed to me. "*Arrivederci*. Until we meet again, Lady Georgiana." And he was gone.

"Belinda," I said as she turned to face me with a big smile on her face. "You have a frightful nerve. How can I entertain this visiting American? I know very little about racehorses, and he'll expect to be meeting with you."

"Don't be silly, darling." Belinda put a comforting hand on my arm and steered me toward the stairs. "He's not really here to buy racehorses. He's in oil or something. I met him at Crockford's when I was having a little flutter last night, and I agreed to go to dinner with him because the poor lamb is in town on business and he hates to dine alone. But of course I couldn't tell Paolo that. He's madly jealous."

"So you've stuck me with an unknown American, who is going to be disappointed that I'm not you and is probably expecting more than dinner."

"Of course not." We had reached the bathroom, from which steam was now billowing. "He's from the Midwest and the only thing that's likely to happen to you is that you'll die of boredom. He'll be so impressed when he finds out that he's dining with the king's cousin. And you'll get a lovely dinner and good wines. I'm doing you a favor, really."

I laughed. "Belinda, when have you ever done anybody a favor? You are one of the world's great manipulators."

"You're probably right." She sighed. "But you will do it for me?" She almost dragged me up the last of the stairs.

I sighed. "I suppose so. What have I got to lose?"

"I don't know. What have you?" She regarded me quizzically. I blushed. "Don't tell me you haven't done it yet! Georgiana, I despair of you. Last time I saw you and Darcy, you appeared to be very chummy."

"The last time I saw him I thought we were chummy too," I said, feeling a black cloud of gloom settling over me. "But he was in hospital at the time, remember. Weak and recovering from a gunshot wound. The moment he came out of hospital he went home to Ireland to recuperate and that's the last I've seen of him. Not even a postcard."

"I don't think he's the postcard-writing type," Belinda said. "Don't worry, he'll turn up again, like the proverbial bad penny. Darcy's as much an opportunist as I am. He's probably found someone to host him on a yacht off the French Riviera."

I chewed on my lip, a bad habit that my governess, Miss MacAlister, had tried to break but never fully succeeded. "The problem is that I'm due up in Scotland soon. That means I won't be seeing him all summer."

"You should have leaped into bed with him when you first had the chance," Belinda said. "Men like Darcy won't wait around forever."

"I know," I said. "It's that Castle Rannoch upbringing. All those ancestors who did the right thing. I kept thinking of Robert Bruce Rannoch, who stood his ground at the battle of Culloden and fought on alone until he was hacked to pieces."

"I fail to see what that has to do with your losing your virginity, darling."

"Duty, I suppose. A Rannoch never shirks her duty."

"And you feel it's your duty to remain a virgin until you either wed or die, do you?"

"Not really," I said. "In fact it seems rather silly when you put it that way. I just had this vision of my mother, leaping from one bed to the next all her life, and I didn't want to turn out like that."

"But think of the fun she's had doing it. And all those lovely clothes she's acquired along the way."

"I'm not like that," I said. "I'm afraid I must take after my great-grandmother, Queen Victoria. I want to find one man to love and to marry. And I really don't care about the clothes."

"I can see that." Belinda eyed me critically. She turned to her maid, who was standing patiently with arms full of towels. "Help Lady Georgiana out of those disgusting wet clothes, Florrie. And then take them away and wash them and bring her a robe."

I allowed myself to be undressed and then lowered myself into the bathtub while Belinda perched on the tub rim.

"So what do you think of Paolo?" she asked. "Isn't he divine?"

"Very divine. Did you meet him in Italy?"

"He came to the villa where I was staying"—she paused for effect—"with his fiancée."

"His fiancée? Belinda, how could you?"

"Don't worry, darling. It's not the same over there. They are Catholic, you know. He's been engaged to this girl for at least ten years. She's very proper and spends half her time on her knees, praying her rosary, but it keeps his family happy, knowing he'll eventually marry someone like that. In the meantime . . ." She gave me a wicked grin.

I felt rather odd, lying in a tub of hot water while Belinda perched on the rim, but she seemed to feel this was quite normal. "This is like old times, isn't it, darling?" she commented. "Remember the chats we used to have in the bathroom at school?"

I smiled. "I do remember. It was the only place we could go where we couldn't be overheard."

"So what have you been doing with yourself?" she asked. "How is your char lady business going?"

"It's not a char lady business, Belinda. It is a domestic service agency. I prepare people's London houses for their arrival. I don't scrub floors or anything like that."

"And the relatives at the palace still haven't found out about it?"

"No, thank God. But in answer to your first question, it's not going at all. I haven't had a job in weeks."

"Well, you wouldn't, would you?" Belinda stretched out her long legs. "Nobody comes to London in the summer. Anybody who can escape from it does so."

I nodded. "I've begun to feel that I'm the only person still here. Even my grandfather has gone to Clacton-on-Sea on an outing."

"So how have you been surviving?"

"Not very well," I said. "I'm pretty much down to tea and toast. I'll have to do something soon, or I'll be joining the lines at the soup kitchens."

"Don't be silly, darling. You could get yourself invited to any number of country houses if you wanted to. You probably are the most eligible spinster in the country, you know."

"I don't know people the way you do, Belinda. And I wouldn't know how to invite myself to someone's house."

"I'll do the inviting, if you like."

I smiled at her. "The fact is that I just don't enjoy sponging off people."

"Well, you could always go home to Castle Rannoch."

"I considered that, which shows you how desperate I've been feeling. But if it was a choice between Fig and starvation, then I think starvation would win."

She looked at me with concern. "My poor, sweet Georgie: no work, no friends and no sex. No wonder you're looking gloomy. We must cheer you up. You'll get a good meal tonight, of course, and tomorrow you can come with me to Croydon."

"Croydon? That's supposed to cheer me up?"

"The aerodrome, darling. I'm going to see Paolo's new plane. He may even take us up."

Having seen the reckless abandon with which Paolo drove a motorcycle, I wasn't too keen to go up in his plane, but I managed a smile. "Spiffing," I said. At least it would be better than sitting at home.

Chapter 3

Rannoch House
August 13, 1932
Weather still muggy.

At ten o'clock the next morning Belinda showed up on my
doorstep, looking fresh and stunning in white linen trousers and a black-and-white-striped blouse. The ensemble
was topped off with a jaunty little black pillbox hat. One
would never have guessed that she had probably been out
all night.

"Ready?" she asked, casting a critical eye over my summer dress and the cloche, from which most of the mud had
been removed. "Are you sure that outfit will be suitable for
flying upside down?"

"I think I'll leave the flying upside down to you," I said,
"and I don't possess any trousers other than the ones I wear
around the estate at home, and they smell of horse."

"We'll have to do something about your wardrobe, darling." She attempted to smooth the creases from my cotton
skirt. "What a pity your mother is so petite, or you could
have all her castoffs."

"She's offered to buy me new clothes on several occasions, but you know my mother. She always forgets and flits away again. Besides, I don't think I'd feel comfortable accepting money that comes from her German boyfriend."

"She's still with her beefy industrialist, then?"

"The last time I heard. But that was a month ago. Who knows."

Belinda chuckled. I closed the front door and followed her to a waiting taxicab.

"So do tell, I'm dying to hear about last night," she said as the cab drove off. "How was your dinner with Mr. Hamburger?"

"Schlossberger," I corrected. "Hiram Schlossberger, from Kansas City. It went exactly as you predicted. He was completely overawed by my royal connections and he would keep calling me 'Your Highness' even though I told him I was only 'my lady' and that we didn't have to be so formal. He was rather a dear, actually, but I'm afraid he was rather boring. He produced snapshots of his wife and children and dog and even the cows on his ranch."

"But you did get a good meal out of it?"

"Delicious. Although Mr. Schlossberger wasn't happy with it. He turned his nose up at the foie gras and the lobster bisque and said all he wanted was a good steak. Then he complained about the size of it. Apparently at home he eats steaks that are so large they hang over the sides of the plate."

"Heavens, that's half a cow. But you had some decent bubbly, I hope?"

I shook my head. "He doesn't drink. Prohibition, you know."

"How ridiculous. Everybody knows that prohibition exists, but everybody drinks anyway. Except him, apparently. So what did you drink?"

I made a face. "Lemonade. He ordered it for both of us."

Belinda touched my arm. "My darling, I am so sorry. Next time I foist off one of my men on you, I'll make sure he doesn't drink lemonade."

"Next time?" I asked. "Do you make a habit of this sort of thing?"

"Oh, absolutely, darling. How else does one get a decent meal occasionally? And one is doing a public service, actually. These poor men come to London to do business and they don't know anybody so they are delighted to be seen with a young society woman who can show them how to behave. Your Mr. Hamburger will be bragging about you for years, I'm sure."

We alighted from our taxicab at Victoria Station and soon our train was huffing and puffing through the drearier parts of south London on our way to Croydon. Belinda had launched into a long description of the villa in Italy. I was half listening as I stared out of the window at those pathetic back gardens with lines of washing strung across them. Because an idea was germinating in my mind. All those men Belinda had mentioned—in London alone on business and having to eat without companionship. What if I started a service to supply each of them with a charming dinner companion of impeccable social pedigree—in other words, *moi*. It would be better than cleaning houses and at the very least would keep the wolf from the door. At best it might prove to be highly successful and I'd be able to buy myself a decent wardrobe and mingle in society a little more frequently.

∞

I had never been to Croydon Aerodrome before and I was surprised at the hustle and bustle and brand-new buildings. As our taxi approached along a leafy lane, a large biplane roared over our heads and landed on the runway. I had never even seen a real airliner land before at close quarters and it was an impressive sight as the great bird touched down on the tarmac, bounced a few times and then went rolling along as an earthbound machine. To me it was quite remarkable that anything so large and clumsy-looking could actually fly.

As we were walking over to the new white terminal building in the art deco style, the airliner came roaring toward us, propellers whirling, making a terrible din. I paused to watch as steps were wheeled up to it and one by one the passengers disembarked.

"That's an Imperial Airways Heracles, just in from Paris," someone behind me remarked.

It all seemed so glamorous and improbable. I tried to picture stepping into that little capsule and being whisked across the globe, above the clouds. My only trips abroad had been across the Channel to Switzerland, thence by uncomfortable train.

"The weather doesn't look too promising, does it?" Belinda said, brushing away the midges that danced in front of our faces. "It feels like thunder again."

It did indeed feel extremely muggy and unpleasant. "Where are we to meet Paolo?" I asked.

"He'll be over by the hangars." Belinda started off for the more ramshackle part of the airport, dotted with huts and bigger buildings that actually housed aeroplanes. We located Paolo standing beside a shiny new aeroplane that looked incredibly flimsy, so I was relieved when he greeted us with, "Sorry about the weather. We will not be going up this afternoon, I fear. The Met boys have warned us of another storm."

"Oh, that's too bad, after we've come all this way," Belinda said. "And I was so looking forward to it."

"You would not enjoy being shaken like a cocktail, *cara mia*, and besides, you would see nothing flying through cloud, and you might get struck by lightning."

"In that case"—Belinda was still pouting—"you had better take us for a good lunch to make up for our disappointment. We're starving."

"There is a restaurant in the passenger terminal," Paolo said. "I cannot vouch for the quality of the food, but you can eat and watch the airliners come in from around the world. It's quite a spectacle."

"All right. It will have to do, I suppose." Belinda slipped her arm through his and then her other arm through mine. "Come on, Georgie. We'll make this man pay for not arranging for good weather, shall we?"

"But I have no control over your British weather," Paolo complained. "If we were in Italy, I could guarantee that the weather would be good. In England it always rains."

"Not always. Two days ago you were complaining it was too hot and sunny," Belinda said.

We passed through the sparkling new building, our feet tapping on the marble floor. I looked up in fascination at the mural that decorated the wall. It depicted the time zones around the world. It was already night in Australia. I experienced a pang of longing. So much of the world waiting to be explored, and the farthest I had been was Switzerland—all very safe and clean.

The lunch was surprisingly good with a well-cooked fillet of plaice and strawberries and cream to follow it. As we lingered over our coffee I stared out of the window with rapt attention, while trying not to notice Belinda and Paolo sharing bites of a strawberry in a most erotic fashion. I had seen the storm clouds building in a great bank of darkness, so I wasn't really surprised by the first clap of thunder immediately over our heads. People who had been standing on the tarmac rushed for shelter as the rains began. Chauffeurs hastily put covers on open motorcars.

"Well, that's put an end to any more flying today," Paolo said. "I hope it stops before I have to ride back to London. Riding a motorcycle in a storm is simply not fun."

"You could get struck by lightning," Belinda said. "I thought you loved danger."

"Danger, *sì*. Getting soaking wet, no."

"You'll have to leave the motorcycle here and come back on the train with us," Belinda said.

"But I could not reach the house where I am staying without my motorcycle," he said. "Where could I spend the night, do you think?"

Of course he knew the answer perfectly well.

"Let me think," Belinda said.

I turned away, wishing I were not the wallflower again. Then somebody shouted, "Look! There's an aeroplane attempting to land."

I peered into the downpour and thought I could make out a blacker speck against the dark clouds.

"He must be crazy to try and land in this," someone else said. "He'll get himself killed."

Everybody rushed to the windows to watch the spectacle. We could see the tiny machine bobbing around, disappearing into cloud one minute and reappearing the next. Then it went into a great bank of darkness. Lightning flashed. Thunder roared. There was no sign of the plane. Suddenly a cheer went up. The little craft came out of the cloud, only a few feet above the runway, and touched down, sending out a sheet of spray behind it.

Everyone streamed out of the restaurant. We followed, caught up in the excitement, and stood under the canopy as the small craft came toward us. It was a biplane, no bigger than a child's toy.

"It's a Gypsy Moth," Paolo said. "Open cockpit, you know. I don't think I'd be brave enough to land a Moth in this kind of storm."

The aeroplane came to a halt. The pilot swung himself out of the rear cockpit and climbed down to applause and cheers. Then he took off his helmet and a gasp went up from the crowd. The pilot was a woman with striking red hair.

"It's Ronny!" Paolo exclaimed, pushing forward through the crowd.

"Ronny? It looks like a girl to me," I said.

"Veronica Padgett, darling." Belinda was following Paolo through the crowd. "You know, the famous aviatrix. She just set the solo record from London to Cape Town."

The pilot was now making her way into the building, graciously accepting the cheers and congratulations as she moved through the crowd.

"Ronny, well done," Paolo called out as she passed us.

She looked up, saw him and gave him a big smile. "What-ho, Paolo. Bet you couldn't do that."

"Nobody in his right mind would have attempted that, Ronny. You're quite mad, you know."

She laughed. She had a rich, deep laugh. "Possibly. I told myself so many times during the last half hour."

"Where have you come from?" Paolo asked.

"Not far. Only over from France. I knew I probably shouldn't have taken off, but I didn't want to miss a party this evening. But the whole thing was utterly bloody. Couldn't see the blasted railway lines in France and then there was fog over the Channel and then I flew into this bank of filthy weather. Bucketed around all over the place. I almost lost my lunch, and my compass was playing up too. No idea where the damned runway was. My God, it was fun."

I looked at her in amazement. Her face was positively glowing with excitement.

"Come on, let's get out of this infernal weather," she said, turning up her flight jacket collar as another clap of thunder sounded overhead and the wind whipped across the aerodrome. As we fell into place behind her, Belinda tapped Paolo on the shoulder. "Are you planning to introduce us or are you keeping her all to yourself?" she asked.

Paolo laughed, a trifle nervously. "I'm sorry, I should have introduced you. Ronny, these are my friends Belinda Warburton-Stoke and Georgiana Rannoch. Girls, this is Ronny Padgett."

I saw Ronny's eyes widen. "Rannoch? Any relation to the dukes of?"

"The last one was my father; the current one is my brother," I said.

"Good God. Then we're almost neighbors. My family place is not too far from you on the Dee."

"Really? It's amazing we've never run into each other before."

"I don't go up there often," she said. "Too damned quiet for my taste. And I'm a good bit older than you. When I was shipped off to boarding school you were probably still crawling around in nappies. And I left home for good when I was sixteen. Didn't want any part of being presented and all that bosh. Since then I've never stayed in one place for long. Born with wanderlust, I suppose. Are you up there much yourself?"

"I have to go up to Scotland in a couple of weeks," I said. "But not to Castle Rannoch if I can avoid it. It's not the liveliest of places these days. I'm due at Balmoral for the grouse shoot."

"Murdering all the poor defenseless little birds," Ronny said. "Barbaric when you come to think of it. But by God it's fun, isn't it? I suppose it must be in the blood, don't you think?"

"I think it must," I said. "I adore hunting but I always feel jolly sorry for the poor fox when it's torn to pieces. I'm not a particularly good shot, so I don't feel sorry for the grouse in the same way. And they are awfully silly birds."

Ronny laughed again. "They certainly are. Maybe we'll bump into each other sometime. If I'm there you can come and shoot with me on the estate."

Belinda, I noticed, was pouting. She was used to being the center of attention.

She tugged at Paolo's arm. "After what Ronny has just achieved, the very least you can do is to fete her with champagne," she said.

"Belinda, I sometimes think you believe that all I am good for is keeping you supplied with champagne and caviar," Paolo said.

"Not at all, you do have other uses." She gave him her cat-with-the-cream smile.

I saw the lingering glance that passed between them. Then he turned to Ronny. "I'm instructed to buy you champagne if they stock a decent bottle at the bar here. Coming?"

She looked around, then laughed again. "Why not? You only live once, don't you? And I've never yet said no to a decent champers." She strode ahead of us, through the crowd and into the main hall of the building. "I don't suppose you've seen my maid, have you?" she asked, her eyes searching the crowd. "Timid little thing. Looks as if she expects everyone to bite her. I told her to meet me here with the dress I plan to wear tonight. She damned well better show up or I'm sunk. I can't go to a party dressed like this."

We made our way toward the bar but there was no sign of a maid. "Probably waiting for me at the hangar, which is where I left the motorcar, thank God. At least it will be dry."

"You have a motorcar, do you?" Paolo asked, eyeing her with interest. "Any chance of a ride into town?"

"Sorry, old thing. I'm heading for deepest Sussex. No use at all."

"Too bad," Paolo said. "I came on my motorcycle and I do so hate getting wet. Now I have no choice but to leave the wretched thing here and go back to London by train."

"What a hardship for you," Belinda said in a clipped voice.

He put an arm around her shoulder. "I didn't mean it like that, *mi amore*. I just meant that once I am in London I will have no means of transport except for those horrible taxicabs that creep around slower than beetles. I'm sure Ronny drives deliciously fast."

"I certainly do, old bean," she said, and laughed again.

We were just entering the bar when a young woman called out, "Miss Padgett!" and came toward us, staggering under a large suitcase. She looked red faced and distinctly flustered. "Oh, Miss Padgett, I'm so sorry I'm late," she gasped. "It started to thunder when I was halfway from the station and I had to take shelter. I'm mortally afraid of thunder, you know. I hope I haven't inconvenienced you."

"Of course you bloody well have," Ronny said. "You can't seem to get anywhere on time. But you're lucky this once. I've been waylaid to drink champagne, so run along to the motorcar and wait for me there."

"The motorcar?"

"It's in the hangar. You know. Number 23? You've been there before. Where I keep the Moth." She turned to us.

"Heavens, it's like talking to a brick wall. I take it you have efficient maids, Lady Georgiana?"

"Please call me Georgie, everyone does," I said. "And at the moment I have no servants at all. I've recently moved to London and frankly I'm still slumming it."

"Splendid idea," Ronny said. "You see, Mavis, Lady Georgiana is the daughter of a duke and she can make do without servants. So you'd better shape up or I may have to follow suit. A new age is dawning, you know."

Paolo had been conferring with the barman, and there was a satisfying pop as the cork flew off a bottle of Bollinger.

"Well, go on then," Ronny said to the long-suffering Mavis, who was now staring at me in fascination. "Take my suitcase and put it in the car, then wait for me there. Oh, and see if you can put the top up. We don't want to get wet."

Mavis attempted a curtsy then staggered off. As she went, Ronny's clear voice echoed across the marble foyer. "I'd sack her in a moment but frankly I know I'd find things like washing and ironing too tiresome."

Chapter 4

Rannoch House
August 13, 14 and 15, 1932
Wet.

"So what did you think of Ronny?" Belinda asked me on the way home.

"Interesting. Different."

"She's certainly her own person, isn't she?" Belinda said. "Heart of a lion, but she doesn't care what she says or whom she insults." She turned to Paolo, who was slumped in the window seat. "I saw you were rather taken with her."

"She amazes me and amuses me," he said, "but as to anything more, she has about as much sex appeal as a plate of spaghetti Bolognese."

"I don't know, spaghetti can be quite sexy, if eaten in the nude." Belinda gave him the most provocative look.

Paolo laughed. "Belinda, you are quite the most shameless girl I know. Angelina would go and say a dozen Hail Marys if a thought like that even crossed her mind."

"That's why I'm more fun than Angelina," Belinda said. "Go on, admit that you have more fun when you are with me."

"Of course I do, but I do not think you will make anybody a suitable wife."

I watched them as the train chuffed toward Victoria. Belinda was going to wind up like my mother, leaping from bed to bed with gay abandon, I decided. The thought seemed to worry me more than it did her.

They dropped me off at Rannoch House then disappeared, presumably for a night of sin. I didn't sleep much either. The thunderstorm had left the air sticky, and even with the windows open it was too hot to sleep. I lay awake, listening to the sounds of the city, and found myself thinking about Belinda and Paolo. What would it be like to spend the night in the arms of a man? Then of course my thoughts turned to a particular man. What was he doing at this moment? Was he really still recuperating at his family's place in Ireland or was he somewhere else, with someone else? One never knew with Darcy.

When I first met him I had thought him a wild Irish playboy opportunist, living by his charm and his wits. But now I suspected he was more than he had told me. In fact I thought he might be some kind of spy. For whom I couldn't say, but definitely not for the communists. He had taken a bullet that almost cost him his life to save the king and queen.

I just wished I knew where he was. I wished I had the nerve to show up on his doorstep. But I was rather afraid of what I might find there. When it came to men, I seriously lacked confidence—probably because the only male I knew until the age of eighteen was my brother.

I fell asleep eventually and woke to the sound of the milkman's horse and the rattle of bottles. The air had cooled overnight and the sweet smell of roses and honeysuckle wafted across from the gardens in the middle of the square. I got out of bed feeling energized and renewed, the black mood of the day before having vanished with the night air. My nature is such that I can never stay down in the dumps for long. And today I had a task ahead of me, one that might set me up with a splendid income for the foreseeable future.

I sat at my desk and composed an advertisement for the *Times*. When I had finished I was rather pleased with myself and wanted to show it to Belinda. But I knew better than to disturb her before eleven o'clock and especially when she was probably not alone. So I printed it out neatly and delivered it to the *Times* office. I thought the girl who wrote the receipt for it looked at me strangely and I wondered if she recognized me. I do appear in the odd photograph in the *Tattler*, since the press thinks of me as an eligible young woman of good pedigree. (Little do they know the state of the Rannoch bank accounts.)

"Are you sure this is what you want it to say, miss?" she asked.

"Yes, quite sure, thank you."

"Very well." She took my money. "So this will appear for the first time in tomorrow's paper and run until you tell us to stop it."

"That's correct," I said. She was still staring at me as I left the office.

I came home full of anticipation and went through my wardrobe for garments suitable for evenings on the town. Luckily I had had a maid for one whole week earlier in the summer, and during that time she had cleaned and pressed my good clothes, so that my evening dresses were not as crumpled as my everyday wear. I sat in front of the mirror and experimented with putting my hair up. (Disaster. I looked like Medusa.) Then I got the scissors and snipped at the ends in the hope of turning it into the kind of sleek bob Belinda wore. Again not too successful. Now all I had to do was wait.

The next morning I ran out to buy the *Times* as soon as the newsagent was open and there it was on the front page in the middle of the other advertisements. *Alone in town on business? Let Coronet Escort Service enhance your evening's entertainment. Our high-class girls make ideal companions to grace your dining and dancing.* I had had to supply a phone number, naturally, and had no choice but to give the Rannoch House number. I just hoped that nobody recognized it and told Binky or Fig. But then I reasoned I wasn't doing anything wrong. That Mr. Hiram Schlossberger had enjoyed every minute of my company the other evening. So why shouldn't similar gentlemen pay for the privilege?

Clearly the idea was not a silly one, because that afternoon I received my first telephone call. The man had a pronounced North Country accent, but I couldn't hold that against him. I thought of all those rich mill owners and people who said things like "Where there's muck, there's brass." Even if his conversation and manners were boorish, he'd pay well. He asked me my price, which no man of breeding would do, and stammered a little when I told him five guineas.

"That's an awful lot," he said. "She'd better be good."

"The very best," I said. "A high-class girl from a good family. You'll be enchanted with her."

"I bloody hope so," he said. "Have her meet me at the Rendezvous Club behind Leicester Square. That's close to where I'm staying."

"Very well," I said. "And what time shall I tell her?"

"Ten o'clock?"

I put down the mouthpiece. It wasn't going to be dinner then, at that hour. Nor a theater. A late supper at a nightclub, maybe? Then dancing, gambling, a cabaret? My heart raced in anticipation. This was the sort of life I'd dreamed of living—out late with the bright young things, coming home at dawn.

I spent a ridiculously long time getting ready, soaking in a hot bath and then actually trying to apply makeup, something I've never really learned to do well. But when I looked in the mirror, I was satisfied with the luscious red lips, even if black mascara on my eyelashes didn't really go with my red-blond hair and coloring and the cocktail dress was not as slinky as I would have liked. It was one that the gamekeeper's wife had run up on her sewing machine for my season. It was a copy of something I'd admired in a magazine, but somehow the combination of Mrs. MacTavish's sewing skills and my taffeta didn't make me quite look the same as the softly draped girl with the cigarette holder in *Harper's Bazaar*. But it was the best I could do and I looked clean and respectable.

My heart thumped wildly all the way in the taxicab. We passed the bright lights of Leicester Square with its theater marquees and bustling crowds and finally pulled up on a dark side street.

"Are you sure this is it, miss?" The taxi driver asked in a concerned voice.

I wasn't sure. It looked awfully dark and lonely. But then I saw a blinking sign over an entrance. Club Rendezvous. "Yes, this is it," I said. "Thank you very much."

"You are meeting somebody, I hope," he said as I paid him.

"Yes, I'm meeting a young man. Don't worry, I'll be fine." I gave what I hoped was a confident smile.

The taxi sped away, leaving me alone in the deserted street. It had rained again and the flashing red sign was reflected in the puddles as I crossed the road. I pushed open the door and found myself facing a flight of steps going down to a basement. Music spilled up to greet me—the wail of a sax-ophone and a heavy drumbeat. I held on to the rail as I went down the steps. This then was a real nightclub. I had never been in a place like this. The stairs were steep with worn carpet on them. And I was wearing my one pair of high-heeled shoes, in my attempt to look glamorous. I haven't mentioned yet that I am apt to be clumsy in moments of stress. Halfway down, my heel caught in a threadbare patch in the carpet. I pitched forward, grasped at the railing and ended up slithering down the last of the stairs, arriving at the bottom in a most undignified way as I cannoned into a potted palm. I hastened to pick myself up before anyone observed this unorthodox entry. I was in a sort of dark an-teroom with an antique writing desk and chair, mercifully unoccupied. The area was separated from the main area by a row of potted palms, one of which now had a frond hanging down, thanks to me. A man had just been emerging from the club beyond the palms. He was staggering slightly as if drunk and started in alarm when I came hurtling down the stairs toward him.

"Let me give you a word of advice, girlie," he said in slurred tones, wagging a finger at me. "Don't drink any more tonight. You've already had enough. Trust me, I know." Then he staggered past me up the stairs.

I collected myself and smoothed down my skirt and my hair before I went through into the club itself. It was dimly lit, with candles on small tables and the only real light com-ing from the stage, where a girl was dancing.

"Can I help you, miss?" A swarthy man in a dinner jacket appeared at my side. He didn't seem to possess a razor.

"I'm meeting someone here," I said. "A Mr. Crump."

"Ah. I see." He gave me something between a grin and a leer. "He's expecting you. At that table on the far right."

The man looked up as I approached him and he rose to his feet.

"Mr. Crump?" I said, holding out my hand to him. "My agency sent me. Coronet Escorts?"

He was a ruddy, bloated sort of fellow with what he probably thought was a jaunty mustache but which looked more like a hedgehog perched on his upper lip. What's more, he was wearing an ordinary day suit and a rather loud tie. I saw him giving me a long once-over.

"You're younger than I expected," he said. "And you're wearing more clothes too."

"I assure you I'm old enough to be a perfect companion for you," I said. "I'm educated and well traveled."

He smirked. "I'm not planning to quiz you on your knowledge of geography." Then he became aware that we were both still standing. "I suppose you'd like a drink before we go?" he said.

"That would be nice. I'd like champagne if they have it." I took a seat at the table.

"Bloody 'ell," he muttered. "You London girls certainly have expensive tastes." I noticed that he had a beer in front of him. He beckoned to a waiter and a bottle of champagne was brought to the table.

"I hope you'll join me," I said, feeling embarrassed now that he'd had to buy a whole bottle when all I'd wanted was a glass.

"Why not? Help us both to loosen up, won't it?" he said and gave me a wink.

The bottle was opened with a satisfying pop. Two glasses were poured. I took a sip then held up my glass to him. "Cheers," I said. "Here's to a lovely evening for both of us."

I noticed he swallowed hard. In fact it almost looked as

if he was sweating. "So I expect you want paying up front, do you?"

"Oh, I don't think that will be necessary," I said. "But I shall expect cash at the end of the evening."

"So what's the plan then? Do we go back to my hotel, or do you have a place where you take clients nearby? I know I should have asked on the telephone but this was all rather last minute, wasn't it? In fact I'd never have thought of it if I hadn't seen your advert this morning. I don't usually do this sort of thing."

I was just trying to digest what he had said when the music picked up in tempo. There were whoops and catcalls coming from the front of the room. I looked up at the stage. The girl was still dancing, but I was suddenly aware that she wore almost no clothing. As I stared in fascinated horror, she opened an ostrich feather fan which she held in front of her, then, to a final drum roll, she produced her brassiere and tossed it into the front rows of the audience.

Suddenly the penny dropped. *My hotel or your place?*

"Wait," I said. "What were you expecting from me?"

"Only the usual, darling," he said. "Same as you do with all the men. Nothing too kinky."

"I think there must be some mistake," I said. "We are a respectable escort service. We provide girls as dinner companions, theater companions, not the sort of thing you obviously have in mind."

"Don't play coy with me, sweetheart," he said. The words were slurred enough to tell me that he had been drinking for some time. He reached across and grabbed my arm. "What are you trying to do, push up the price? I wasn't born yesterday, you know. Come on, drink up your bubbly and we'll go back to my hotel, or you'll be charging me by the hour."

I attempted to stand up. "I'm afraid there's been a horrible misunderstanding here. I think I'd better go."

His grip on my arm tightened. "What's the matter, girlie, don't you fancy me, or what? Isn't my brass good enough for you?" The smile had disappeared from his face. He was blowing beery breath in my face. "Now you come with me like a good girl or you know what I'll do? I'll have you arrested for soliciting."

He stood up and attempted to drag me with him.

"Let go of me, please," I said. I sensed people at the tables around us watching. "Just let me go and we'll forget the whole thing."

"No, we bloody won't," he said. "I've had to pay for a bottle of champagne. And we made an agreement, me and your agency. We struck a bargain and Harold Crump doesn't take kindly to people who try to back out of business deals. Now stop playing the prissy little miss and get moving."

"Didn't you hear the young lady? She will not be coming with you," said a voice behind me.

I recognized that voice and spun around to see Darcy O'Mara standing there, looking amazingly dashing in a white dinner jacket and bow tie, his unruly black hair combed into submission, apart from a wayward curl that fell onto his forehead. It was all I could do not to throw myself into his arms.

"And who are you, butting in like this?" Mr. Crump demanded, blustering up to Darcy only to find he was several inches shorter.

"Let's just say that I'm her manager," Darcy said.

"Her pimp, you mean."

"Call it what you like," Darcy said, "but there's been a mistake. She should never have been sent out tonight. Our agency only deals with clients of the highest social echelon.

We have a new girl answering the telephone and she omitted to put you through our normal vetting process. And now I've seen your behavior, I am afraid there is no way I could allow one of our girls to go anywhere with you. You simply don't pass muster, sir. You are, to put it bluntly, too common."

"Well, I never did," Mr. Crump said.

"And you're not going to now," Darcy replied. "Come, Arabella. We're leaving."

"Here, what about my champagne?" Mr. Crump demanded.

Darcy reached into his pocket and threw down a pound note on the table. Then he took my arm and half dragged me up the steps.

"What the hell do you think you were doing?" he demanded as we stepped out into the night. His eyes were blazing and I thought for one awful moment that he might hit me.

"That stupid man got it wrong." I was near to tears now. "I advertised my services as an escort. He must have misunderstood. He thought I was—you know—a call girl."

"You advertised your services as an escort?" Darcy's fingers were still digging into my upper arm.

"Yes, I put an advertisement in the *Times* and called myself Coronet Escorts."

Darcy spluttered. "My dear naïve little girl, surely even you must have realized that the words 'escort service' are a polite way of advertising something a little more seedy? Of course he thought he was getting a call girl. He had every right to think so."

"I had no idea," I snapped. "How was I to know?"

"Surely you must have had your suspicions when you saw that club. Nice girls do not go to places like that, Georgiana."

"Then what were you doing in it?" I demanded, my relief now turning to anger. "You walk out of my life. You don't bother to write. And now I find you slumming it in a place like that. No wonder you're not interested in me. I don't take my clothes off in front of a group of men."

"As to what I was doing there . . ." he said. I thought I detected the twitch of a smile on his lips. "I had to meet a man about a dog. And I can assure you that I didn't bother to look at what was taking place on the stage. I've seen far better and had it offered for free. And as to why I disappeared and didn't get in touch—I'm sorry. I had to go abroad in something of a hurry. I just got back yesterday. And you're damned lucky I did, or you'd still be trying to fight off that troglodyte."

"I would have managed," I said huffily. "You don't always have to step in and rescue me, you know."

"It seems that I do. You're simply not safe to be allowed out alone in the city," he said. "Come on. We're going to Leicester Square where we can pick up a taxicab, and I'm sending you home."

"What if I don't want to go home?"

"You have no choice, my lady. Exactly what would your family think if you were snapped by a passing newspaperman, coming out of a seedy London gentlemen's strip club? Now walk."

He propelled me along the pavement until he flagged down a taxicab. "Take this young lady back to Belgrave Square," he said in an authoritative voice I had never heard from him before. He bundled me into the cab. "And you remove that advertisement from the *Times* the first thing tomorrow morning, do you hear?"

"It's my life. You can't dictate to me," I snapped because I thought I might cry any moment. "You don't own me, you know."

"No," he said, looking at me long and hard. "But I do care about you, in spite of everything. Now go home, have a cup of cocoa and go to bed—alone."

"Aren't you coming with me?" My voice quivered a little.

"Is that an invitation?" he asked, the scowl vanishing for a second before it resumed, and he said, "Regrettably I still have business to conclude. But I expect we'll run into each other on some future occasion in a place that is more suitable." Then he leaned into the cab, grasped my chin, drew me toward him and kissed me hard on the mouth. Then he slammed the taxicab door, and I was driven off into the night.

Chapter 5

Rannoch House
August 16
Cooler, more normal weather.
Internal turmoil not cooler at all.

I managed to make it all the way home without crying. But as soon as I shut the big front door behind me, the tears started to roll down my cheeks. It wasn't just the fright and embarrassment of what happened and what might have happened, it was the knowledge that I had now definitely lost Darcy. I went up to bed and curled into a tight little ball, wishing I were somewhere safe, with someone who loved me, and coming to the realization that I actually had nobody, apart from my grandfather, that I could count on.

I awoke to the sound of distant knocking. It took me a moment to realize that someone was hammering on my front door. It was only nine o'clock and I pulled on my robe and went downstairs cautiously, wondering who it could be at this hour. Certainly not Belinda. Hope rose for an instant that it might be Darcy, coming to apologize for his boorish behavior last night. But when I opened the door a young policeman was standing there.

"I've been sent from Scotland Yard to speak to Lady Georgiana Rannoch," he said, eyeing my night attire and wild hair. "Is she available, please?"

"I am Lady Georgiana," I said. "May I ask who has sent you from Scotland Yard and what this is about?"

"Sir William Rollins would like to have a word with you, my lady."

"Sir William Rollins?"

He nodded. "Deputy commissioner."

"And why does Sir William wish to speak with me?"

"I couldn't tell you, my lady. He doesn't confide in ordinary coppers. I'm told to go and fetch you, and I go. Now if you could hurry and get dressed, he doesn't like to be kept waiting."

I tried to think of a crushing retort. He was, after all, speaking to the daughter of a duke and second cousin to the king. I opened my mouth to say that if Sir William Rollins wished to speak to me, he could present himself at Rannoch House. But I couldn't make the words come out. In fact my legs were a trifle shaky as I went back upstairs. What could Scotland Yard possibly want with me? And not just Scotland Yard, but somebody frightfully high up there? In my past dealings with the Metropolitan Police I had had to contend with a truly obnoxious inspector and a rather smarmy chief inspector. Clearly this was something more serious, then, but I couldn't for the life of me think what. . . . Unless . . . Surely they couldn't have found out about last night? And even if they had, I had done nothing against the law—had I?

I grabbed the first dress I could find in my wardrobe that looked vaguely presentable, ran a brush through my hair, cleaned my teeth and splashed water on my face. Then I came downstairs again to face whatever I had coming to me.

I found it hard to breathe as the squad car whisked me toward Whitehall and entered into the forecourt of Scotland Yard. The door was held open for me and I tried to enter with my head held high, only to trip over the doormat and come flying into the foyer at a full stagger. (That tendency to clumsiness in moments of stress again, I'm afraid.)

Even more humiliating for me, a young, fresh-faced bobby grabbed me and saved me from crashing into a glass partition. "Keen to be arrested, are you, miss?" he said, giving me a cheeky grin.

I tried to give him a look that would have done my great-grandmother credit when she pronounced the words "We are not amused," but somehow I couldn't make my face obey me either.

"This way, your ladyship," my original escort said, and ushered me into a lift. It seemed to take an eternity to go up. I found I was holding my breath, but by the time we reached the fifth floor, I had to gasp. At last it juddered to a halt. The constable pulled back the concertina door and I stepped out into a deserted hallway. At the end of the hall he pressed a button. A door opened and we were admitted to an outer office where two young women were busy typing. This was different from my previous experience of Scotland Yard. The floor was carpeted, for one thing, and the rich, herby smell of pipe tobacco hung in the air.

"Lady Georgiana to see Sir William," the young policeman said.

One of the young women got up from her desk.

"This way, please. Follow me." She looked and sounded the epitome of efficiency. I bet she'd never tripped over a rug in her life.

She led me down another hallway and tapped at a door.

"Come in!" a voice boomed.

"Lady Georgiana, Sir William," the woman said in her efficient voice.

I stepped inside. The door closed behind me. The pipe smell was revealed as coming from a big, florid man who sat behind the desk. He spilled over the sides of a large leather chair, the meerschaum clenched between his teeth. As I entered, he removed it from his mouth and held it poised in one hand. If I had summed up the typist as efficient, I could sum him up in one word too: powerful. He had fierce eyebrows, for one thing, and the sort of expression that indicated he didn't like to be crossed, and rarely was.

"Lady Georgiana. Good of you to come so quickly." He held out a meaty hand.

"Did I have a choice?" I asked, and he laughed heartily, as if I had made a good joke.

"I'm not arresting you, you know. Please. Take a seat." I sat.

"Then would you like to tell me what I'm doing here?" I asked.

"You don't have an inkling?"

"No. Why should I?"

He leaned back, eyeing me across his large mahogany desk. "Some disturbing news has just come to light," he said. "Our vice squad keeps an eye on the newspapers for potentially illegal and antisocial activities. When an advertisement showed up in no less than the *Times* yesterday, they checked on the telephone number given in the advert. They couldn't have been more surprised to find out that the number was that of your London residence—a telephone owned in the name of the Duke of Glen Garry and Rannoch. So we immediately came to the conclusion that there had been a misprint in the newspaper and we contacted the Times to tell them so. We were then informed that there was no misprint."

He paused. Those alarming eyebrows twitched with a life of their own, like two prawns. "So I thought you and I had better have a little chat and settle this matter before it goes any further. Would you like to clarify things for me?"

I was currently staring in fascination at the eyebrows, while wishing that the floor would open up and swallow me.

"It was all a hideous mistake," I said. "I merely intended to start a small escort service."

"Escort service?" The eyebrows shot up.

"Not what you're thinking. Well-bred girls who would be available as dinner or theater partners for men who didn't like to dine alone. Nothing more. Perhaps my wording was inept?"

He shook his head, chuckling now. "Oh dear, oh dear me. Your wording couldn't have been more obvious if you'd written 'Call Fifi for a good time.' But I must say I'm relieved that you haven't actually joined the oldest profession yet."

I could feel my face positively glowing with the heat of embarrassment.

"Absolutely not. And I assure you I will be withdrawing the advertisement this morning."

"Already done, my dear," he said. "But in future I must warn you to be a little more prudent if you desire to go into business. Check with someone older and more worldly wise so that you don't make any more embarrassing blunders, eh?"

"I will," I said. "I'm sorry. It really was innocently intended. I'm a young woman trying to earn a living like everybody else in this city, you know. I thought I had found a niche and leaped in to fill it."

"I'd stick to the more acceptable professions in future. All I can say is you're lucky our man happened to pick up on that advert so quickly. Can you imagine what a field day the gutter press would have had if they'd come upon it first? The tart with the tiara? The Buck House brothel?"

He watched me wince at each of these epithets. I could tell he was rather enjoying himself.

"I've told you it won't happen again," I said. "And fortunately the press has not found me out."

"All the same," he went on slowly, "I think it might be wise if you left the city immediately. Take the next train to your home in Scotland, eh? Then if by any chance any nosy parker did stumble upon yesterday's paper and called the number, they would realize that Rannoch House was empty and closed up for the summer and that there had been a mistake. We'll brief the *Times* to verify that the telephone number was their error."

He looked at me inquiringly. I couldn't do anything but nod in agreement. He obviously had no idea that going home to Scotland meant facing a dragon of a sister-in-law who would want to know what I was doing landing on their doorstep with no warning. But I did see his point. I went to stand up, presuming the interview was at an end. Sir William put his pipe to his lip and took a long draw on it.

"One other small thing," he said. "Do you happen to know a woman by the name of Mavis Pugh?"

"Never heard of her."

"I see. Only yesterday evening a young woman was found dead on a byway close to Croydon Aerodrome. It appeared that she had been run over by a fast-moving vehicle—a motorcycle by the looks of it. We assume it was just a tragic accident. The lane was leafy and shady, and it was just after a sharp bend. Maybe she stepped out at the last minute and he didn't see her. But he didn't stop to report it either. And we've turned up no witnesses."

I tried to keep my face interested but detached. I tried not to let Paolo come into my mind. "I'm very sorry for the woman, but I don't see what this has to do with me," I said. "I can assure you that I've never ridden a motorcycle in my life and was nowhere near Croydon Aerodrome last night, as the owner of a seedy nightclub can verify."

"Nobody is suggesting you were," he said. "I asked because her handbag was thrown across the road by the impact. Some of the contents wound up in the ditch. Among them was a half-finished letter, apparently to you. The writer was using a cheap ink and most of it had washed away but we could read 'Lady Georgiana' and the words 'Older brother, the Duke of . . .' "

"How extraordinary," I said.

"So if you don't know this woman, we wondered why she was writing to you." His eyes didn't leave mine for an instant. In spite of his age, and he must have been over fifty, his eyes were extraordinarily bright and alive. "We wondered, for example, whether she might have been thinking of blackmailing you."

"For what? My brother and I are virtually penniless. He at least owns the property. I own nothing."

"The lower classes don't think like that. To them all aristocrats are wealthy."

"I can assure you that I am not being blackmailed by anybody. Was this woman known to be of the criminal classes?"

"No," he said. "She was a lady's maid."

Then a memory stirred within my brain as I put together the words "Mavis" and "lady's maid." "Wait," I said. "Was she by any chance in the service of Veronica Padgett, the famous lady pilot?"

"Aha." He gave a smug smile. "Then you do know her?"

"I encountered her once, a few days ago at Croydon Aerodrome. She had come to meet her mistress and bring clothes for a party. Miss Padgett was cross with her because she was late. She pointed me out and said that Lady Georgiana could manage without a lady's maid and she was thinking of following suit, so this young woman would have known who I was. But I didn't have any direct communication with her."

"You say her mistress was cross with her? Maybe she was writing to you to apply for a job."

"Possibly," I said. "But I got the feeling that Miss Padgett was just needling her, not really threatening to dismiss her. What does she say about it?"

"She was quite upset, actually. She was down at a house party in Sussex and she had left her maid in London. She had no idea what the maid would have been doing near the aerodrome when her mistress wasn't planning to return to London for several days and had given her maid no instructions to leave the residence."

"I wish I could help you, Sir William," I said, "but as I just told you, I had no dealings with this person."

"You're a friend of this Miss Padgett, are you?"

"Not at all. I only met her once and then by chance. She happened to land her aeroplane at Croydon Aerodrome when I was visiting with friends. She knew one of our party and we went to drink a glass of champagne with her while she waited for her maid."

"I see," he said. There was a long pause. "Just an unfortunate coincidence," he went on, "but it's lucky that you're leaving London, or this might turn into another whiff of scandal that we simply can't allow."

"Is that all?" I asked. I felt as if my nerves were close to snapping. Honestly, I'd done nothing wrong and I was beginning to feel as if I were a prisoner in the dock and the black cap might be produced at any minute.

He nodded. "Well, that seems to be that, then." He glanced at his watch. "If we made a dash for King's Cross, we might still catch today's Flying Scotsman. It leaves at ten o'clock, doesn't it?"

"Today's Flying Scotsman?" I stared at him, open-mouthed. "I will need some time to pack, you know. I can't just up and go to Scotland."

"Have your maid do it for you, and she can follow on a later train. Surely you have the bulk of your clothing at Castle Rannoch?"

Now I was feeling both angry and flustered. "Contrary to popular belief, all aristocrats are not rich enough to own a vast wardrobe. The few items of clothing I possess are with me in London."

"But you can do without them until tonight. I'll have my man drive you via Belgrave Square so that you can give your maid instructions and pick up the odd toiletry."

"I have no maid at the moment," I reminded him.

"No maid? You've been living in Rannoch House alone?" His manner implied that I had indeed been operating the suspected house of ill repute.

"I can't afford a maid," I said. "Which is why I've been trying to find work."

"Dear me." He gave an embarrassed sort of cough and tapped his pipe into the ashtray. "And I suppose I can't expect you to travel by a slow train to Edinburgh, and the overnight Pullman into Glasgow won't work then?"

"I can't make an easy connection from Glasgow, nor expect our chauffeur to meet me there," I said.

"Very well, it had better be tomorrow then. I'll have my girl book your seat. And I can't urge you strongly enough to talk to nobody in the meantime."

"I presume you want me to telephone my brother to let him know I'm coming?" I said.

"Don't worry, that's been taken care of," he said.

I felt myself flushing red again, wondering just what had been said. Would it be clear to all that I had been sent home in disgrace like a naughty schoolgirl? Sir William rose to his feet. "Very well, you'd better get going. Don't answer the telephone whatever you do, and if you can draw the blinds and make the house appear to be unoccupied, so much the better. My man will call for you in the morning."

Annoyance was gradually overtaking fear. This man was ordering me around as if he was my superior in the army.

"And if I choose not to go?" I demanded.

"I should have no alternative but to bring the matter to the attention of Their Majesties. I should hope you'd wish to spare them any embarrassment. Besides, I understand you are expected at Balmoral in the near future anyway. You are merely putting forward your arrival by a few days. Simple as that. Off you go then. Enjoy the grouse shooting, you lucky devil. Wish I could be up there instead of stuck behind this desk."

And he gave me a hearty laugh, playing the benevolent uncle now that I was following his wishes. I nodded coldly and left the room with as much dignity as I could muster.

Chapter 6

Rannoch House
Still August 16

I felt as if I was about to explode as I let myself into Rannoch House under the watchful eye of the young constable. In truth I suspect that the anger I felt was a result of my embarrassment and humiliation. I just prayed that Sir William hadn't revealed my gaffe to Binky and Fig. Binky would think it was a huge joke, but I could just picture Fig giving me that withering look and going on about how I'd let the family down and suggesting it was my mother's inferior blood coming out again. This of course turned my thoughts to my grandfather. He was the one person I would dearly have loved to see at this moment because I needed a good hug. Belinda would be no use, even if she wasn't currently in Paolo's arms. She'd think the whole thing was screamingly funny. "You of all people pretending to be a call girl, darling," she'd say. "The one remaining virgin in London!"

But my grandfather was not on the telephone and I didn't think Sir William would take kindly to my gadding around on a tube train. So I packed the sort of clothes one needs in Scotland, then sat in the gloomy kitchen below stairs, sipping a cup of tea. At that moment the telephone rang. I jumped up but remembered the instruction not to answer it. A little later it rang again. Now my nerves were seriously rattled. Had the press twigged to me after all? Or was it a potential client who had discovered my advertisement in yesterday's newspaper? I moved uneasily about the house, occasionally peeping through the closed blinds of the front bedroom to see if any reporters had stationed themselves in the square.

Then at about five o'clock there was a loud knock at the front door. I rushed to the bedroom window and tried to see who was there, but the front door is under a covered portico. It could have been Belinda of course, but the knock had somehow sounded mannish and demanding. It came again. I held my breath. If it was someone from Scotland Yard, then it was their own silly fault that I wasn't answering the door. I was obeying instructions. I watched and waited and eventually I saw a man walking away from the house. An oldish man, not too well dressed. Then suddenly there was something about the walk I recognized. Forgetting all instructions, I rushed down the stairs, flung open the front door and sprinted down the street after the retreating figure.

"Granddad!" I shouted.

He turned around and his face broke into a big smile. "Well, there you are after all, ducks. You had me worried for a moment there. Did I wake you from a little nap?"

"Not at all," I said. "I was instructed not to open the door. Come inside and I'll tell you all about it."

I almost dragged him back inside Rannoch House, glancing around for reporters lurking in the bushes inside the gardens. I know the gardens are private and require a resident's key to enter, but reporters are notoriously resourceful and can leap iron railings when required.

"What's this all about, my love?" he asked as I shut the front door behind us with a sigh of relief. "Are you in some kind of trouble? I suspected as much when that bloke told me you'd been to my house—the one day I was away, of course. Went on the annual outing to Clacton."

"How was it?" I asked.

"Smashing. All that fresh sea air did a power of good to these old lungs. I felt like a new man by the time we came home."

I looked at him critically. I knew his health hadn't been good for some time and he didn't look well. A stab of worry shot through me that I might lose the one rock in my life, coupled with a pang of regret that I wasn't in a position to do more for him. I wished I could send him to the seaside for the summer.

"So what's up, ducks?" he asked me. "Come and make a cup of tea and you can tell your old granddad all about it."

We went down to the kitchen and put on the kettle while I told him the whole story. "Blimey," he said, trying not to grin, "you do get yourself into a right pickle, don't you? Escort service? High-class girls?"

"How was I to know?" I demanded hotly.

"You weren't. Brought up too sheltered, that's your trouble. But next time you have any bright ideas, you run them past your old granddad first."

"All right." I had to smile.

"Anyway, no harm done," he said. "You're lucky you got out of it as easily as you did."

"I wouldn't have if Darcy hadn't been at the nightclub," I confessed. "He stepped in and rescued me. And the bad thing is that somehow Scotland Yard got wind of this and they are shipping me off to Scotland posthaste, just in case any reporters stumble upon it."

"That's going overboard, isn't it? What if a reporter did stumble upon it? You'd just say it was a poorly worded advertisement."

"Scotland Yard is getting the *Times* to say the telephone number was an error. They think I'd be embarrassing the Crown."

"No more than their own son is embarrassing them," Granddad said. "Has he still got that married American woman in tow?"

"As far as I know. I must say the press is being wonderfully discreet about it. It hasn't made the papers at all."

"Because Their Majesties have requested it be kept hush-hush."

The kettle boiled and I made tea while Granddad perched on a hard kitchen chair, watching me. "So you're to be shipped back to Scotland, are you? To Balmoral or to your brother?"

"Castle Rannoch. My Balmoral invitation is not for over another week."

"I can't see your sister-in-law throwing out the red carpet for you."

"Neither can I," I said. "In fact I'm rather dreading it, much as I adore being in Scotland at this time of year."

"Don't you let her push you around," Granddad said. "It's your home. You were born in it. Your father was a duke, and the grandson of the old queen; hers was just a baronet who got his title for lending Charles the Second money to pay his gambling debts. Remind her of that."

I laughed. "Granddad, you're awful. And I believe you're a bit of a snob at heart."

"I know my place and I don't claim to be what I'm not,"

he said. "I don't have no time for people who give themselves airs about their station."

I gazed at him wistfully. "I wish you were coming with me," I said.

"Now can you see me huntin' and shootin' and hobnobbing with the gentry?" He chuckled, and the chuckle turned into a wheezing cough. "Like I said, I know my place, my love. You live in your world and I live in mine. You go home and have a lovely time up there. I'll see you when you get back."

Chapter 7

The Flying Scotsman, traveling north
August 17, 1932
Going home. Excited and dreading it at the same time.
Lovely day. Bright and warm.

The next morning I sat in a first-class compartment on the Flying Scotsman as the countryside flashed past, bathed in sunlight. It was all very pleasant and rural, but my head was swimming with conflicting emotions. I was going home—back to a place I loved. Nanny still lived in a cottage on the estate, my horse was waiting for me in the stable, and my brother would be pleased to see me, even if Fig wasn't. The thought of Fig clutched at my stomach. I wasn't afraid of her, but it is never pleasant to know that one is not wanted. I wondered what Sir William had said to her. Would she know that I'd been sent home in disgrace?

Outside in the corridor I was conscious of a bell ringing and a voice announcing the first sitting for luncheon. Luncheon in the dining car was something I would not normally have allowed myself in my present impecunious state, but today I felt I deserved it. After all, for the foreseeable future I'd not be fending for myself, and someone at Scotland Yard had paid for my train ticket. I got up, glanced in the mirror to make sure I looked respectable then came out of my compartment into the corridor, almost colliding with a person emerging from the next compartment. He was a rather good-looking young man, tall, with blond hair, brilliantined into a set of pretentious waves, and wearing a sporty-looking blazer and slacks.

"Frightfully sorry," he muttered, then he appeared to really notice me. His eyes traveled over me in the way that eyes usually traveled over Belinda. "Well, hello there," he said in what I suppose was a slow, sexy drawl. "I say, what a lucky coincidence to find someone like you in the next compartment. Here was I, steeling myself for eight hours of boredom and the crossword puzzle. Instead I bump into a frightfully pretty girl, and what's more, a pretty girl who appears to be alone." He glanced up and down the empty corridor. "Look here, I was on my way to the cocktail lounge. Care to accompany me for a drink, old bean? One simply can't survive without a gin and tonic at this time of day."

Part of me was tempted to go with him; the other part was affronted at the way he had been mentally undressing me. This didn't happen to me often and I wasn't sure whether I should enjoy it or not. As always in moments of stress, I reverted to type. "It's frightfully kind of you, but I was on my way to the dining car."

"It's only the first sitting. Nobody goes to the first sitting except for aged spinsters and vicars. Come on, be a sport. Come and keep me company with a cocktail. It's a train, you know. The rules of society are bent when traveling."

"All right," I said.

"Jolly good. Off we go then." He took my elbow and steered me in the direction of the cocktail bar. "Are you going up to Scotland for the grouse shoot?" he asked as we maneuvered unsteadily forward against the rocking of the train.

"I'm going to visit family," I said over my shoulder, "but I expect I'll do a little shooting. How about you?"

"I may do a little shooting myself but I'm particularly going to watch a chum of mine try out his new boat. He's designed this fiendish contraption with which he plans to break the world water speed record. He's going to be trying it out on some ghastly Scottish lake, so a group of us decided to come along as a cheering section."

"Really?" I said. "Where shall you be staying?"

"I've managed to wheedle a sort of invitation to a place nearby called Castle Rannoch," he said. "I was at school with the duke, y'know. I must say the old school tie works wonders everywhere. But I can't say I'm looking forward to the castle with great anticipation. Positively medieval by the sound of it. No decent plumbing or heating and family ghosts on the battlements. And the live occupants sound equally dreary, but it really will be dashed convenient for all the excitement so I expect I'll be able to stomach it for a few days. How about you? Where are you staying?"

"At Castle Rannoch," I said smoothly. "It's my family home."

"Oh, blast it." He flushed bright pink. "Don't tell me you're Binky's sister. I really have bally well put my foot in it, haven't I?"

"Yes, you do seem to have," I said. "Now, please excuse me. I don't want to miss the first sitting at luncheon with the vicars and spinsters." I spun away from him and stalked off fast in the opposite direction.

The dining room was quite full by the time I arrived, and not just with the threatened spinsters and vicars, but I was found an empty table and handed a menu. I noticed a man seated opposite me staring with interest. He was an older military type—slim, upright bearing and neat little mustache, and I wondered if he made a habit of picking up young women on trains. In fact he half rose to his feet, as if to come in my direction, when he was beaten to it by another man.

"I'm frightfully sorry," the latter said in high, breathless tones, "but the whole wretched place appears to be occupied so I wondered if you'd mind frightfully if I joined you. I promise that I don't slurp my soup or drink my tea from the saucer."

He was the complete physical opposite of the other man— short, chubby and pink, with a dapper little mustache and a carnation in his buttonhole. His dark hair was carefully combed to cover a bald spot. Completely inoffensive in any case and he was giving me a hopeful smile. He could even have been one of the aforementioned vicars, traveling minus dog collar.

"Of course," I said. "Do sit down."

"Splendid. Splendid," he said, beaming at me now. He took out a crisp white handkerchief and mopped his brow. "Warm on this train, isn't it? They'll all get a frightful shock when they reach Scotland and the usual howling gale is blowing."

"Do you live in Scotland?" I asked.

"Good lord, no. I'm a cosmopolitan bird myself. London and Paris, that's me." Then he extended a pink, chubby hand. "I should introduce myself. I'm Godfrey Beverley. I write a little column for the *Morning Post*. It's called 'Tittle Tattle.' All the juicy gossip about what's going on around town. You've probably heard of me."

A small alarm bell was going off in my head. This man was part of the press. Was he ingratiating himself to me so that he could get the inside scoop on my current rapid departure from London?

"I'm sorry," I said smoothly, "but we take the *Times*, and I pay no attention to gossip."

"But my dear young lady, you must be one in a million if you don't find gossip utterly delicious," he said, looking up expectantly as soup plates were delivered to our table.

"Ah, vichyssoise—my favorite," he said, beaming again. "I've heard they do a decent meal on this train these days. So much better than when they used to stop for lunch at York and we all had to cram down awful sausage rolls in twenty minutes. And I didn't get a chance to ask you your name, my dear."

I tried to come up with an innocuous name and was just about to say Maggie McGregor, which was the name of my maid at home, when the maitre d' appeared at our table. "Some wine for you, your ladyship?" he asked.

"Uh, no, thank you," I stammered.

"Your ladyship?" My table companion was gazing at me in eager anticipation. He put a hand to his mouth like a naughty child caught at the biscuit barrel. "Oh, heavens above, how silly of me. Of course. I recognize you now from your pictures in the *Tattler*. You're Lady Georgiana, aren't you? The king's cousin. How absolutely crass of me not to recognize you. And here I was thinking you were an ordinary wholesome young girl going home from boarding school or university. You must have thought me frightfully presumptuous, trying to sit at your table. And how gracious you were about it too. Please do forgive my boorishness." He half rose to his feet.

"Not at all," I said, smiling to calm his fluster. "And please do stay. I hate to eat alone."

"You are too, too kind, your ladyship." He was positively bowing now.

"And I am an ordinary wholesome young woman," I said. "I am going home to visit my family."

"To Castle Rannoch? How delightful. I shall be staying at my favorite inn, not far from you. I always like to go up to Scotland during the season. Everybody who is anybody is there, of course, and there is always the chance that your esteemed family members will appear from Balmoral and mingle with humble commoners like myself from time to time." He paused to work his way through the soup. "I presume you have been invited to Balmoral?"

"Yes, one is always expected to put in an appearance each season," I said, "but I plan to spend a few days at home on the family estate first."

"They must all miss you so much when you are away," he said. "Have you been traveling in Europe?"

"No, I've been in London for most of the time," I said, then I remembered that he was Mr. Tittle Tattle. "Of course one visits friends frequently at their country houses. I'm a country girl at heart. I can't stay in the city for too long."

"How true, how true," he said. "So do tell me with whom you have stayed recently. Any juicy scandals?"

"Not since the German princess," I said, knowing he would be fully conversant with that one.

"My dear, wasn't that awful? You are so lucky to have escaped with your life, from what one hears."

The empty soup plates were whisked away to be replaced with roast pheasant, new potatoes and peas. Godfrey Beverley beamed again. "I have to confess that I do adore pheasant," he said, and tucked in with relish.

"So tell me," he asked after he had demolished most of the food on his plate, "what is this we hear about your esteemed cousin the Prince of Wales and his new companion?

Is it true what they are saying, that she is a married woman? Twice married, in fact? And an American to boot?"

"I'm afraid the Prince of Wales does not confide in me about his lady friends," I said. "He still sees me as a schoolgirl."

"How shortsighted when you have blossomed into such a lovely young woman."

I was about to remind him that he had also taken me for a schoolgirl, and he must have remembered at the same moment because he became flustered again and started playing with his bread roll. The plates were removed and a delicious-looking queen pudding was placed in front of us.

"I wonder if *she* will be up in Scotland?" he asked in conspiratorial undertones.

"She?"

"The mysterious American woman about whom the rumors are flying," he whispered. "She certainly wouldn't be invited to Balmoral, but I do hope to catch a glimpse of her. They say she is the height of fashion—which reminds me, have you seen much of your dear mother lately? I am inordinately fond of your dear mama."

"Are you?" My hostility toward him melted a little.

"Of course. I adore that woman. I worship the ground she treads upon. She has provided me with more material for my columns than any other human being. Such a deliciously naughty life she has led."

The hostility returned. "I see very little of her these days," I said. "I believe she is still in Germany."

"Oh no, my dear. She's been in England for the past couple of weeks at least. I spotted her at the Café Royal the other evening. And she sang with Noel Coward at the Café de Paris the other night. There is a rumor he's writing a play for her. You wouldn't happen to know if that's true, would you?"

"You obviously know more about her than I do," I said, feeling ridiculously hurt that she had been in London and hadn't contacted me once. Not that she had contacted me for months on end when I was growing up or away at school. The maternal instinct never ran strongly through her veins, I suspect.

I managed to eat my meringue without shattering white bits all over me and also managed a couple of polite answers to Mr. Beverley's persistent questions over coffee. With great relief I drained my cup and called over the steward to pay my bill.

"Already taken care of, your ladyship," the steward said.

I looked around the car, a little flustered over who might have been treating me to lunch. It certainly wasn't Mr. Beverley. He was counting out his money onto the tablecloth. Then I decided that perhaps Sir William might have arranged this, trying to soften the blow of my having to leave London in disgrace, I suppose.

I rose and nodded to Mr. Beverley, who also staggered to his feet. "My lady, I can't tell you what a pleasure it was to make your acquaintance," he said. "And I do hope that this will be the first of many meetings. Who knows, perhaps you will be free to take tea with me one day while I am at the inn. There is a delightful little teahouse nearby. The Copper Kettle. Do you know it?"

"I usually take tea with the family when I am home," I said, "but I'm sure we'll bump into each other at some stage, if you are planning to stay in Scotland long. Maybe at one of the shoots?"

At this he turned pale. "Oh, deary me, no. I do not relish killing things, Lady Georgiana. Such a barbaric custom."

I almost reminded him that he had tucked into the pheasant with obvious relish and that somebody had had to kill it at some stage, but I was more anxious to make an exit while I could.

"Please excuse me," I said. "I was up very early this morning and I think I need to rest after lunch." I gave him the gracious royal nod and retreated to my compartment. Really this had been a most tiresome two days. It was with great expectation that I thought of home.

Chapter 8

Still on the train
August 17

The compartment was warm with afternoon sun and I was replete with a good lunch. I must have dozed off because a small sound woke me. The slightest of clicks, but enough to make me open my eyes. When I did, I sat up in alarm. A man was in my compartment. What's more, he was in the process of closing the curtains to the corridor. It was the military-looking man who had been eyeing me closely in the dining car.

"What do you think you are doing?" I demanded, leaping to my feet. "Please leave this compartment at once, or I shall be obliged to pull the communication cord and stop this train."

At that he chuckled. "I've always wanted to see that done," he said. "I wonder how long it takes to stop an express going at seventy miles an hour? A good half mile, I'd guess."

"If you've come to rob me, I have to warn you that I am

traveling with nothing of value," I said haughtily, "and if you've come to assault me, I can assure you that I am blessed with a good punch and a loud scream."

At this he laughed. "Oh yes, I see what they mean. I think you'll do very well." He sat down without being asked. "I assure you that I mean you no harm, my lady, and I ask you to forgive the unorthodox method of introduction. I tried to introduce myself to you in the dining car but that odious little man beat me to it." He leaned closer to me. "Allow me to introduce myself now. I am Sir Jeremy Danville. I work for the Home Office."

Oh, golly, I thought. Someone else from the government making sure I got home safely and caused no royal scandal. He probably wanted to know what I'd told Godfrey Beverley.

"I caught this train deliberately," he said, "knowing that we could talk without danger of being overheard. First I want your word that what I am going to say to you will never be repeated to anyone, not even to a family member."

This was unexpected and I was still in the process of waking up from my doze. "I don't see how I can agree to something when I have no idea what it is," I said.

"If I told you it concerns the safety of the monarchy?" He looked at me long and hard.

"Very well, I suppose," I said.

I began to feel a little as Anne Boleyn must have done when she was summoned to the Tower and discovered it wasn't for a quiet dinner party. It crossed my mind that someone might have telephoned the queen over my little gaffe and I was about to be dispatched posthaste to be lady-in-waiting to a distant relative in the Outer Hebrides.

Sir Jeremy cleared his throat. "Lady Georgiana, we at the Home Office are not unaware of the part you played in uncovering a plot against Their Majesties," he said. "You showed considerable spunk and resourcefulness. So we decided you might be the ideal person for a little task involving the royal family."

He paused. I waited. He seemed to expect me to say something but I couldn't think of anything to say as I had no idea as to what might come next.

"Lady Geogiana," he resumed, "the Prince of Wales has recently had a series of unfortunate accidents—a wheel that came loose on his car, a saddle girth that broke on his polo pony. Fortunately he was unharmed on both occasions. These could, of course, be deemed unlucky coincidences, but as we looked at them more closely, we found that the Duke of York and his other brothers had also experienced similar unlucky accidents. We have come to the conclusion that someone is trying to harm or even kill members of the royal family, or more accurately heirs to the throne."

"Golly," I exclaimed. "Do you think it's the communists at work again?"

"We did consider that possibility," Sir Jeremy said gravely. "Some outside power trying to destabilize the country. However, the situation and nature of some of these accidents draw us to a rather startling conclusion: they appear to be what one might call 'an inside job.' "

I went to say "golly" again and swallowed it down at the last moment. It did sound a trifle schoolgirlish. "You mean someone has infiltrated the palace?" I said. "I suppose that's not completely impossible. After all, one of the communists managed it in Bavaria."

"We don't think it is the communists this time," Sir Jeffrey said bluntly. "We think it's closer to home."

"Someone connected to the family?"

He nodded. "Which makes our surveillance rather difficult. Naturally we have our special branch men protecting the Prince of Wales and his brothers to the best of our ability, but there are times and places when we can't be present. That's where you come in. They're all currently at Balmoral for the grouse shooting."

"Well, that's all right then, isn't it?" I looked up at Sir Jeremy. "They'll be safely out of harm's way up there."

"On the contrary. The Prince of Wales had a near miss while out driving only yesterday when the steering locked on the shooting brake he was driving."

"Gol—gosh," I stammered.

"So you see we were glad to know that you were on your way home. You are part of their inner circle. You can move freely among them. You'll be the ideal person to keep your eyes and ears open for us."

"I'm not actually invited to Balmoral for another week," I said.

"That's no problem. Castle Rannoch is close enough, and several members of the Balmoral shooting party are currently staying with your brother. We'll let Their Majesties know that you will be arriving early and will be joining the shoot as part of your brother's house party."

House party! That certainly didn't sound like Fig. Surely no guests would stay long enough at Castle Rannoch to shoot anything, particularly if Fig displayed her usual meanness and allowed only half a slice of toast each for breakfast and two inches of hot water in the bathtub. Another thought struck me.

"Do Their Majesties know about this?"

"Nobody knows except for a handful of our men," Sir Jeremy said. "Not even the Prince of Wales or his brothers suspect that these are anything more than accidents. In fact the Prince of Wales made a joke that he should probably check his horoscope before venturing out. And nobody is to know. Not the slightest hint, you understand. If this is true, then we are dealing with a cunning and ruthless person, and I want to make sure that we nab him before he manages to do some real damage."

"And you have no idea who this person might be?"

"None at all. We've conducted a thorough check into the backgrounds of all the royal staff, in fact into all those who might have access to the Prince of Wales and his brothers. And we've come up empty."

"I see. So you weren't exaggerating when you said it was one of us. You really meant one of our inner circle."

"As you say, your inner circle." Sir Jeremy nodded gravely. "All we ask of you is to keep your eyes and ears open. Our man on the spot will make himself known to you and you can report anything suspicious to him. Naturally we do not expect you to place yourself in any kind of danger. We can count on you, can't we?"

It was hard to make my tongue obey me. "Yes. Of course." It came out as a squeak.

Chapter 9

Castle Rannoch
Perthshire, Scotland
August 17

Night had not quite fallen as our aged Bentley turned into the driveway leading to Castle Rannoch. The sun sets very late in summer in Scotland and although I could see the lights from the castle winking through the Scots pine trees, the horizon behind the mountains still glowed pink and gold. It was a rare glorious evening and my heart leaped at the familiar surroundings. How often had I ridden my pony along that track. There was the rock from which Binky dared me to dive into the loch, and there was the crag that I alone had managed to climb. Beyond the fence our Highland cattle looked at the motorcar with curiosity, turning their big, shaggy heads to follow our progress.

All the way home my spirits had been rising as we left the city of Edinburgh and climbed through wooded countryside before emerging onto the bleak, windswept expanse of the Highlands, with peaks rising around us and burns dancing in cascades beside the road. Whatever might happen next, I was home. As to what might happen next, I decided to put it from my mind tonight. It was all too worrying, and what's more I was starting to smell a rat. I had a distinct impression that I was being used. The convenient way I was summoned to Sir William, shamed into agreeing to retreat to Scotland immediately, only to find Sir Jeremy on the train—it was all too pat. Did the police really scan the advertisement page in the *Times* every day? Did they really check on every suspicious telephone number? And was it really such a sin to run an escort service? Then something occurred to me that made me go hot all over: Darcy. I knew he did something secret, which he wouldn't discuss. In fact I suspected he was some kind of spy. Had he tipped off the Home Office about my little gaffe, thus giving them a brilliant excuse to pack me off to Scotland without alarming me unduly?

They could have just summoned me to the Home Office and told me what they wanted me to do, but then I suppose I could have refused. Under this little scheme I was a sitting duck for their plans, with no way of wriggling out of the journey. And it seemed more and more likely, as I played everything over in my head, that Darcy was the one who had instigated the whole thing. Some friend, I thought. Betraying me and then setting me up for a difficult and maybe dangerous assignment. I am well rid of him.

The tires of the Bentley scrunched on the gravel as the car came to a halt outside the front door. The chauffeur jumped out to open my door but before it was fully open the castle door opened, light streamed out and our butler, Hamilton, appeared.

"Welcome home, my lady," he said. "It is so good to have you back."

So far, so good. At least someone was pleased to see me.

"It's good to be back, Hamilton," I replied and went up

the worn steps and in through the big front door. After a small anteroom lined with stags' heads, one steps into the great hall, the center of life at Castle Rannoch. It rises two stories high with a gallery running around it. On one side is a giant stone fireplace big enough to roast an ox. On the wood-paneled walls hang swords, shields, tattered banners carried into long-ago battles, more stags' heads. A wide staircase sweeps up one side, lined with portraits of Rannoch ancestors, each generation hairier as one went back in time. The floor is stone, making the hall feel doubly cold and drafty, and there are various sofas and armchairs grouped around the fire, which is never lit in summer, however cold the weather.

To outsiders the first impression is horribly cold, gloomy and warlike, but to me at this moment it represented home. I was just looking around with satisfaction when Fig appeared in the gallery above.

"Georgiana, you're back. Thank God," she said, her voice echoing from the high ceiling. She actually ran down the stairs to meet me.

This was not the reception I had expected and I stared at her blankly as she ran toward me, arms open, and actually embraced me. She'd called me by my name so she couldn't have mistaken me for anyone else. Besides, Fig doesn't make anyone welcome, ever.

"How are you, Fig?" I asked.

"Awful. I can't tell you how frightful it's been. That's why I'm glad you're here, Georgiana."

"What's wrong?" I asked.

"Everything. Let's go into Binky's den, shall we?" she said, slipping her arm through mine. "We are not likely to be disturbed there. You'd like something to eat, I suspect. Hamilton, could you have the drinks tray and a plate of those smoked salmon sandwiches brought through for Lady Georgiana?"

All right. This was Scotland, after all. My sister-in-law had been bewitched, or taken by the fairies and a changeling left in her place. But since she was offering me smoked salmon and the drinks tray, who was I to refuse? She steered me across the great hall, down the narrow passage to the right and in through an oak-paneled door. The room had the familiar smell of pipe smoke and polished wood and old books: a very masculine sort of smell. Fig indicated a leather armchair for me and pulled up another one beside me.

"Thank God," she said again. "I don't think I could have endured it for another day alone."

"Alone? What's happened to Binky?"

"You didn't hear about his dreadful accident then?"

"No. What happened?"

"He stepped on a trap."

"An animal trap?"

"Of course an animal trap."

"When did MacTavish start using animal traps on the estate? I thought he was always so softhearted."

"He doesn't. He swears he never laid the trap, but he must have done, of course. Who else would put a bally great trap on one of our paths, and especially a path that Binky always walks in the morning?"

"Crikey. Is Binky all right?"

"Of course he's not all right," she snapped, reverting to type for the first time. "He's laid up with a dashed great dressing over his ankle. In fact he was extremely lucky he was wearing those old boots that belonged to his grandfather. I kept telling him to throw them away but now I'm glad he didn't listen to me. Anything less stout and the trap would have had his foot off. As it was the trap wouldn't close completely and he got away with nasty gashes down to the bone and a cut tendon."

"Poor old Binky. How terrible for him."

"Terrible for him? What about terrible for me with all these awful people in the house?"

"What awful people?"

"My dear, we have a house full of disgusting Americans."

"Paying guests?"

"Of course not paying guests. What on earth gave you that idea? Since when did a duke take in paying guests? No, these are friends of the Prince of Wales, or rather a certain woman among them is a friend of the Prince of Wales."

"Oh, I see. Her."

"As you say, 'Her.' The prince is at Balmoral, of course, and his woman friend would certainly not be welcome there, so the prince asked Binky if he could offer her hospitality so she'd be close enough to visit. And you know Binky—always too softhearted. Can't say no to anybody. And he looks up to the prince, always has done. So of course he said yes."

I nodded with sympathy.

"And the prince suggested that maybe we build a little house party around her and her husband—oh, did I mention that she still has a husband in tow? Mooches around like a lost sheep, poor fellow. Spends his time playing billiards. Can't even shoot. So Binky goes ahead and invites some people to make up a house party—the cousins, of all people, to start with."

"Which cousins?"

"On the Scottish side. You know that dreadful hairy pair, Lachan and Murdoch."

"Oh yes. I remember well." Lachan and Murdoch had always rather terrified me with their wild Highland appearance and behavior. I remember Murdoch demonstrating how to toss the caber with a fallen pine tree and hurling it through a window.

"Well, my dear, they haven't improved with age, and you have no idea how much they eat and drink."

I had a pretty good idea, if Murdoch's caber tossing was any indication. We broke off as there was a discreet tap at the door and Hamilton entered, bearing a tray with a neat pile of sandwiches decorated with watercress, a decanter containing Scotch, and two glasses.

"Thank you, Hamilton," I said.

"My lady." He nodded, smiling at me with obvious pleasure. "May I pour you a little sustenance?" and without waiting for the go-ahead, he poured a liberal amount into one of the tumblers. "And for you, Your Grace?"

"Why not?" Fig said. This was also unusual. She normally drank nothing stronger than the occasional Pimm's on summer outings. But she took hers instantly and had a jolly good swig. I tucked into a sandwich. Local smoked salmon. Mrs. McPherson's freshly baked bread. I couldn't remember tasting anything more divine. Hamilton retreated.

"But that's not the worst part of it," Fig said, putting her empty glass back on the tray with a loud bang.

"It's not?" I wondered what was coming next.

"The dreadful American woman arrived and guess what? She's brought her own house party with her. The place is positively crawling with Americans. They are eating us out of house and home, Georgiana, and you have no idea how demanding they are. They want showers instead of baths, for one thing. They told me that baths are quite unhygienic. What can be unhygienic about a bath, for heaven's sake? It's full of water, isn't it? Anyway, they had the servants rig up a shower contraption in the second-floor bathroom, and then it fell on some woman's head and she was screaming that she'd been scalded and got a concussion."

I gave a sympathetic grin.

"And what's more, they are always taking showers and baths. They want them every day, can you imagine? And at all times of the day and night. I told them that nobody can possibly get that dirty in so short a time, but they bathe every time they come in from a walk, before dinner, after dinner. It's a wonder they're not completely washed away. And as for drinking . . . my dear, they want cocktails, and they're always experimenting with new cocktails. They used Binky's twenty-year-old single-malt Scotch to make some drink with orange juice and maraschino cherries. I'm only glad that Binky was lying in agony upstairs and didn't see them. I tell you it would have finished him off on the spot."

For the first time in my life I looked at my sister-in-law with some sympathy. She was definitely looking frazzled. Her short, almost mannishly bobbed hair was usually perfectly in place and it currently looked as if she'd come in from a gale. What's more she had spilled something down the front of her gray silk dinner gown. Tomato soup, I'd gather.

"It must have been terribly trying for you," I said. "And as for poor Binky . . ."

"Binky?" she shrieked. "Binky is lying up there being fussed over by Nanny and Mrs. MacTavish. All he has is a mangled ankle. I have Americans."

"Chin up. It can't be for too much longer," I said. "Nobody stays in Scotland for more than a week or so."

"By the end of a week or so we shall be destitute," she said, her voice dangerously near to tears. "Eaten out of house and home, literally. I'll have to take in paying guests to make ends meet. Binky will have to sell of the rest of the family silver."

I put out a tentative hand and rested it over hers. I believe it was the first time I had willingly touched her. "Don't worry, Fig. We'll think of something," I said.

She looked up at me and beamed. "I knew I could rely on you, Georgiana. I am so glad you're here."

Chapter 10

As we emerged from Binky's den and came down the corridor to the great hall, a noisy party was coming out of the drawing room, at the far end of the opposite hallway.

"And so I said to him, 'You simply don't have the equipment, honey,' and he said, 'I've got a bloody great big one, and what's more, when it's revved up, it goes like a ramrod.' He thought we were still talking about the boat."

There was a roar of laughter. Even though they were still a good distance away and bathed in shadow, I recognized the speaker before I could get a good look at her. It was, of course, the dreaded American woman, Mrs. Wallis Simpson. As she came closer I noticed that she was looking rather thin, angular and masculine in a metallic pewter-gray evening dress and matching metallic helmet. And old. She was definitely beginning to look her age, I thought with satisfaction.

"Wallis, honey, you are shameless." The speaker was an

older woman, dressed in sober black. She was statuesque in build and towered over Mrs. Simpson, but she carried herself well with a regal air, rather like a larger version of Queen Mary. "How you can tell tales like that in public I don't know. Thank heavens Rudi is not still alive to hear."

"Oh, don't come the countess with me, Merion," Wallis Simpson said. "I remember you when you were plain old Miss Webster, remember? You took me for root beer floats at Mr. Hinkle's soda fountain in Baltimore when I was just a toddler, and you flirted with that young guy behind the counter!"

"Who is that?" I murmured to Fig, indicating the older woman.

"Oh, she's the Countess Von Sauer."

"I thought you said they were all Americans."

"They are. She's part of the Simpson woman's party. She was originally called something perfectly ordinary like Webster but she did her tour of Europe and snagged herself an Austrian count. I don't think the Simpson woman has forgiven her for one-upping her on the social scale."

"She's trying hard enough to remedy that now," I muttered to Fig.

"She certainly is. The Prince of Wales has been over here to visit almost every evening. I told him I didn't approve and he said I was a prude. When have I ever been a prude, Georgiana? I consider myself as broad-minded as anybody. After all, I did grow up on a farm."

"Fritzi, honey, I left my wrap. Be an angel and fetch it for me or I shall freeze." The countess turned to a large, pink young man who was trailing at the back of the party. "It's positively frigid in here. It makes our Austrian castle feel like the Côte d'Azur."

"Mama, you're always forgetting things. I shall be worn

to a rail if you keep me running around like this. Do you know how far it is to your room from here? And all those horrible stairs?"

I turned to Fig again.

"She's also brought her reprobate son with her," she muttered. "He piles his plate with all the good sandwiches at tea and he pinches the maids' bottoms."

"Hasn't the keep-fit movement reached Austria yet?" one of the men in the party asked. "Babe can't start the day without her gymnastics and dumbbells, can you, Babe, honey?"

"I sure can't," a petite, bony woman replied.

At that moment they emerged into the great hall and Wallis Simpson noticed me. "Why, it's the actress's daughter," she said. "What a surprise. When did you get here?"

I was still feeling angry on behalf of Fig and Binky and wasn't about to take any of her cutting remarks. "Actually it's the duke's daughter," I said, "and the current duke's sister, and the king's cousin and great-granddaughter to Queen Victoria, and you are currently a guest in my ancestral home."

"Ouch," said a man who had been lingering at the back of the party. I recognized him as Mr. Simpson, the invisible and until now silent husband. "I reckon you've met your match there, Wallis."

"Nonsense," she said with a guttural chuckle. "It's lack of sex. It makes people touchy. We should do the kind thing and get her hitched up with a gamekeeper while she's up here. Think of Lady Chatterley."

And they went into peals of laughter again.

"Who is Lady Chatterley?" Fig whispered to me.

"A character in a book, by D. H. Lawrence. It's banned over here. He had it printed in Italy, and there are smuggled copies all over the place."

"And what's so terrible about it?"

"The lady and the gamekeeper have a continuous roll in the hay together and describe it with four-letter farm words."

"How disgusting," Fig said. "I bet the writer has never seen a real gamekeeper, or he'd never have thought they had sex appeal. They smell of dead rabbits, for one thing."

"One of these days you'll go too far, Wallis," Mr. Simpson said sharply.

She glanced up at him, then put a hand up to his cheek and chuckled again. "I don't think so. I believe I know exactly how far I can go."

The big man in the party now came over to me, his hand extended. "So you're the young lady of the family, are you? Glad to meet you. I'm Earl Sanders. This is my wife, Babe."

I shook hands all around. I noticed Mrs. Simpson didn't offer hers.

"So who is up for whist or bridge?" Wallis Simpson asked. "Or shall we be devils and play roulette?"

"I'm afraid we don't possess a roulette wheel," Fig said frostily. "If we choose to gamble, we go to Monte Carlo."

"Don't worry, Earl's brought his own," Mrs. Simpson said. "He can't go more than a day without gambling, can you, Earl honey?"

"The question is where are we going to play without freezing to death and without having the cards blown away by a howling gale?" the Countess Von Sauer asked. "Surely not in here."

"I was sensible enough to bring my mink," Babe said. Her morning keep-fit regimen was certainly paying off. She hadn't an ounce of spare flesh on her and made the angular Mrs. Simpson look positively feminine. No wonder she was cold. She turned to her husband and retrieved the fur from him, wrapping it snugly around her shoulders. "I even wore it in bed last night. My dears, the draft from that window. It wouldn't close properly and there was a hurricane blowing."

"Will the drawing room not do?" Fig asked. "I can have the servants move back the sofas and set up tables."

"There are some rather loud young men in there, smoking up a storm and working their way through the whiskey decanter," Mrs. Simpson said.

"See, what did I tell you?" Fig muttered.

"Then it will have to be in here," Fig said out loud. "I'll call the servants."

"How about that nice little room that looks out on the lake?" Babe suggested. "The one where we had coffee this morning."

"But that's the morning room." Fig sounded horrified.

"So is it a crime to go in there after noon?" Wallis Simpson asked with amusement. "Really, I find all these British rules too, too fascinating."

"I suppose you can use it if you insist upon it," Fig said. "It's just that we never do. Not after luncheon."

"It's probably haunted," the big man chuckled. "The ghost only appears after the stroke of twelve midday. Babe swears she saw a white figure floating down the corridor upstairs."

"That would be the White Lady of Rannoch," I said. "Did you hear her moaning? She often moans."

"Moans?" Babe looked apprehensive.

"Frightfully," I said. "She was thrown in the loch with a great stone tied to her for being a witch. The locals also say that they see bubbles coming up from the loch and that could be the White Lady returning. Of course, it could be just the monster."

"Monster?" The countess sounded alarmed now.

"Oh yes. Didn't you hear we have a famous monster in the loch? It's been there for hundreds of years."

"Mercy me," the countess said. "I think I might skip the cards tonight and go straight to bed. Fritzi, would you pop up ahead of me and make sure there's a hot water bottle in the bed and that my nightdress is wrapped around it?"

"Of course, Mama." He nodded dutifully and went.

"Well, I need my nightly gamble," the big man said. "You guys go take a look at that morning room place and I'll go fetch the roulette wheel."

They disappeared. Fig looked at me. "Now you can see for yourself," she said. "Torment, utter torment. Did you ever hear of anyone wanting to use the morning room after luncheon?"

"Never," I agreed.

"You'd think the one who became a countess would know better, wouldn't you? She does have a castle in Austria."

"And the other man is an earl, isn't he?" I commented, watching his large retreating rear.

Fig broke into tense laughter. "No, that's just his Christian name. I made the same mistake and called his wife 'countess' and she thought it was a hoot." She went to walk ahead then turned back to me. "But tell me, what was all that about the White Lady of Rannoch? I've never heard of her."

"I made her up," I said. "It occurred to me that if you want the Americans to leave, you should make them want to leave. The occasional nighttime haunting by the family ghost might help to do the trick."

"Georgiana, you are wicked," Fig said, but she was beaming at me with admiration.

"And we can institute some other measures to make them

uncomfortable," I said. "Turn down the boiler, for one thing. We did that at Rannoch House when we wanted the German baroness to move. They won't stay if they can't get their hot showers."

"Brilliant!" Fig was still beaming.

"And does Fergus still play the pipes?" I asked, referring to one of our grooms who led the local pipe band.

"He does."

"Have him play them on the battlements at dawn, like they used to do in the old days. Oh, and serve them haggis for breakfast. . . ."

"Georgiana, I—I mean, we couldn't. Word would get back to the Prince of Wales and he'd be angry with Binky."

"What for?" I asked. "We're just carrying on our normal family traditions to make them feel welcome."

She stared at me hopefully. "Do you really think we dare?"

"Let me put it this way: how long do you want them to stay here?"

"We'll do it," she exclaimed. "We'll turn it into a castle of horrors!"

The sound of laughter erupted down the hallway from the direction of the drawing room. "And I should go and remove the whiskey decanter from those two cousins of yours," she said. "They break things when they get drunk."

"I suppose I should come and say hello," I said hesitantly.

"You should." Fig strode ahead. She pushed open the drawing room door. Two young men in kilts looked up as we came in. The room was in a fog of cigar smoke—Binky's cigars, I suspected.

"Och, hello, Cousin Fig. Come and join us," one of them said. "We're just celebrating the removal of the American terror."

"And finishing Binky's good Scotch, I notice," Fig said, holding up an almost empty decanter. "When it's gone there isn't any more, you know. We're absolutely paupers, Murdoch."

Murdoch's eyes drifted past her to see me standing in the doorway. "And who's yon bonnie wee lassie?"

"This is your cousin Georgiana," Fig said. "Georgiana, these are your cousins Lachan and Murdoch. I don't believe you've met for many years."

Two giants with sandy hair rose to their feet. They were both wearing kilts. One had a red beard and looked like the Rannoch ancestors come to life. Then I looked at the other. He was clean shaven and was—well, rather good-looking. Tall, muscled, rugged. Like a Greek god, in fact. He held out his hand to me. "No, this is never little Georgie. Remember when you used to make me play at being your horse and carry you around the estate on my back?"

"Oh, that was you." I smiled, the memory returning. "I do remember when Murdoch threw that tree trunk through the window."

"Och, he does things like that," Lachan said, still smiling down at me and still holding my hand. "So come and sit down, have a wee dram, and tell us what you've been doing."

"I've just had a drink with Fig," I said, in case she thought I might be joining the enemy. "And I've been leading a blameless life in London. How about the two of you?"

"Running the estate, mainly," Murdoch said. "We can't afford the manpower any longer so we both have to work like dogs to make a go of it."

"Apart from the times you're away at your Highland Games," Lachan pointed out.

"I win prizes at those Highland Games. Didn't I win us a pig last year? And a barrel of whiskey?"

"You did. But then you also went down to Aintree for the races and then to St. Andrew's for the golf," Lachan said with a grin.

"Well, that's business, isn't it?" Murdoch replied. "I have to go to Aintree to watch our racehorses."

"While I'm stuck at home dipping the sheep."

"Of course, I'm the elder."

"But I'm the smarter."

"You are not. Whatever put such an idea into your thick head?"

They had half risen to their feet. Fig looked at me nervously, suspecting this might come to blows. "Georgiana, you really should look in on your brother before he goes to sleep."

"Of course," I said. "Excuse me, won't you?"

"Come back when you're done," Lachan said. As I went out I heard him say, "Whoever thought that wee Georgie would turn out so nicely?"

And for the first time in ages I smiled to myself.

Chapter 11

Castle Rannoch
August 17
Now very late in the evening.

"So that's the sum total of your house party?" I asked Fig as we started to climb the staircase to Binky's room. "Two wild cousins? In which case it's lucky Mrs. Simpson brought her own friends."

"Of course that's not the sum total," Fig said. "We have two more young men staying here. I don't know where they've disappeared to."

"No other women?"

"It is a shooting party, after all," Fig said. "I believe Binky did ask a couple of females but they were busy."

I grinned to myself. It would indeed take a brave young woman to endure Castle Rannoch. "Not too many women are interested in shooting, I suppose," I said kindly.

"I can't see why not," Fig said. "I absolutely adore it."

"So who are these young men?" I asked, feeling suddenly hopeful at being the only unattached female in the group. "Anyone I know?"

"Well, you must know Prince George."

"The king's youngest son?" I asked. "Oh yes, I know him well enough." As I said it I remembered a rather disreputable party at which His Highness had begged me not to mention to anyone that I'd seen him there.

"An ex–navy officer and quite handsome," Fig went on. "A good catch for you, Georgiana."

Again I kept quiet about the look that had passed between him and the performer Noel Coward, and the fact that I'd seen him slip into the kitchen at that party, where I later found cocaine being used. Not such a good catch, in fact. But quite pleasant, as relatives went.

"I expect the king and queen have someone of higher rank than me in mind for their son," I said tactfully. "A European alliance at this unsettled time."

"Speaking of which," Fig said, and stopped short. Voices were coming down the upper corridor toward us. Male voices. One of them had a strong foreign accent.

"Shall we attempt to ascend that mountain tomorrow, do you think?"

I froze on the stairs. "No, not him!" I hissed as I recognized that voice. It was my nemesis Prince Siegfried, of the house of Hohenzollen-Sigmaringen, whom everyone expected me to marry. Since I referred to him as Fishface and knew that he prefered boys, I was less than enthusiastic about this. A horrible thought crossed my mind that this whole thing was a plot. I'd been whisked back to Scotland not to solve any crime but to be thrust together with the man I so vehemently avoided. If I spotted a priest while I was in the same room as Siegfried, I resolved to run.

"Prince Siegfried, you mean?" She looked innocently at me. "You don't like him? He has beautiful manners and he's connected to all the great houses of Europe. He might even be king someday. If anything happens to his brother."

"Like being assassinated, you mean?"

"Well, yes, but . . ." She stopped, as the speakers had come into view. They were chatting merrily and stopped in surprise when they saw us.

"Good heavens, it's Cousin Georgie," Prince George said. "When did you get here?"

"Just arrived, sir, " I said.

"I didn't know you were expected. How jolly," my cousin went on. "And look here, you don't have to call me 'sir' when we're alone. I know my father expects it at all times. Mother even makes the granddaughters curtsy to her each morning. They just can't see that all these stuffy rules are obsolete. This is the jazz age. People should be free, shouldn't they, Siegfried?"

"Not too free," Siegfried said. "Within our class, maybe. But as for encouraging the lower classes to be too familiar, I am afraid I am against it." He bowed to me and clicked his heels. "Lady Georgiana. We meet again. How delightful." He sounded about as delighted as one who has been presented with a plate of rice pudding.

"Your Highness." I nodded in return with an equal amount of enthusiasm. "What a pleasant surprise to find you here."

"So you've come to join the shooting party, have you?" Prince George asked.

"I have. Is Binky still arranging a shoot here or are you going over to Balmoral to join theirs?"

"We've been over to Balmoral a couple of times. Binky's a bit out of commission at the moment, as you've probably heard. We've just been cheering him up, haven't we, Siegfried?"

"What? Oh *ja*, absolutely."

"So why aren't you staying at Balmoral?" I asked the prince.

"Too impossibly stuffy, and Mummy going on at me to hurry up and get married. And then all the tension with David. They've heard that the Simpson woman is here, of course, and, like our great-grandmother, they are not amused." He grinned.

"Well, would you be?" I said. "The Prince of Wales will be king someday. Can you imagine a Queen Wallis, if she ever casts off her current husband?"

The prince chuckled. "I do get your point. David simply doesn't take the job seriously. He's a good enough chap, kind and generous, y'know, but he finds the affairs of state too boring and I can't say I blame him."

"You're lucky," I said. "The job won't come to you unless there is another huge flu epidemic or a massacre." I had been exchanging banter but as I said it I felt a cold shiver pass over me. Could it be true that somebody was trying to eliminate those who stood between him and the throne? I'd have to look at the succession list in the morning and see who that could possibly be. Certainly not Prince George. Being king would put an end to his current lifestyle.

"You're looking awfully pensive," he said. "Come down and have a nightcap with us. Are your fearsome cousins still ensconced in the drawing room?"

"They are."

"My God, what brutes. Throwbacks to the stone age, didn't we agree, Siegfried?"

"Oh yes, absolute brutes. We risk our lives every time we encounter them."

I stifled a giggle, as they both seemed rather enchanted with this.

"I'm on my way up to see Binky," I said, "but I'll no doubt see you in the morning. Your Highnesses." I inclined my head again.

Siegfried clicked his heels and we passed on the stairs.

"You see, Georgiana, two charming young men and you hardly say two words to them, much less flirt," Fig admonished. "You have to learn to flirt, my dear, or you'll wind up an old maid."

I stole a quick glance at her solid, angular face. I was dying to ask if she had ever flirted with Binky and if she had, why he hadn't run screaming in the opposite direction. Apart from her pedigree she didn't seem to have much going for her.

We continued along the hallway. Cold drafts swept past us, stirring the tapestries and making me think that I could easily do more with this White Lady of Rannoch idea. From outside the castle came the sound of a screech owl. Definitely a place that lent itself beautifully to ghosts and ghoulies and long-legged beasties and things that go bump in the night. At the far end Fig opened the door cautiously. "Binky, are you awake?" she whispered. "I've brought someone to see you."

My brother raised himself from his pillows and turned to look in our direction. "Georgie," he exclaimed with delight, and held out his hand to me. "What a lovely surprise. And how good of you to come. You heard about your poor brother's accident and rushed to his side, did you? I call that splendid family loyalty."

Whatever Fig had been told of the reason for my sudden arrival, she had kept wisely silent. I went over and kissed his forehead. He looked rather pale, and there was an improvised cage over his left ankle that was swathed in white linens.

"I'll leave you two to chat then," Fig said. "I'm off to bed. Those Americans have completely worn me out."

"Sleep well, old thing," Binky called after her. He looked back at me. "She's been having a beastly time of it. Glad you're here to keep her company."

"How about you? I hear you've turned poacher," I said. "Messing around with traps."

"I like that. I nearly lose my foot and my sister makes jokes about it."

"Only because I'm worried about you," I said. I perched on the bed beside him. "What a rum thing to happen, Binky."

"It most certainly was. I still can't fathom it. I mean, if someone wanted to come and poach on our estate, they wouldn't bother to walk a couple of miles from the boundary, would they? They'd nip under the fence and lay their traps in the woods where they wouldn't be noticed. This was left out among the heather on that little path up the mountain that I like to take in the mornings. You know, the one that gives the good view over the estate and the loch."

I nodded. "I used to ride up there sometimes. Lucky you weren't on horseback or it would have snapped the horse's leg."

"It damned near snapped mine," Binky said. "In fact if I hadn't been wearing what grandfather used to call his 'good stout brogues,' I'd have lost my foot, I'm sure of it. As it is, I have to keep soaking it and having revolting poultices to prevent infection, but luckily no bones were broken."

"Have you any idea who'd want to do a thing like this?" I asked.

"Some idiot who thought that the animal he was trying to trap habitually used that particular path," Binky suggested. "But as to what animal that could be, I've no idea. We've a couple of grand stags on the property at the moment but nobody could be crass enough to bring down a stag in a trap, could they?"

"If they were hungry enough and poor enough, I suppose."

"But the risk of being seen when he went to collect the stag would be enormous. Besides, how could he drag it off the property? He'd be almost in full view of the castle all the way."

"It does seem strange," I agreed. "You don't think . . ." I paused, weighing whether to say this. "You don't think the trap was meant for you?"

"For me?"

"Everyone knows you like to take that walk in the mornings."

"For me?" he repeated. "Someone wanting to harm me? But why? I'm a harmless sort of chap. No enemies that I can think of."

"Perhaps someone wants to inherit Castle Rannoch," I said, but my voice trailed off at the end. "So who would inherit Castle Rannoch if you died?"

"Why, Podge, of course," he said.

Oh, golly, Podge, his son. Was he in danger too, and how could I warn his nanny without alarming her too much?

"And after Podge?"

"That pair who are working their way through my whisky. Murdoch's the elder and then Lachan." He looked at me and laughed. "But you're not suggesting that they had something to do with this? Murdoch and Lachan? We've played together since we were boys."

"Perhaps it was just a horrible practical joke that went too far," I said.

"A practical joke? To set a trap that could take someone's leg off? Not my idea of a joke."

"I agree," I said, "but they do seem like a wild pair. Perhaps they didn't think the trap was very strong."

"They know all about traps," Binky said. "They had trouble with poachers a while back and they told me they were thinking of setting mantraps. I talked them out of it."

"So this wasn't a mantrap."

"Oh no. Definitely meant for an animal." He looked up at me sharply and then laughed. "What on earth put that into your head, Georgie? I mean to say, we're no longer in the times of the clan wars. I can't see any brazen Campbell sneaking onto the estate to have off my leg, nor any member of the Clan Rannoch trying to take over the castle. Who'd want it, for God's sake? There's no income from it. We had to sell off a good part of the land to pay the death duties, and all that's left just produces enough for our daily needs. And as for living in the castle—well, I can understand those Americans complaining like billy-o. Of course the plumbing needs updating, and of course it would be a good idea to have central heating put in, but we've simply no money to do it."

"Perhaps somebody wants the title," I suggested. "It's rather fun to be Your Grace, isn't it?"

"If you want to know the truth, it's damned embarrassing to be a penniless duke," Binky said. "I'd rather be just a plain farmer on a prosperous farm, like our cousins."

I left him soon after and went to bed. I had always thought of my room as friendly and cozy, but as I lay there and listened to the moan of the wind around the castle walls, I decided I was downright chilly. I'd have given anything for a hot water bottle, but of course it would be letting the family down to admit to being cold and asking for one. Four months of London living had made me soft.

So I curled into a tight little ball and pulled the quilt over my head. But sleep wouldn't come. I had forgotten the country could be so noisy. The lapping of the loch, the creak of the pine trees in the night wind, the shriek of a rabbit as it was taken by a fox, the baying of a distant hound all kept me from slumber. Those and my racing brain. Somebody had wanted to kill or maim Binky, that was obvious. And he was an heir to the throne—albeit only thirty-second in line. Which would rule out both Murdoch and Lachan. They came from the nonroyal side of our family and all they'd inherit was the dukedom. But they'd have to finish off little Podge first. I shivered. If I did anything at all, it would be to protect him.

Chapter 12

Castle Rannoch
August 18, 1932

I woke with first light. Dawn comes early in the Highlands and the slanting rays of sun were painting a bright stripe on my wall. The dawn chorus in the forest was deafening. Falling back to sleep was impossible. Besides, such a morning made one want to be up and out, and I wanted to see for myself where that trap had been set.

I washed and put on my jodhpurs and hacking jacket. Nobody else was stirring in the house, apart from the occasional maid who bobbed a curtsy and shyly whispered, "Welcome home, my lady," as she went about her early duties. I made my way to the stables and a great surge of happiness shot through me as I saw my horse, Rob Roy, his face poking over the door of the loose box. He gave a whicker of surprise at seeing me. I'd always thought he was particularly intelligent. When I tried to put on his saddle, however, it became obvious that he hadn't been ridden for some time.

He was incredibly skittish and I had to calm him down before he'd let me tighten the girths.

When I mounted he danced like a medieval charger until I gave him his head and then he took off like a rocket. For a while I let him run, feeling the exhilaration of speed as we shot across the parkland behind the castle. When the manicured lawns turned to springy turf and a path wound through pine forest, I reined in Rob Roy and we slowed to a walk. I didn't want him stepping on another trap! As we emerged from the woodland and the path started to climb through the heather and bracken, I looked down at the castle and grounds below me. The loch was hidden in early morning mist, which curled up the shoreline, making the castle look as if it was floating on a cloud. Then through the mist I saw a movement and heard the soft thud of hooves on a dirt trail and the clink of bit and harness. Another rider was out early. I noted the graceful movement of horse and rider, fluid as if they were one being. Who could it be? The rider, a young man with dark hair, resembled nobody staying at the castle. Then of course my suspicions were roused. Was this the trap setter, returning to inflict more damage?

I swung Rob Roy around and plunged down through the heather to cut him off. He was moving too fast and had passed by the time I reached the path on which he was traveling. I spurred Rob Roy into a flat-out gallop, trying not to lose the other rider in the mist that now swirled around us.

"Hey," I shouted. "You there. Hold up a minute."

He reined in and spun the horse around so that it danced like a medieval charger, rising on its back legs.

"This is private land," I shouted as I closed in on him. "What do you think you are doing here?"

"As to that, I might ask you the same question," he said. "Last time I saw you it was in a sleazy London nightclub."

"Darcy!" I exclaimed, recognizing him as the mist parted. He was wearing a white shirt, open at the neck, and his dark hair was windblown even wilder than usual. On that dancing horse, against the backdrop of heather and mountains, he looked like a Brontë hero and I felt my heart hammering. "Don't tell me you're staying at the castle and nobody told me."

"I'm not actually." He urged his horse toward mine. "I'm staying with a group of friends a couple of miles away. They're renting a house on Lord Angus's estate. They're testing a new speedboat. They want to break the water speed record. And I didn't realize that I'd strayed off Lord Angus's land, so for that I apologize. I was just enjoying the speed of a good horse after all that time cooped up in the city."

"I know, it feels glorious, doesn't it?" We exchanged a smile. I couldn't help noticing how Darcy's dark eyes lit up when he smiled and I felt a little flutter in my heart.

"But what about you?" he asked. "When did you get here?"

"I arrived last night," I said. "I decided to come and help Fig with her party of Americans."

"I see. I must say that was noble of you." He looked amused and suddenly I remembered what I had deduced on the drive from the train. He knew why I was here. Someone must have tipped off Scotland Yard or the Home Office or the special branch or whoever they were to my misdeeds at the nightclub. That constable had come too early in the morning for this to have been reported in a normal fashion during normal office hours. So it had to have been a late night or early morning telephone call. Who else but Darcy himself could have made that call? If he was, as I suspected, a spy of some sort, he'd be chummy with those shadowy people in the special branch.

"It was you, wasn't it?" I blurted out.

"What was me?"

"You tipped off Scotland Yard about my embarrassing evening at the nightclub. You betrayed me. You tricked me into coming up here so that I could be a spy for Sir Jeremy Whatever-His-Name-Is."

"I have no idea what you're talking about, my dear."

"I'm not your dear," I said, feeling my cheeks burning now with anger. "Obviously you don't care a damn about me. You only show up when I'm useful to somebody in the government. I'm fed up with being used."

"I'd volunteer to use you more often, but you don't give me the chance," he said, that wicked smile spreading across his face and his eyes flirting.

"Oh, most amusing," I snapped.

"Just trying to make you see that you are upsetting yourself over nothing," he said.

"Over nothing? I like that. You pretend to be interested in me one minute, then you disappear for weeks on end with no communication whatsoever, then you betray me to Scotland Yard. Well, I've had enough. I can't trust you, Darcy O'Mara. I don't want to see you again."

I spun Rob Roy around and urged him into a gallop. I knew we were going too fast for the twists and turns of the path, but I didn't care. I just wanted to go fast enough to obliterate all thoughts and feelings.

I didn't once look back, so I don't know if he attempted to follow me or not. Probably not. What was one girl less to a man like Darcy? As I neared the castle I decided to pay a call on Nanny. She had now retired to a little cottage on the estate and I was pretty sure she'd be up at this early hour. Of course she was, and she greeted me with a beaming smile and open arms.

"I had no word that you'd be coming, my dove," she said in her soft Scottish voice, hugging me to her ample bosom. "Well, this is a lovely surprise."

She had shrunk, I noticed. I'd always thought of her as a big woman but she now only came up to my shoulder. She bustled about, pouring me a cup of tea and ladling out a big bowl of porridge.

"You came because of your poor brother, I suppose," she said. "We were all stunned to hear it. Who could have done such a wicked thing?"

"Who indeed," I said.

"Some lad on the estate trying to make an extra shilling or two by catching the occasional rabbit, maybe," she suggested.

"Rather a big trap if he was after rabbits," I pointed out.

"I'd hate to think it was someone who bore a grudge against His Grace," she said.

I looked up sharply. "Do you know of anybody who bore a grudge?" I asked.

She shook her head. "He's well liked around here."

"Has anyone been dismissed recently?"

She thought. "The head gillie did have to let a boy go for helping himself to shot," she said. "Young Willie McDonald. Always was a nasty piece of work, that one."

Willie McDonald, a nasty piece of work, I thought. Of course, that made much more sense then any conspiracy theory against the royal family. I should have a chat with Constable Herries at the local police station and suggest he put the fear of God into young Willie to get him to confess.

"So how is your poor brother faring?" Nanny asked, as I tucked into the porridge.

"He seemed cheerful enough last night. Of course I haven't taken a look at the wound."

"The gamekeeper's wife has been dressing it for him. She said it looked verra nasty." (She rolled her *r*'s in the true Scottish manner.) "We're just praying it doesn't turn septic. And your poor brother, laid up when he's got a houseful of people he should be entertaining."

"I think he's rather glad to avoid some of them," I said and she chuckled.

"I saw that American lady going off with the prince the other morning," she continued. "My, but she gives herself airs and graces, doesn't she?"

"Some people are already worrying that she sees herself as queen someday."

"But she already has one husband, doesn't she? And to think that the British people would stand by and let a woman like that be queen. They'd never allow it."

"Let's hope it never comes to that. I'm sure the Prince of Wales will do his duty in the end and not let us down. He's been raised to be king, after all."

She nodded and sat, staring into the fire.

"So how have you been keeping?" I asked her.

"Not too bad, thank you. A touch of rheumatics now and then. And lonely sometimes, stuck away out here. Your brother visits me, but apart from that . . ."

"What about your neighbors?"

"Gone," she said. "The cottages on either side of me both stand empty now. They've cut back on estate workers since all that land was sold off, you know. And your brother only employs a handful of gillies on the estate too. The old men are retiring and there's no young men to fill their shoes. They don't want this type of hard work anymore. They're off to the cities. Not that there *are* many young men now. Not since the Great War took them away."

While she was speaking my brain was racing. Empty cottages on either side of her. Suddenly I had a good idea about who could fill one of those cottages, at least for a while. My grandfather could come up here to get the fresh air he needed and he could help me with my current assignment. I resolved to write to him immediately.

As soon as I left Nanny I checked out those empty cottages and decided that one of them would do very nicely. It appeared to be fully furnished and not too dusty. It also had a pleasant little kitchen that looked out over the lake. I could picture my grandfather sitting there with his cup of tea. I closed the door carefully then mounted and rode back to the castle. I left Rob Roy in the hands of the groom and went in to see about breakfast. All that Highland air had given me a marvelous appetite. There was only one occupant in the dining room—a young man sitting at the long table, tucking into a large helping of kedgeree and scrambled eggs. He rose as I came in, then his eyes lit up.

"Well, hello there," he said. "We meet again, I see."

It was the objectionable young man from the train.

"What are you doing here?" I asked.

"I think I mentioned that I had an invitation to stay," he said.

"You also mentioned that the castle was positively medieval and the hosts boring, if I remember correctly," I said coldly.

"Yes, well, that was rather crass of me, wasn't it?" he said. "I'm sorry that we got off on the wrong foot. You see, it never occurred to me that you were Binky's sister. I mean, dash it all, he'd always talked of you as a skinny, mousy little thing. So I never dreamed that this gorgeous creature could be associated with Castle Rannoch."

"Flattery will get you nowhere with me," I said.

"Really? It usually works rather well, I find. But I should introduce myself. I'm Hugo. Hugo Beasley-Bottome."

"Dear me," I said. "I bet you were teased about that name at school, weren't you?"

"Beaten to a pulp, constantly. Your brother was one of the house prefects when I first arrived and he was rather kind to me, so I've always, y'know, looked up to him." He gave what he hoped was a winning smile. "And I only know you as Binky's sister."

"I'm Georgiana," I said, not prepared to give him the more familiar form of my name.

He held out his hand. "Delighted to meet you, old bean. I understand poor Binky is laid up with a mangled foot. Rotten luck, what? But I look forward to being shown around by you."

"You wouldn't like it," I said. "It's positively medieval."

His fair skin flushed at this. "Oh, look here. Couldn't we forget that disastrous first meeting and start all over?"

I had taken an instant dislike to him but upbringing won out and forced me to say graciously, "Of course."

"You've been out riding already." He looked me up and down again in that frankly appraising way I found disturbing. He was mentally undressing me again.

"No, I always sleep in my jodhpurs," I said.

He laughed. "Oh, *très* droll. I like a girl with wit. I say, do have some breakfast and join me. I hate eating alone."

I remembered how those words had brought nothing but trouble to me. It was because Belinda had told me that men who came to London hated eating alone that I had come up with my stupid idea of an escort service in the first place. I was tempted to say I wasn't hungry and leave him to it, but the thought of a good breakfast, after months of austerity, toast and tea, was too enticing.

"Please do sit down," I said. "Your kedgeree is getting cold."

I went over to the sideboard and helped myself to kidneys, bacon and fried eggs. If this was economizing, then Binky and Fig weren't doing too badly.

"So where do you live, Mr. Bottomly-Beasley?" I asked.

"It's Beasley-Bottome," he corrected. "And my family has a place in Sussex. I have a pied-à-terre in London."

"And do you work?"

"Oh, rather. Boring desk job, actually. Pencil pusher. My older brother will inherit the estate and there's not much money in the family, so I was cast out upon the cruel world."

We actually had a lot in common and he was attractive in a film-starrish sort of way, so why couldn't I warm to him? After all, he had been to the right sort of school. He was one of us and I did need a husband. But there was just something about him—the exaggerated cut of his jacket, maybe, and the brilliantine in his hair, and those bedroom eyes, and the way he called me gorgeous when I wasn't. Healthy or "not bad looking" at best.

Fortunately before I had to make more polite conversation with Hugo Beasley-Bottome animated voices down the hall heralded the arrival of the Americans.

"And I had just got myself lathered up nicely when the hot water gave out," came a voice. I think it must have been Babe's. "I had to finish my shower in freezing cold water. My dears, it was not a pleasant experience, I can tell you."

"Positively primitive," Mrs. Simpson said, "but I understand from a certain person that Balmoral is even more so.

And they have a bagpiper at dawn there every morning—can you imagine?"

"Bagpiper at dawn?" I said brightly as they came into the breakfast room. "Oh, we do that here, as well. In fact, it's done at all the Scottish great houses."

"Well, I've never heard him."

"No, I gather he's been laid up with bronchitis and hasn't had the wind to play the pipes for the past week. We really miss him."

They stopped as Hugo rose to his feet yet again and introductions were made all around. Hugo was almost oozing charm and the Americans were easily won over.

"How nice that you've joined us, Mr. Beasley-Bottome," Babe said. "You'll liven up our little party no end." And her eyes held his for longer than was socially acceptable. I began to think that bed hopping might well be a national sport across the Atlantic, until I remembered my very correct man from Kansas.

"So what do we have planned for today, Wallis honey?" Countess Von Sauer asked.

"I believe I'm going on a little jaunt in an automobile. You'll just have to amuse yourselves," Wallis said.

"I tell you what," Hugo announced brightly. "Why don't you come with me down to the loch? My friends are testing a new speedboat and may be going to have a go at the world water speed record. It should be ripping fun."

"That does sound like a good idea, doesn't it, Earl?" Babe said. Anything to be with Hugo, I suspected. "We could take a picnic. I just adore picnics. It looks as if it's going to be a fine day."

"Lady Georgiana, why don't you ask your cook if she could pack a picnic for us," the countess suggested.

"And should we take our bathing things?" Babe asked.

"The loch is freezing and there is the monster," I said, giving her an encouraging smile.

"Does this monster actually appear in broad daylight?" Fritzi, the countess's wayward son, asked. "I mean, is it an established phenomenon? Have they been sacrificing virgins to it for generations?"

"Oh, absolutely," I said.

"Lucky it wasn't in Baltimore," Wallis Simpson muttered. "They'd have run out of virgins too quickly."

Again the group tittered.

"In which case I'll bring my gun along," Earl said. "I've always wanted to bag a monster. It will look great stuffed on the wall beside that marlin."

I left them making noisy preparations and bumped into Fig. She was pleased to hear about the picnic and the prospect of a day free from Americans. "And sandwiches cost so much less than a proper lunch," she said. "Maybe Mrs. McPherson can make pasties. She's such a dab hand with pastry, isn't she?"

"And I notice the hot water boiler has already been turned down," I added in a low voice. "It was commented on. Babe had to finish showering in cold water."

She gave me a conspiratorial smile. "And I'm just about to go and see Fergus about playing the pipes in the morning. He'll love it that we've reintroduced that old custom. And I must remember to suggest the haggis for dinner tonight. I wonder if Cook will have time to make it. What goes into it exactly?"

"It's a sheep's stomach with the rest of the intestines minced up with oatmeal and sewn into it."

"Is it? How disgusting. I know it's always served on Burns Night and New Year's Eve but I only eat the required mouthful myself. I don't suppose Cook has the odd sheep's stomach on hand."

"And it has to boil for hours," I pointed out.

Fig made a face again. "Well, let's hope she can procure one by tomorrow. The mere description ought to drive them away." She went to walk away then looked back at me. "This has to work, doesn't it, Georgiana?"

"One hopes so," I said.

Chapter 13

Castle Rannoch and a lochside jetty
August 18
Calm and pleasant weather to begin with . . .

I weighed up whether to join the picnic party. Frankly a day in the company of Earl and Babe was not exactly enticing, but it would give me an excuse to find Constable Herries and have a little chat with him about Binky's accident. Before we left I had a couple of tasks to complete. One was the letter to my grandfather and the other was a visit to Podge. I found him playing in my old nursery, surrounded by toy soldiers and a fort, while his nanny sat mending an item of clothing.

He jumped up when he saw me, scattering soldiers underfoot. "Aunt Georgie!" he cried and flung himself into my arms. "Look at my toy soldiers. They used to belong to Papa. And the fort. He's letting me use them because I'm old enough now. Come and play with me."

We played a pleasant game while I tried to think what I could say to warn his nanny without being too dramatic. I did point out to her that there might be more illegal traps on the estate, so that Podge should never be allowed to stray far from the house and that she should keep a good eye on him at all times.

"I always do, my lady," she said in a shocked voice. "He's not allowed to run wild, you know. If he goes out, he goes out in his pram."

Podge looked wistfully toward me as I left. I remembered how lonely nursery life had been and how I'd longed for a little sister or brother. Of course I hadn't realized in those days that my mother was just not the breeding kind, and besides, by the time I was old enough to think about a brother or sister, she had already bolted to another man. I went up and dressed for the picnic.

After much preparation and many last-minute forays for forgotten items, we loaded into the shooting brakes and headed for the lochside. The two princes had decided to go off climbing together. There was still no sign of the wild cousins, so it was just Hugo and I with the remaining Americans. Countess Von Sauer and her son went in the first car with Earl, so I found myself stuck with Hugo and Babe.

"Well, this is cozy, isn't it?" Hugo said, pressing his knee rather too closely against mine and slipping an arm around my shoulder as the car drove away. I gave him a frosty stare and was glad that the ride would be a short one. It was easy to locate where the action was on the loch as the speedboat had attracted quite a crowd of local spectators. As we pulled up at the jetty and got out, we could see the long, thin boat, painted bright blue, being towed back to shore by a rather more sturdy vessel, full of people.

"What happened?" Hugo shouted, going onto the dock to meet the approaching vessel.

"Damn thing became airborne at one twenty," someone shouted back. "He was lucky it didn't flip over."

"What the hell are you doing back here?" someone shouted from the boat. "I thought you'd gone."

"Couldn't keep away, old chap," Hugo shouted back. "Missed your delightful wit."

The boat docked and the party came ashore. Suddenly there was an excited squeal and someone was running down the dock toward me.

"Georgie, it is you!" she exclaimed, arms open. It was Belinda.

"Good heavens, what are you doing here?" I asked in amazement.

"I was about to ask you the same question," she said, enveloping me in a cloud of Chanel perfume as she hugged me. I hadn't recognized her earlier as she was wearing a most un-Belinda-like outfit of beige twill trousers and open-necked shirt with a brown pullover, but her face was still perfectly made up.

"I arrived last night," I said. "I came to help Fig." This had now become the obvious excuse.

"Darling, I never thought I'd hear you say those particular words," she said. "I thought you loathed Fig."

"I do, but she's in a bit of a pickle at the moment. Binky's laid up and the house is full of Americans, including the dreaded You-Know-Who."

"Is she here?" Belinda looked around. "Well, I never."

"Not at this moment. She's gone off driving with a certain prince. Mr. Simpson is over there—the one with the sulky expression on his face."

"I'm not surprised. Wouldn't you be sulky if your wife only dragged you around for respectability and then kicked you out of the bedroom at night to dally with a prince?"

"I'm not sure he actually comes to her bedroom at night, but I wouldn't want to be an object of pity like poor old

Simpson. So what are you doing up here?" I saw the answer to that question making his way down the dock toward us.

Belinda looked up at Paolo adoringly. "I'm here because of Paolo, silly. He's the one who's driving the boat. He's going to break the world speed record. Isn't it too, too thrilling?"

"It sounds rather dangerous to me," I said.

"Of course it is. Paolo's only happy doing something dangerous," she said.

The rest of the boaters now came down the dock toward us, deep in discussion, and words like "thrust" and "velocity ratio" floated in the clear Highland air.

"I think you know almost everybody, don't you?" Belinda waved in their general direction. "Paolo, look who it is. It's Georgie."

"Well, that's not too surprising, seeing that it's her family home on the other side of the loch," Paolo said, and kissed my hand. "You arrived just too late to see my impression of a water bird. I was airborne for several seconds, you know. Quite exhilarating."

"It's supposed to stay in the water, or rather on it," an American voice said behind him. The speaker looked ridiculously young and terribly earnest, peering owlishly through round spectacles.

"That's the designer, Digby Flute," Belinda muttered to me. "Father owns film studios in Hollywood. Pots of money. He's tried breaking the record himself twice and nearly killed himself each time."

"So now he wants Paolo to kill himself instead? That's nice of him."

Belinda smiled. "He's improved his design and it has a new engine, built in Germany. In fact, speaking of Germany, guess who's designed and supplied the engine."

She gestured to a big, blond and very Germanic-looking man who was picking his way toward us from the shore.

"Max!" I exclaimed. "Does that mean my mother is somewhere in the vicinity?"

I hadn't quite finished this sentence when I saw her. She was standing deep in conversation with two other people I recognized and one I didn't. The first was a large, pink and frightfully rich young man called Augustus Gormsley, usually known by his nickname of Gussie. The second was Darcy. And with them was a girl I had never met before: darkly exotic looking, slim, petite and at this moment regarding Darcy with smoldering brown eyes. My first temptation was to duck behind a pine tree and disappear, but I was too late. Gussie spotted me.

"I say, it's your daughter, old bean," he said to my mother and then beckoned me over. "What-ho, Georgie."

I had no alternative but to join them. "Hello, Gussie. Darcy. Hello, Mummy." I managed to sound calm and civil. "What a surprise to see you here."

"Hello, darling." My mother and I exchanged the usual air kisses. "You're looking rather pale," she said. "Aren't you well?"

"It's been a trying summer so far," I said. "I didn't expect to see you here. Where are you staying?"

"At Balmoral, darling, where else?"

I couldn't have been more surprised if she had told me a hermit's cave on the mountain. "Balmoral? I didn't realize you were pally with Their Majesties these days."

"Not me, Max. He took the Prince of Wales shooting at his lodge in the Bohemian Forest last winter and the prince is returning the favor. Besides, it's all in the family, you know. Max is connected through his Saxe-Coburg-Gotha line."

"Goodness, I didn't realize he had royal blood. So should I have been calling him Your Highness all this time?"

It occurred to me that I hadn't really called him anything because his English was very limited, so it probably hadn't mattered.

"No, darling. The Saxe-Coburg-Gotha lot were on his mother's side, so he's just plain Herr, more's the pity. I do rather miss being a duchess. One got such good service in Paris, where such things matter."

"I'm sure there are plenty of dukes floating around for you to snag," I said.

"The trouble is that I've become rather attached to Max," she said. "He does have his faults—like not being able to speak English and preferring to live in Germany with all those dumplings. But he is rather sweet and cuddly, isn't he?"

It was like asking if a grizzly bear was sweet and cuddly. I refrained from commenting. "So you've come to join the royal shooting party?"

"And of course Max is interested in seeing how his engine is performing." She giggled. "Frankly, between the two of us, his engine performs remarkably well for his age."

She smiled coyly and held out her hand as Max came toward her. "You remember my daughter Georgiana, don't you, Max darling?"

Max clicked his heels and gave me a nodding bow.

"I hear you've come to shoot with the prince," I said, pronouncing each word slowly.

"*Ja.* Shoot wiz prince. Is *gut.*"

"And he came to your hunting lodge last winter?"

"*Ja.* Vee shoot vild boar. Big tooths."

"Tusks, Max. Boars have tusks," my mother corrected. She patted his hand. "His English is improving wonderfully, don't you think?"

"Definitely," I said.

Paolo and the young American descended on us and started talking about engines and thrust again.

"This is the part I find horribly boring," my mother said. "I think I shall go back for a lie-down, if one is allowed to lie down at Balmoral. It's all horribly hearty and outdoorsy, isn't it?"

I felt a ridiculous wave of disappointment that my mother hadn't seen me for months and now had no wish to spend any time with me. I should have become used to it by now, but I hadn't. "You could go and cheer up poor Binky," I said and related the saga of his accident.

"If I can sneak in without encountering the dreaded wife," she said, "maybe I'll do that. I've always had a soft spot for your brother." And off she went. He wasn't her son, of course, but she had briefly been his stepmother and I knew he was fond of her.

I stood watching her go with that strange hollow longing that always came over me when I met my mother. And then I realized that she had left me with three people I had no wish to talk to: two men who had behaved badly and a dark, sultry girl who was far too beautiful and sexy. Was she now my replacement in the girlfriend stakes? I could feel Darcy's eyes on me, and forced myself not to look around. I was trying to move away, giving the impression that there was somebody I simply had to speak to, when I was snagged by Gussie.

"Long time no see, Georgie," he said. "How have you been?"

"Well enough, thank you, Gussie," I replied coolly. He seemed to have forgotten that the last time we met, I had had to fight him off, while he tried to remove my knickers.

He moved closer to me. "You know I was hoping we

could maybe pick up where we left off last," he said, proving that he hadn't forgotten at all.

"You mean when I was saying 'Get off me, you brute' and you weren't listening?"

He chuckled. "All the girls say no, but they don't really mean it. It's just to appease their consciences. Afterward they can say 'I tried to fight him off but he was just too strong for me.' "

"I really meant it."

"Oh, come on, Georgie," he said, turning slightly pinker. "Everyone likes a bit of the old rumpy-pumpy from time to time, surely. I mean, it's awfully good fun, isn't it?" He looked at my face. "You mean you don't? You haven't?"

"Frankly that's none of your business," I said haughtily. "But if you really must know, I intend to wait until I meet someone I can love and respect," I said.

"Good God." He studied me as if I were some kind of exotic species of unknown animal. "Oh, well, let me know if you find such a being. And if not, I'm always available if you change your mind."

Darcy and the dark girl were moving off. My gaze followed them.

"Now there's someone who doesn't follow your rules," Gussie said.

"Who is she?"

"Name's Conchita. Spanish, I believe, or is it Brazilian? Father owns plantations. Oodles of money. Paolo persuaded her to invest in this latest madness. She and the Yank are funding it, and Paolo's driving it."

"And what about you?"

"Oh, I've just come along for the excitement," he said. "And I promised Father I'd write him up a column for one of his daily newspapers. Oh, there's Hugo come back," he added. "I knew he couldn't stay away long."

I spotted Hugo Beasley-Bottome, moving through the crowd as if looking for someone. "He's been up here before, has he?"

"Oh yes. Pops up and down all the time. He was staying with us at the house until a few days ago. I didn't realize he'd come back."

"He's staying at Castle Rannoch now," I said.

"I say, is he? I wonder why he decided to change his abode. I don't think anyone in our party upset him and the food's halfway decent and there's plenty of booze."

"He inveigled an invitation out of my brother, so he said. Even though he was damned rude about the place. Called it positively medieval."

"Well, it is, isn't it?"

"I suppose so, but then why go out of his way to stay with us?"

Gussie followed Hugo's progress through the crowd. "Of course we all know what he's doing here and where he'd like to stay, but he hasn't received an invitation."

"Where's that?" I asked, immediately thinking of Balmoral.

"The Padgetts', of course."

"Padgetts?"

"Yes, you know. Major and Mrs. Padgett. They live on the edge of the Balmoral grounds. He's the master of the estate or whatever the official title is. He's been in the royal service for donkey's years. He used to be rather important at one stage, one of the favorites of Queen Victoria and then King Edward. Now he's more or less retired—they only bring him out on rare ceremonial occasions."

"Oh yes. I believe I have met him. But why would Hugo want to stay there?"

"Because of Ronny of course, old thing. He has what the Americans call 'hot pants' for her. She's not shown any interest in him but he doesn't give up."

"Oh, of course. Ronny Padgett," I said, finally putting two and two together. "I met her at the aerodrome. She said her family lived up here, but I had never connected her with the major at Balmoral."

"Well, she's up here now. She comes and goes in that little plane of hers. Lands on the lakes, so hold on to your hat if you're picnicking on the shore. She comes in awfully low."

I laughed. At least Gussie was one of my social set. He was amusing. One knew where one stood with him. It was unfortunate that I wasn't attracted to him. He'd have made a good catch and I might have enjoyed a luxuriously decadent lifestyle with him. I looked around. Darcy and the dark lady had now completely disappeared. But I did spot Constable Herries keeping an eye on things from the road above. I excused myself and made my way up to him.

"How are you, Constable?" I asked.

He touched his helmet. "Well enough, my lady. I'm sorry to hear about His Grace's accident."

"Nasty business," I said. "I wondered whether you had made any inquiries about it?"

"Inquiries, my lady?"

"Into who might have set such a trap on Castle Rannoch land?"

He leaned his red, whiskered face closer to me. "I suspected it was someone from the estate who just wanted to snare the odd rabbit and now dare not come forward and own up."

"What if it was deliberately set by someone with a grudge against us?"

He gave me a startled look. "Now who would ever do a thing like that?"

"I understand that a boy called Willie McDonald was let go recently. Have you spoken with him?"

"You'd have a job speaking with him, my lady. He went off and joined the Royal Navy. He said that leaving the estate was the best thing that ever happened to him and now he was free to see the world."

"Good for him," I said. Back to square one.

Chapter 14

Beside a loch in Scotland
August 18
Weather brisk (which is Scottish terminology
for blowing a howling gale).

We ate our picnic in the shade of a large Scots pine tree. My mother returned from visiting Binky up at Castle Rannoch and came to join us as the picnic was being set up.

"How utterly beastly for poor Binky," she said. "He looks awfully pale. I suggested he go to my little pied-à-terre on the Riviera to recuperate but he claims he has no money to travel."

"That's true. He doesn't," I said. "Father saddled him with enormous death duties."

"Typical of your father," she said. "Utterly useless and never thought about anyone but himself. If he'd truly adored me, I would have stayed, but he preferred all those horrible outdoor sports, like shooting and fishing, to staying home and amusing me." She broke off and touched my arm. "Who is the rather divine-looking blond boy?"

"That? His name is Huge Beasley-Bottome."

My mother burst out laughing. "What an unfortunate name. So tell me about him."

"He seems to be a sponger. He was with the motorboat party and now he's invited himself to Castle Rannoch."

"So no money then?"

"Not your type at all," I said. "Decades too young and penniless, I suspect."

"But darling as one ages, one likes them young. So good for the ego, even though they've no staying power at that age."

"What do you mean?"

She looked at me strangely. "They go off like rockets, darling. Really, didn't I manage to give you the slightest hint of the facts of life when you were growing up?"

"You were never there," I said. "My education was hopelessly lacking. I didn't even manage to find a friendly gamekeeper."

She laughed again. "You'd better make up for lost time, hadn't you? Isn't there a likely male in the picture?"

"Not at the moment," I said, glancing around to see if Darcy was still anywhere around, but he and the señorita had disappeared.

"Too bad. I expect you'll find one soon," my mother said languidly, her gaze moving to Hugo as she spoke. "I might as well join you for lunch."

"You can't afford to make Max jealous, can you?" I said. "Think of all those lovely Parisian gowns."

"When Max is talking about engines, he wouldn't notice if a zeppelin dropped on his head." She lowered herself onto the best rug and stretched out luxuriantly. "So what are we eating?" she said. "Don't tell me that Mrs. McPherson has made pasties."

The Americans eyed her with suspicion.

"Don't mind little *moi*," she said, waving a gracious hand in their direction. "I eat like a sparrow."

"Pardon me, but I don't think we've met." Babe lowered herself to the rug beside my mother.

"My mother, the former Duchess of Rannoch," I said hastily, and saw Mummy frown. She hated to admit she had a daughter of my age.

"And you were the famous actress Claire Daniels, weren't you?" Countess Von Sauer exclaimed.

"Once upon a time I suppose I had my modicum of fame," Mother said with brilliantly pretended humility.

Of course, after that she was the center of attention.

Unfortunately the wind had come up and was blowing dust and pine needles onto the food, while the speed racers were testing their engine, emitting the occasional loud roar that jangled all our nerves and made conversation difficult. Mother, of course, made herself the center of attention instantly. She turned the full force of her dazzling charm onto Hugo so that he was transformed into her lap dog. I even began to feel a little sorry for him. As for the Americans, it was as if they were in the presence of a visiting goddess, which I suppose she was.

I sat on the two inches of blanket my mother was not occupying, staring out across the lake, simply not able to get into the swing of their conversation. Too many worrying thoughts were buzzing around my head. These thoughts ranged from Sir Jeremy's mandate to Binky's trap to Darcy and the mysterious dark woman. What was I supposed to do about any of the above? And why was I supposed to step in and rescue other people when nobody seemed to show any interest in me whatsoever? I was looking along the edge of the lake—I suppose that subconsciously I was trying to catch a glimpse of Darcy and see if he'd actually gone off with that Conchita woman—when I sat up, suddenly alert. Someone was creeping through the stand of fir trees on the point behind us. I watched as the figure darted from tree to tree, obviously not wanting to be seen. And he was coming closer. Thoughts of the trap and the reported accidents to the royal heirs instantly flashed across my mind.

Suddenly I'd had enough. If this person was cowardly enough to plan horrid little accidents and set a trap for my brother, then I was going to put a stop to him right now. I stood up and started to wander apparently aimlessly, bending to pick a sprig of heather here and there, but all the time making my way closer to those trees. When I was close enough, I darted behind the nearest pine then moved from tree to tree, just as our stalker was doing. I caught sight of him again as he crept through deep shadow to the next large pine.

Right, my lad, I thought. He was making quite a bit of noise. He would have been useless stalking a deer. I, in contrast, moved silently. He had no idea I was behind him until I leaped out and pounced.

"Got you!" I shouted, grabbing at the collar of his jacket. "All right. Let's take a look at you then, you miserable specimen." In truth I was rather relieved to find that he was a miserable specimen. I don't know what I would have done if I'd leaped out on a hulking six-footer armed with a gun or knife. As it was he gave a little squeak, tried to flee and was yanked backward by me, almost sitting down in the process.

"The constable's just up there on the bank," I said. "He'll be here in two seconds if I call him, so you'd better confess."

"My dear young lady, I've done nothing wrong. Unhand me, I beg you," he said. I recognized the voice at the same moment I staggered with him into a patch of sunlight.

"Mr. Beverley!" I said in a shocked tone. "What were you up to?"

"Your ladyship! Nothing, I assure you nothing at all," he

said, most flustered now as I released my hold on him. "I was just trying to—well, you know, it's silly really, but I have always had a crush, as it were, on your dear mother. I couldn't believe my luck when I saw she was here. So I was seizing the chance to get a little closer to her, that's all."

"You were spying on her. You were going to eavesdrop and then reveal all in your column. I know how you newspapermen work."

"Oh no, I assure you."

"You do run a gossip column, don't you?"

"Yes, but . . ."

"So you were just doing your job and going to report gossip."

He looked red faced and crestfallen now, like a deflated balloon. "Well, I do have to confess . . ."

"You're very lucky I don't turn you in to our police constable," I said. "I could, you know. Someone has been setting traps on our estate. You could well be a prime suspect."

"Oh no. I'd never do anything violent," he said, fluttering his hands in distress. "You know I abhor violence."

"Very well," I said. "I'll let it go, just this once, but if I catch you spying on us again, then I will have no qualms about turning you over to our constable."

"I don't suppose there is any chance, is there, that I might just be allowed to greet your divine mama? I've worshipped her from afar for so long now." He gazed at me hopefully, like a dog begging to be taken on a walk.

I looked over at the rugs where my mother was still holding court. "Why not?" I said. I took him by the hand and led him across to our group.

"Mother, I'd like you to meet one of your biggest fans," I said. She deserved a little punishment for the way she ignored her only daughter.

Godfrey Beverley stepped forward, bowing like a medieval vassal. "Such an honor, Your Grace—well, I know it's not really 'Your Grace' any longer, but I still think of you as nobility, you know."

"Indeed." Mother's mouth was set in a firm line. "How do you do? Mr. Beverley, isn't it?"

"You remembered. How flattering."

"How could I forget? All those witty little columns . . ."

I moved off, leaving them to it. A few moments later Mummy showed up at my side again, looking absolutely furious. "How could you desert me and leave me with that odious little man?" she demanded.

"Oh, Mummy, I'm sure he's harmless. He said he was completely infatuated with you. So I thought I'd make his day and bring him to meet you."

"Oh, you've made his day, all right," she said. "And as for harmless, he's one of the most vicious little serpents I've ever come across. He just loves to unearth nasty snippets of gossip about me to put in his column. And you know what the next one will be, don't you?"

When I didn't respond she went on. "He had somehow found out that we were staying at Balmoral and he said wasn't it amazing how broad-minded and modern the royal couple had become, allowing us to live in sin under their roof, as it were? Insufferable little smarmy prig. I could kill him."

I should point out that under moments of extreme stress my mother reverts to type, and she did have a grandmother who sold fish in the market.

"He's probably watching from the bushes," I said, trying not to smile. "Don't let him see that he's upset you."

"That's probably what he does for sexual thrills—watches from the bushes," she snapped. "He's certainly never been near a woman in his life, or a man either. I bet he does needlepoint in his spare time."

I could see that she was really riled. "Why don't you come back to the castle for some tea?" I asked.

She shook her head. "I'm sure I'm getting a migraine after that encounter. I really do need to lie down or I'll look like an old hag by dinner." She returned to our party to announce her departure, but it seemed that everyone was restless by this time and wanted to go back to the castle. Maybe the strength of the wind and the blowing dust had become too much for them. The mechanics working on the boat were busy covering it in a tarpaulin, and Gussie came down the dock to us.

"They can't do any more today with this gale blowing," he said. "They might end up with dirt in the engine."

I didn't like to tell him that this wasn't a gale, just a normal afternoon breeze for our part of Scotland, where the strong westerlies from the Hebrides are funneled through a gap in the Grampians. I wondered why they had picked our particular loch for their speed trials. It wasn't calm at the best of times.

"I tell you what," my mother said, looking around at her adoring fan club, which by now included Hugo. "Why don't we all come up to Castle Rannoch to join you for dinner tonight? I'm sure there will be plenty of food. There always is and I know it would cheer up Binky to see old friends. Maybe we can have him carried down to dinner."

Everyone seemed to think this was a good idea. I was just trying to picture Fig's face when she found that at least half a dozen more people would be descending on us. I dragged Mother aside. "Why on earth did you suggest this? You know what Fig's like. She'll have hysterics."

Mummy smiled. "Precisely. That will teach her to be rude to me," she said.

"When?"

"Earlier today. When I arrived at the castle I met her coming down the stairs and she asked me in extremely uncivil tones what I wanted. I reminded her I used to be Binky's mother and do you know what she said? 'Yes, but not for long, was it?' What a spiteful tongue that woman has. She deserves an unexpected dinner party."

"It's all right for you," I said. "You're not the one who has to break the news to her."

She chuckled. "Think of poor Binky. He desperately needs cheering up."

"I don't know if the sight of more people eating his food will do the trick," I had begun to say, when the sound of an engine made us turn around.

"I thought they'd finished with that bloody boat," my mother said, then realized that the sound was not coming from there. Suddenly a small plane appeared, approaching low through the gap in the mountains. It roared over our heads, almost clipped the top of the tallest pines, skimmed over the surface of the lake, bounced a few times then touched down, sending out a sheet of spray behind it.

"Good-o. Ronny's here," Hugo exclaimed, my mother clearly having been discarded for the moment.

I was amazed to see that Ronny's aeroplane, if it was indeed the same one, now had floats instead of wheels.

As we watched Ronny's plane come to a halt, the countess gave a sudden scream. "Look. The monster!"

Excitement broke out on the shore as great black ripples came toward us. People tried to flee, knocking others out of their way in their fear. Then Constable Herries's voice came loud and clear.

"That's no monster. It's just the way the wind comes down from the pass and creates a particular series of waves. It's blowing extra hard this afternoon. We've seen it before and I expect we'll see it again. Now everyone calm down and go home. Monster indeed. There's no monster in this loch."

The crowd dispersed, muttering excitedly. Some were convinced they'd seen a head rise from that wave. I wasn't sure I hadn't seen something myself. Babe and the countess twittered as they were herded back to the cars.

"What if it comes on land? What if it swallows up that boat?" the countess said. "Fritzi darling, I expect you to protect me."

Her son didn't look as if he relished the prospect of fending off a large monster.

"I think we should sacrifice Lady Georgiana to appease it," Hugo said. The laugh broke the tension, but I sat in the car with my cheeks bright red. Was it so obvious to the world that I was still a virgin?

Chapter 15

Back at Castle Rannoch
August 18
Late afternoon.

As I had predicted, Fig did not take the news of the extra dinner guests with great enthusiasm.

"How many people, did you say?" she demanded, her voice close to a shriek. Clearly she had never had a governess to constantly remind her that a lady never raises her voice. "Coming here? Tonight? Why in God's name didn't you stop them?"

"How could I stop them without looking terribly petty or telling them we currently had the Black Death?" I said. "They decided among themselves that they were enjoying each other's company so much that they'd all like to dine together."

"Then let them all dine together somewhere else," she snapped.

"But they wanted to cheer up Binky," I said. "They suggested he be carried down to join us."

"It's those blasted Americans, isn't it?" (I had tactfully forgotten to mention that the idea was entirely my mother's.) "They act as if they own the place. That Babe creature actually gave Hamilton a lecture about the lack of hot water this morning. She said it wasn't good enough. Not good enough? I ask you. The nerve of it. That woman spends all too much time in the bathroom, if you ask me. It's not healthy."

Fig was clearly in a state now.

"It will be all right," I said. "I'm sure Cook can whip up a big hearty soup or something as a first course to fill them up."

"Would you go and tell her, Georgiana? I really don't think that I can face her at the moment."

"If you like," I said, having been a real favorite of Cook's during my childhood.

"I'm so glad you're here," she said yet again. Wonders would never cease.

As I had suspected, Cook took the news more calmly than my sister-in-law had done, but she clearly wasn't pleased. "Eight more for dinner, you say? What does Her Grace think I am, a miracle worker? A conjurer? I'm supposed to produce a few rabbits out of a hat?"

I gave a sympathetic smile.

"She barely gives me enough money to feed the regular household and now I'm supposed to whip up banquets out of thin air?"

"Just do your best, Mrs. McPherson," I said. "They'll realize that this is all very last minute and they can't expect haute cuisine."

"It would never have been haute cuisine at the best of times," she said dourly. "Good plain food, that's what I do. None of this fancy French muck—snails covered in garlic." She made a disgusted face. "What's wrong with good local beef and Scottish salmon fresh from the stream?"

"Nothing at all," I said. "You're a wonderful cook, Mrs. McPherson. Everybody says so."

"Och, get away with you." She gave an embarrassed chuckle. "Well, it will have to be neeps and tatties for them tonight. I've nothing else."

"Neeps and tatties?" I asked. She was referring to the Scottish peasant dish made with potatoes and turnips. Filling but not exactly elegant.

"Aye. Like I said, I'm no miracle worker. That roast should be big enough for a slice or two each but we'll need to fill them up somehow. Do them good. They can sample our traditional Scottish fare. And lucky for you I made a nice rich broth with that leftover lamb from the other night. I can thicken that up into a soup. I don't know about the fish course, though. It's too late for the fishmonger to deliver anything. I can't divide loaves and fishes meant for twelve and make enough for twenty."

"I'm sure they won't necessarily expect a fish course, Mrs. McPherson," I said.

"They'd be getting one at Balmoral, wouldn't they?"

"It's only my mother and Herr Von Strohheim who are currently staying at Balmoral. The rest of them are in a house on Lord Angus's estate. I don't suppose they've a decent cook there, which is why they all jumped at the chance to come here and sample your cooking."

Mrs. McPherson was softening. "Maybe I'll see if we've enough smoked trout to go around," she said. "I was keeping it for a luncheon salad, but no doubt we can obtain more. And the boys have brought in a bushel basket of berries to make a crumble, so we'll get by, I suppose. We usually do."

"You're very kind, Mrs. McPherson," I said. "Her Grace will be so impressed."

She sniffed. "That one is only impressed when I cut

corners and save her a penny or two," she muttered. "In the old duke's time there would have been none of this penny-pinching."

"He did go bankrupt," I pointed out.

"Her Grace also requested a haggis when she came to see me today," Cook said. "Is that another of her economy ideas?"

I laughed. "No, she's hoping to scare away the Americans. She says they're eating her out of house and home."

"Och, so that's it?" She started to laugh, her ample bosoms shaking up and down like a jelly. "Well, you can tell her that I make the best haggis in this part of Scotland so they're liable to like it and ask for more. I've the sheep's stomach already boiling away ready to stuff tomorrow."

I left her and returned upstairs quite cheered. It was good to be home again. The whole party assembled in the great hall for tea, the cousins and the princes having returned from their various outdoor pursuits. The wind that had picked up at lunchtime had heralded the arrival of bad weather and was now howling down the chimneys while rain peppered the windows. Our guests were clearly feeling the cold and gazed hopefully at the empty fireplace. Fig was pretending that she was comfortably warm and didn't need to light the fire, proving that she was as good an actress as my mother. It really was awfully dismal in the great hall. I was longing to go upstairs for a second cardigan but I couldn't let the side down. In truth I was glad one of the dogs was leaning against my leg.

I was quite enjoying studying Fig. I could see that she was considerably put out watching Earl spreading heaps of her special Fortnum & Mason jam with gay abandon on his scone. Suddenly there were raised voices in the entrance hall and Mrs. Simpson swept in, looking less amused than my austere great-grandmother had done. Her usually immaculate coiffure was windswept and her silk outfit was streaked with rain.

"Wallis honey, you look terrible." The countess rose to greet her.

Obviously Wallis didn't appreciate the remark. She already knew she looked terrible and didn't need anybody to point this out.

"Come and have a cup of tea to warm you up before you go change." The countess took her arm and led her over to us.

"We've had an absolutely beastly day," Wallis said. "And the storm was the least of it. My dears, something terrible happened. We were lucky to escape with our lives."

"What on earth do you mean?" Babe asked.

"We were on our way back here, driving down the pass, when a damned great boulder came flying out of nowhere and struck us. Luckily it landed on the bonnet. A couple of feet in the wrong direction and David and I should both have been crushed. I tell you, my heart has only just started beating again. David was wonderfully calm. He said these things happen in the Highlands. 'Then I can't think why you choose to spend any time up here,' I said. 'I've never seen a more godforsaken place to begin with.' He wasn't thrilled with that remark and we had words. So all in all a most trying day."

She took the teacup that was offered her and sipped gratefully. The other Americans made a terrific fuss of her. Even her husband was nice to her. But my thoughts were racing again. Another accident that could have killed the Prince of Wales. Then a new thought struck me. Maybe we had got it wrong: maybe it wasn't the prince who was the target. Maybe someone was trying to eliminate Mrs. Simpson. I had seen enough American gangster films to know that people paid other people to take out an enemy. What if someone in the royal circle wanted to remove her permanently from the prince's life? Or on the other hand, what if her husband was angry enough with the way he was being cheated to want to get rid of her without paying alimony?

I decided I should make discreet inquiries to find out if Mrs. Simpson had been present when the other accidents happened to the prince. I noticed Lachan and Murdoch exchange an amused glance as she swept from the room. Then they too got up and excused themselves. One by one the party dispersed to go and rest before dinner or, in the case of Babe, to have yet another bath before dinner. I resolved to go and see exactly where this boulder fell onto the car and if it was possible that someone could have given it a convenient push. It was not unheard of for rocks to fall down mountainsides, but the chances of timing a rock to fall on a car would be slim, I should have thought. But I couldn't deny that it was yet another accident.

I went up to change for dinner. I was in the upstairs bathroom when I heard voices. I should probably clarify that I am not in the habit of hearing voices. The plumbing system at Castle Rannoch is eccentric, to say the least. It was added a few hundred years after the castle was built, of course. One of the features of the plumbing is that voices are carried by the pipes from one part of the castle to another. Two men were talking in low tones, in what sounded like Scottish accents.

"So are you going to tell her?" I heard one voice whisper.

"Are you mad? We'd be chucked out on our ear. She'd see to that. And I can't afford anything to come between me and my goals right now. This place is ideal for it. You must see that."

"What if somebody saw?"

"Then we plead ignorance. We didn't mean it, did we?"

And the sound of chuckling reverberated in the pipes.

Chapter 16

Castle Rannoch
August 18
Evening.

I stood there, not noticing the rain and wind blowing in on me. (Oh, didn't I mention that it's a Castle Rannoch tradition to keep bathroom windows open at all times? Guests find this somewhat startling and hard to endure—especially when coupled with the tartan wallpaper and the groans and creaks emitted by the pipes.) A conspiracy then. It had never occurred to me before that maybe there could be Scottish nationalists at work in the castle—men who wanted home rule, like Ireland, or maybe wanted to replace the primarily German strain of monarchy with the old Stuart dynasty. Rannoch seemed an odd place to be harboring such feelings, as our family traced its ancestry back to the Stuarts on the old duke's side as well as to the currently reigning monarch through my grandmother.

I went back to my bedroom deep in thought. When my maid, Maggie, came to dress me for dinner and was anxious to chatter about castle gossip, I was happy to oblige her.

"So is anyone new on the staff since I went away?" I asked.

"Why, you've only been gone a few months, your ladyship," she said, chuckling. "Nothing's changed here, you know."

"So how many men actually work in the house these days?" I asked. "Hamilton and His Grace's valet and Frederick and the under footman. Is that it?"

She looked at me strangely. "Yes, that would be it, apart from the gardener's boy who comes in to help with the boots and bringing up the heavy stuff from the cellar."

"And what about on the whole estate, how many men would you say there were?"

She laughed. "Are you thinking of taking yourself a local husband, my lady?"

"No, just trying to work something out," I said. "There would be the grooms, and the gardeners and the gillies, wouldn't there?"

"And don't forget the gamekeeper and field hands and the shepherd, and old Tom."

Quite a few then, but only four who would be allowed in the castle. Except that some of them did come into the castle from time to time. Fergus came in to play the pipes on special occasions. The gardeners brought in firewood; the gamekeeper and the gillies delivered fish and birds. But would any of them dare to meet in a castle bathroom? Hardly likely.

"So do you think that anybody here would have home rule feelings?"

"What do you mean, my lady?"

"Wanting to do away with the king and queen and turn Scotland into a separate state."

"Why would anyone want to do that?" She looked perplexed.

"Some people feel that way."

"Not anybody around here. We think the world of the king and queen. In fact, everyone in these parts knows someone or has a relative who works on the Balmoral estate and they can't speak highly enough of Their Majesties."

When I came down to dinner, I found Binky had been carried down and was now reclining in an ancient bath chair that looked as if it once transported our venerable great-grandmother the queen. He was holding court, chatting to our visitors who had already arrived. I was uneasy to see that Darcy was among them, as was the dark and sultry Conchita, dressed in a slinky scarlet gown with a black fringed Spanish shawl over it. So was Ronny Padgett, looking remarkably civilized and feminine in a long bottle-green dinner dress with a white silk wrap and white elbow-length gloves. I went over to talk to her immediately so that I didn't find myself in a group with Darcy. I told myself it shouldn't matter that Señorita Conchita was making cow eyes at him, but it did. I suppose it's not that easy to fall out of love so quickly.

"I saw you land on the loch this afternoon," I said. "I didn't realize your plane could land on water."

"I had fins made for the Moth so that I can fly up here," she said. "The lochs are the only places nearby flat enough to put down a plane."

"It must be a wonderful feeling to fly," I said.

"I'll take you up some time if you like," she said. "Just let me know when. I'm here for a while. At least until they put that boat through its paces." She leaned closer to me. "Between ourselves I'm hoping to be given a chance to break the record myself. I'm sure I'd do a damned sight better than that foreign idiot Paolo. But then, he's got the money and we Padgetts are as poor as church mice."

"Really?" I looked surprised.

"Yes, Father has a grace-and-favor position at Balmoral these days. There were times when he was in the thick of things. He had been promised a knighthood at least for services to Queen Victoria and King Edward, but he suffered some kind of ill health and was sent up here to recuperate. And here he's stayed. It's rather lonely for my mother. We really are in a godforsaken spot in the middle of nowhere."

"Don't they come down to London?"

"Not often. We no longer have a London house and my little matchbox is too small to accommodate them properly."

A memory stirred in my head at the mention of her London flat. "By the way, I was awfully sorry to hear about your maid."

She nodded. "Yes, it was a rum do, wasn't it? Poor little thing. She was still a country girl at heart. Hadn't a clue about traffic. Always wandering across the road without looking, even in London. Although what she was doing at Croydon Aerodrome on that particular evening I simply can't fathom. I'd told her to wait at the flat in London for my instructions and I wasn't planning to return for several days." She broke off and looked at me with interest. "So how did you come to hear about her accident?"

"The police mentioned it to me," I said. "It seems that there was a half-finished letter to me in her purse when she was killed."

"A letter to you? How extraordinary—what did she want?"

"I've no idea," I said. "It had fallen into a ditch and most of the ink had washed away, but it was clearly addressed to Lady Georgiana and I suspect I'm the only person with that name in London. The police thought that maybe she was asking me for a job."

"A job—with you? Why would she be doing that?"

"I thought perhaps because you were threatening to dismiss her."

"Dismiss her?"

"You told her to watch her step when I saw you together."

She looked at me and laughed. "That's the way I always spoke to her. She knew that. It's just the way I am. And I was actually quite fond of her, clueless though she was. I tell you, I'd like to catch the blighter that mowed her down. I'd strangle him with my bare hands."

"If she'd wandered out into the road, as you say, he probably couldn't have avoided hitting her."

"But then why bugger off and leave her there to die? Why not summon the police and admit to it like a man?"

"Frightened to, maybe? Maybe he had black marks against him for reckless driving before and feared his license would be taken from him."

She nodded. "Poor old Mavis." She sighed. "And dashed inconvenient for me. Now I'm up here with no maid, only an idiot local girl who tried to iron my leather jacket."

Hugo moved in on us. "I watched you land that plane this afternoon, Ronny. I must say you are magnificent. So when are you going to take me up?"

"If you're not careful, Hugo, I might just tip you out," she said, laughing. "I do love barrel rolls, you know. They are a great way to get rid of unwanted suitors."

So the attraction was not mutual.

"How can you afford to run a plane?" I blurted out before I remembered that a lady never mentions money.

She shrugged. "I have sponsors. And one of the reasons that I enter all these damned air races is that they come with very nice cash prizes. I'm going to try solo to Australia this autumn. It's never been done by a woman and the *Daily Mail* is coming up with a fat check if I succeed."

"Do you have a good chance of succeeding?"

"Fair to middling, I'd say. There's a lot of desert to be flown over. You come down in the middle of the Arabian Desert and that's pretty much it. Nobody's likely to find you before you run out of water." She looked around the room. "Speaking of which, I'm dying of thirst. Isn't there anything stronger than sherry around here?"

And she wandered off, leaving me alone. I wondered if I actually envied her or pitied her. It would be wonderful to be so daring and independent, of course, but then I pictured the loneliness and the likelihood of dying in the desert and was glad that I didn't have her nerve.

Hugo was still lingering nearby. He sidled up to me. "I say," he said, "this old place is rather fascinating, isn't it? Awfully rich in history. So tell me, does it have a laird's lug? I've heard about them but I've never actually seen one."

"Yes, it does, actually."

"And what exactly is it? A place where the laird could spy on his guests, isn't it?"

"Exactly. A little secret room built into the walls, where the laird could listen through slots to hear if anyone was plotting against him."

"Dashed interesting. You wouldn't like to take me to see it, would you?"

I gave him an exasperated look. "I thought you were supposed to be keen on Ronny, Hugo. And now you're trying to lure me off somewhere secret? I'd stick to one girl if I were you."

"No, I really am interested in Scottish history," he said.

I laughed. "I'll have one of the servants show you the

laird's lug tomorrow if you're keen on Scottish history."
Then I moved to join Belinda and Paolo, who were talking
with Max and Digby Flute, the young American.

Belinda intercepted me halfway across the floor. "Darling, talk to me about something normal," she said. "I
shall scream if I hear the words 'torque' and 'thrust' again.
Strangely enough I found the use of the word 'thrust' quite
titillating until now, but not when it so clearly applies to a
boat engine."

"They're still at it, are they?"

"Nonstop." She sighed. "And speaking of that—what is
up between you and Darcy? You're not exactly acting like
dearest chums, are you?"

"Absolutely not," I said. "He did something—well, for
which I can't forgive him."

"The lovely señorita, you mean? My dear, he hasn't been
near her, and it's not for want of trying on her part."

"No, it was something in London. He—" I stopped, un-
able to talk about it. "Let's just say that he is not my favorite
person at the moment."

"Such a pity when you're both in the same place for once
and the atmosphere is so romantic up here. Oh, and talking of romance, take a look at the dreaded Mrs. Simpson. I
think she was expecting another dinner guest and he hasn't
turned up."

I followed her gaze to the group around Binky. Mrs. Simpson was standing close to him, only half paying attention to
a story he was telling. She kept glancing up nervously, or
was it impatiently? Lachan and Murdoch had now joined
us, looking resplendent in full Highland dress. They stood
a little apart, deep in conversation, and suddenly it dawned
on me that they were two men with slight Scottish accents.
Could they have been the ones I overheard in the bathroom?

Surely they weren't Scottish nationalists out to kill the heir to the throne? But then they did have Stuart blood in them. I went over to join them.

"We didn't see you all day," I said brightly. "Where did you disappear to?"

"We were after a damned fine stag that your brother told us about," Lachan said, smiling down at me. "We didn't mention it to the others because they'd have ruined everything, tramping through the bracken like a herd of elephants and alerting every creature within miles."

"So did you find the stag?"

"We did," Murdoch replied. "Up on the flanks of Ben Alder. But it's a canny beast. It never let us get close enough for a good shot."

The flanks of Ben Alder, I thought. A perfect location to spy on the road down the pass and give a signal to someone that a car was approaching. . . . I looked up at Lachan's jolly, weathered face and twinkling blue eyes and tried to picture him calmly eliminating the heirs to the British throne. It seemed impossible, but then I'd been taken in before. I knew enough to realize that criminals do not look guilty.

Hamilton was approaching with the drinks tray. Lachan and Murdoch made a beeline for it. I was still watching them when Darcy appeared at my side.

"So are you going to sulk and ignore me forever?" he asked in a low voice. "Aren't you being rather childish?"

"I'm just tired of never knowing where I stand with you," I replied. "You disappear for weeks at a time. You flirt with other women. You probably do much more than flirt."

I saw the smile twitch at his lips. "You have to take me the way I am."

"I need someone I can rely on," I said.

Lachan had poured himself a generous Scotch and turned

back to me. "What can I get for you, Cousin Georgie?" he asked.

"That's very kind of you, Lachan," I said. "A sherry would be nice."

"Sherry? That's for old ladies. Come and let me pour you a dram of Binky's single malt." He put a big arm around my shoulder. I let myself be led away from Darcy. Luckily an interruption occurred at that moment with the announcement of the Prince of Wales. So that's why Mrs. Simpson had been so jumpy earlier.

Now she's in a pickle, I thought. Her husband is here. Fig was moving through the crowd like a sheepdog, trying to line us up to go in to dinner. "We won't process in until the piper gets here," she said, "but here's how the order of procession should go. Since Binky can't be part of it, His Royal Highness should escort me, Prince George should escort Lady Georgiana, Prince Siegfried with Countess Von Sauer, Herr Von Strohheim with—" She broke off as she looked at my mother, obviously trying to remember what her current name was. It was still Mrs. Clegg, as her Texan millionaire husband did not believe in divorce, but Fig wasn't to know that. She moved on hastily down the rest of the line. Mrs. Simpson was paired with Darcy and did not look pleased.

"These customs are so quaintly old-fashioned, aren't they?" she said to her lady friends, loud enough for those around her to hear. "So backward. No wonder Britain is being left behind in terms of world progress."

"They do rule half the globe, Wallis honey," Babe pointed out.

"One wonders how, with all these inbred families and their stupid customs. It really irks me to see that woman go ahead of me." She leaned out of the line to glare at my mother. "I mean, she's no longer a duchess, is she?"

She had meant my mother to hear. Mummy turned around to her and gave her a sweet smile. "Ah, but I usually try to discard mine before I move on to the next one. You are planning to discard this one, aren't you? Or are you worried he'll want too much alimony?"

There was the hint of a twitter from the other women but Mrs. S looked daggers at my mother as she turned back serenely to Max and slipped her dainty hand through his arm. Darcy caught my eye and gave me a wink. I had returned the smile before I remembered that I wasn't speaking to him.

Chapter 17

Castle Rannoch
August 18
Evening. Blowing a gale outside. Not much warmer in.

Suddenly the most awful wail echoed through the house. The countess grabbed at Siegfried's arm. "What is it? Is it the ghost? The White Lady of Rannoch?"

"Och, it's only the piper," Murdoch said. "Come to pipe us in to dinner."

And it was. Old Fergus looking very grand in his kilt and bonnet. We lined up behind him and marched down the hall to the banqueting room. The room, with its rough stone walls and high arched windows, can be austere at times but tonight it was ablaze with candles. Their light sparkled from the silverwear and highlighted the starched white tablecloth, stretching down the length of the room. Fig had certainly pulled out all the stops. I sat in the middle of the table, between Lachan and Prince Siegfried. Babe sat opposite and was clearly fascinated by Lachan's Highland dress.

"So is it true what they are saying, that Scotsmen wear nothing under their kilts?" she asked.

"If you care to reach under the table you can feel for yourself," Lachan said. Babe shrieked with laughter.

"I was hoping to serve you our traditional haggis tonight," Fig said. "But unfortunately—"

"Unfortunately we weren't able to catch any today during our hunting expedition," Murdoch interrupted.

"Catch them? I thought haggis was a type of sausage thing," Hugo said.

"Oh aye, it is. That's how you serve it after you've caught it," Lachan said earnestly. "You mince it up and make a sausage of it, but before that it's a canny wee beast. Ferocious for its size."

"Mercy me," said the countess. "And what does it look like?"

"Verra hairy," Lachan said. "With pointy little teeth, and it lurks in the heather and goes for the ankles of bigger prey. In fact if I hadn't seen Binky's trap with my own eyes, I'd have thought he'd been attacked by a band of haggis."

Those of us in the know were trying not to laugh, but Babe and the countess were gazing at Lachan, quite fascinated.

"We could take you on a haggis hunt tomorrow if you like," he suggested. "We saw haggis tracks today when we were out on the moor."

"That would be just fascinating, wouldn't it, Earl?" Babe said.

I waited for someone to burst out laughing and tell them the joke, but nobody did.

"So how was the climbing today, young fellows?" the Prince of Wales asked. I noted he had been seated nowhere near Mrs. Simpson and she, as a result, was sulking. "Did you plant the flag on any summits and claim them for England?"

"That would hardly be wise, seeing that we're in Scotland," Prince George replied. "But alas we reached no summit. We stupidly left the ropes and climbing paraphernalia behind. Didn't think we'd need it, you see, until we came to this great overhang. Well, we weren't prepared to tackle that with no ropes and pitons so we had to retreat."

"You should take Georgiana with you," Binky said. "She knows these munros better than anyone."

"Munros?" Gussie asked. "What the deuce is a munro?"

"Local name for a peak over three thousand feet," Binky said. "Georgie used to be up and down these munros like a bally mountain goat, didn't you, old bean?"

I felt all those eyes on me, staring at me as an object of curiosity.

"You make me sound like the wild woman of the glen," I said.

I noticed Mrs. Simpson give Earl a dig in the side and mutter something.

"We would be honored if you would accompany us tomorrow, Lady Georgiana," Siegfried said. "Your expertise would be most welcome. And we shall bring ropes this time and by the grace of God we shall conquer the summit."

He made it sound as if he was talking about Mont Blanc and not a Scottish hill only three thousand feet high, most of which involved simple scrambling.

Dinner passed pleasantly enough. The soup was delicious, there was enough beef to go around and even the neeps and tatties were commented upon as tasty. Talk turned to the speedboat and the monster. Binky's opinion was that someone had resurrected the old legend to drive tourist trade up here.

"I've lived here all my life and never heard it mentioned until recently," he said, "and I've certainly never seen it."

"But you have to agree that the way the water in that lake moved suddenly, looked awfully like a big creature swimming," the countess exclaimed. "What about that wake? Something had to have made those ripples."

"A plane had just landed," I pointed out, "and the loch goes from shallow to very deep just about there, so the waves do behave strangely with the right wind conditions."

"I'm sure I saw a head," the countess said. "A very large head."

"Maybe it's a submarine, spying on your speedboat," the Prince of Wales said, turning to Digby and Paolo. "A rival for the world speed record, maybe."

Dinner concluded with berry crumble and fresh cream followed by Welsh rarebit. We women followed Fig dutifully from the room to the drawing room, where coffee was waiting. Conchita came over to join me.

"We have not yet been introduced," she said, those dark eyes flashing. "You are the daughter of this house?"

"I'm the sister of the current duke," I said. "I'm Georgiana Rannoch."

"And I am Conchita da Gama. From Brazil."

"What are you doing in Scotland?"

"I make friends with Paolo in Italy. He needs money to pay for racing boat. I have much money," she said. "My father, he own rubber plantations in Brazil and now he find oil on his land. Very lucky, no?"

No wonder Darcy was interested, I thought. He was penniless like me. She'd be a very desirable catch.

It was as if she was reading my thoughts. "This Mr. Darcy O'Mara," she said, her eyes straying to the door, "he is handsome, do you not think? And the son of a lord, and Catholic."

I could see where this line of thought was going. "And penniless, I'm afraid," I said.

"No problem." She waved her hand. "I have enough

money to do what I want. But I do not understand. He tells me there is already a lady he admire."

Irrationally a great surge of hope rose in my heart. Then, of course, I wondered if I was the lady to whom he was referring. Obviously not, judging by the way he had treated me in London. The men soon joined us, or at least some of them did. Mr. Simpson was nowhere in evidence. The Prince of Wales headed straight for the arm of Wallis Simpson's chair when she patted it as if summoning a dog. Dancing was suggested. The rugs were rolled back in the great hall, someone set up the gramophone and we started, as always, with the Gay Gordons. I don't suppose the person who suggested the dancing had realized what she was in for. Lachan came to claim me and I was delighted to be able to shine for once. Scottish dances are one thing I do know how to do well.

After that Lachan grabbed Ronny to join us for the Dashing White Sergeant, which requires one man and two women. Murdoch attempted to drag Belinda and Fig onto the floor but most of the others looked on this time, Highland dances being unfamiliar to them. I was conscious of Darcy watching me from the shadows. Was I the lady he was talking about, I wondered, or had he just said that to dissuade the affectionate Señorita Conchita? From what I had seen, he hadn't been pushing her away too hard. Did I want him to like me? I wondered. He was in every way unsuitable husband material. I'd probably not even be allowed to marry him, since he was Catholic—forbidden to those in line to the throne of England.

The dance ended. A Paul Jones was suggested and everyone was urged onto the floor. We ladies moved in a clockwise direction while the men circled around us counterclockwise. The music stopped and I found myself with Lachan again. This time it was a waltz. He held me tightly. Darcy passed us, dancing with Conchita who was flirting shamelessly. I looked up at Lachan and gave him an encouraging smile. His grip on me tightened, almost crushing me.

"You've turned out quite nicely, Cousin Georgie. A nice trim wee waist, good sturdy limbs and not a bad figure. And you're not my first cousin, are you?"

"No, our grandfathers were brothers, I believe, which would make me a second cousin."

"Well, that's good to know." He spun me around dizzily.

"I believe you judge women like heifers," I said, and he laughed loudly.

The music summoned us back to the Paul Jones. The men and women circled each other again until I found myself opposite Earl. He was about to put his arm around my waist when Darcy stepped in rapidly. "My dance, I think," he said, and snatched me from under Earl's astonished nose.

"That's not quite cricket," I said. His tight hold on me was quite unnerving.

"Cricket is a very boring game, don't you think?" he whispered, his lips inches away from mine. "I much prefer other, more energetic sports." He swept me across the floor in a slow fox trot. "So you're talking to me again now, are you?"

"I forgot." I turned my head away.

He was holding me very close. I could feel the beat of his heart against mine and the warmth of him against my cheek.

"Are you going to stay angry at me forever?" he asked.

"I don't know. Did you tell Conchita that I was your girlfriend?"

"Well, I had to say something. She was all over me."

"So I was just an excuse again. I seem to be part of your life when it's convenient." I tried to lean away from him but his hand on the middle of my back was unrelenting. And he was laughing. "So you've decided that your hairy cousin is a better catch?"

"He may be."

"Don't be ridiculous. You're too damned sensitive, you know."

"Sensitive? I like that. You come and go as you please. You tell me——" I broke off. Had he ever actually told me he loved me? I wasn't sure.

"I can't be around all the time, Georgie. You should realize that," he said softly into my ear. His lips were brushing my cheek as he spoke and all the time he was steering me toward the edge of the dance floor. Then he fox-trotted me down the nearest hallway, in which, due to Fig's economy measures, no lamp was burning.

"There, that's more like it, isn't it?" he said. He pulled me to him and his lips searched for mine. I wanted to kiss him but I kept reminding myself why I was angry with him in the first place.

"First I want you to admit that it was you who telephoned that frightful priggish man at Scotland Yard about my embarrassing evening," I managed to say, turning my face to avoid his lips.

"Oh, God, not now, Georgie. Don't you want to kiss me?"

"Not until . . ." I said, weakening as his lips were now nuzzling at my ear and continuing down my throat.

"Not now?" he whispered as his lips moved across my chin and brushed my own lips with a feather-light kiss.

"This isn't fair," I said.

"Don't you know that all's fair in love and war?" he said, whispering the words one at a time, in between imprisoning my lips between his own. I felt the warmth of his body, pressing hard against me. Oh, God, I wanted him.

"Now, do you want me to kiss you or not?"

"All right, just shut up and kiss me," I said and turned my face to him.

I was no longer conscious of time or space. When we broke apart we were both breathing very hard.

"Georgie," he whispered, "is there somewhere we could go that's a little more comfortable than a cold and drafty hallway?"

"There's nowhere exactly comfortable in Castle Rannoch," I said, "and the only place that could be described as warm is the linen cupboard. I used to curl up there with a book and a torch when I was a child."

"The linen cupboard. Now that sounds intriguing." He gave me what could be described as a challenging grin. "Do you think it's large enough for two people?"

"Darcy!" I was half shocked, half excited.

"You could show me," he whispered, pulling me close to him and nuzzling at my neck again. "Or surely Castle Rannoch must possess a famous bedroom in which Mary, Queen of Scots, was born or Saint Margaret died."

I laughed uneasily, my sense of propriety fighting with my rising passion. "Neither. If you want to know, Castle Rannoch possesses the most uncomfortable beds in Scotland— probably in the civilized world."

"It's amazing that any Rannoch offspring were ever conceived then."

"I was conceived in Monte Carlo," I said. "I don't know about Binky. I think Rannochs always go away to get that sort of thing done."

"Then you'll just have to show me the linen cupboard." He slipped an arm around my waist, holding me very close to him as he steered me to the back stairs. We went up one flight, pausing for a couple of kisses along the way. My heart was really racing now. Darcy and I, alone together just as I had pictured it. I was not going to get cold feet this time!

We were just starting on the second flight of stairs when a piercing scream echoed through the castle. Then another. The screams were coming from the floor above us. We broke apart and rushed up the next flight of stairs, Darcy leading the way and taking the steps two at a time. Feet echoed below us as people came up the main staircase.

We were halfway up the second flight when we met the countess, staggering toward us, her face a mask of pure terror. "I saw her," she gulped. "The White Lady of Rannoch! She came wafting down that hallway."

We piled into the hallway but of course there was nothing to be seen. Ghosts don't usually wait around for an audience. The men opened doors, one by one, but there was no sign of a ghost.

As we turned to come back down, Fig drew me aside. "Well done, Georgiana," she said. "Brilliant, positively brilliant."

"It would have been brilliant," I whispered back, "but it wasn't me."

Chapter 18

Castle Rannoch
Late evening, August 18, 1932,
followed by early morning August 19.

It was a subdued group that assembled downstairs in the drawing room. Countess Von Sauer was sipping brandy and recounting her horror to anyone who would listen.

"It was coming down the hall toward me—a white disembodied face and light hair and hands, that's all I saw— and it was sort of wafting. Then I suppose I screamed and it just—melted away. Vanished. I won't feel safe sleeping here again, I can tell you that. Fritzi, you'll just have to find us a hotel."

"At this time of night, in the middle of nowhere, Mama?" Fritzi looked worried. "I tell you what. I'll sleep on a mattress on the floor of your room and we'll look for a hotel in the morning."

"I'm sure you're quite safe, Countess," Binky said. "Georgiana and I have lived here all our lives and have never met a hostile ghost yet."

"But that's because you're family members," the countess

wailed. "Everyone knows that family ghosts are only hostile to strangers."

"If you ask me, it was someone playing a practical joke," the Prince of Wales said, looking around at the assembled group. "And if it was someone here, it would be the honorable thing to own up right now."

Our guests looked at each other but nobody spoke.

"Then let us think back to see if anyone was missing from the room when the countess screamed," the prince went on.

"Mr. Simpson, for one," my mother couldn't resist saying.

"Well, honey, he had a headache and went up to bed," Mrs. Simpson said, smiling serenely. "And I don't think he could be mistaken for a white lady, even in the poorest light. He's rather tall, you know. And he has dark hair." Her gaze fell on me. "But I did notice Lady Georgiana leaving the room . . . with Mr. O'Mara."

"I can assure you we had other things on our mind than playing at ghosts," Darcy said. I felt myself blushing like a schoolgirl.

I looked around the room. "And where's Hugo?" I asked.

"Yes, where is he?" someone else said. "He was dancing in the Paul Jones a little while ago."

We looked up as footsteps were heard coming down the stairs. All eyes watched as Hugo came down. He did have very light hair, worn rather long.

"Where have you been?" Earl demanded.

Hugo looked suitably confused. "Can't a chap bally well go to take a leak without having to get permission first?"

"Which bathroom did you use?" Fig demanded.

"Why this interest in my call of nature?" Hugo grinned. "In answer to that, the closest one, just off that hall to the left."

"It was a real ghost, I know it," the countess insisted. "Real people can't just vanish."

I watched Hugo as he took his place among the guests, chatting easily as if nothing had happened. He did have light hair, and he wasn't that tall. Was this his idea of a joke or something more serious? I resolved to keep a closer eye on him. The party broke up soon after. The mood had been broken and nobody showed any interest in dancing again. Off they went and we were left with our house guests plus the Prince of Wales, who showed no intention of leaving in the near future. One by one they went off to bed, with Fritzi promising faithfully to stand guard at his mother's bedside all night.

"Well, that was a rum do, wasn't it?" the prince said, when the Americans and Hugo had also gone to their rooms, leaving only essentially family members. "It's been a rum day altogether—what with that dashed great rock crashing onto my car and now this."

"And don't forget Binky's foot getting caught in a trap," Fig said, looking with concern at her husband. "One might almost think that someone is out to do us harm."

There, she had expressed it out loud. I looked from one prince to the other, and then at the two Scottish cousins. The Prince of Wales laughed. "I don't believe that any communist or anarchist would go to the trouble of setting traps and arranging for rocks to land on cars," he said. "One good bullet would do the trick much more cleanly."

He was right about that, of course. If someone did want to do away with the prince, or with the heirs in general, then these were petty accidents with small chance of success, when a bullet or bomb could be guaranteed to kill. It was being done with monotonous frequency to one European royal family after another.

"Maybe it's all someone's idea of a joke," Binky suggested.

"It would have to be someone with a rather twisted sense of humor," Fig said bitterly.

I just happened to glance across at the cousins and I saw a smirk pass between them. Was this really their idea of a joke? I worried about this later as I lay in bed. They were poor, by their own admission, so I could understand if they wanted to do away with Binky and get their hands on this estate. But they had no connection to the Prince of Wales, and why would anyone want to frighten the countess? The latter was the most easily explained, of course. She had proved herself to be of a nervous disposition. It was she who had seen the monster in the lake. Maybe she had caught sight of Hugo heading for a bathroom and decided she was seeing a ghost.

Of course then my thoughts turned to Hugo. Why had he decided to invite himself to Castle Rannoch when I'm sure the rented house was more pleasant and full of young people like himself. Was he really so besotted with Ronny Padgett that he followed her everywhere? Could he be the one with a grudge against our family? The whole thing was too ridiculous. Then I remembered the feel of Darcy's lips on mine and the delicious anticipation of the linen cupboard, and fell asleep with a smile on my face.

I was woken by the most ungodly sound—a half-strangled scream, an unearthly wail. I leaped out of bed and ran to the window because the sound seemed to be coming from outside. It was still only half light. Then the sound came closer and of course I realized what it was. It was old Fergus piping in the day around the castle, as had been done for the past six hundred years. I slipped on my dressing gown and went out into the hallway. I could hear voices coming from the other side of the stairwell, where the Americans were housed. Animated voices in considerable distress.

"You heard it too, did you? Unearthly, that's what it was. A soul in torment. I knew this place was haunted from the moment we came here."

I crossed the landing and found Babe and Earl, the countess and Fritzi huddled together in their nightclothes. The countess looked up, saw me and screamed. "It's the White Lady!" she exclaimed, clutching at Earl.

"It's only me, Countess."

"It's young Lady Georgiana," Earl said. "You heard it too, did you? Confounded noise woke me up. What was it, some kind of animal in distress?"

"No, it was only our piper, resuming his morning round of the castle. He's been off sick but now it sounds as if he's back in fine form."

"Bagpipes, you mean?"

"Of course. You are in Scotland, you know."

"But it's not even light yet."

"Precisely. Bagpipes at dawn. That's the tradition here."

"You mean every morning from now on?" Babe looked shocked.

"Every morning. And I expect he'll entertain us at dinner too, now he's back."

"Oh, my God." Babe put her hand to her head. "Where are my headache powders, Earl? And I need an ice pack."

"An ice pack?" I asked. "It's summer. You won't find any ice."

"Is there no ice in the whole of Scotland?" Earl demanded.

"Pretty much."

"Earl, I don't know how much longer I can take this,"

Babe said. "I mean, Wallis knows I'd do anything for her, but this is beyond human endurance."

"I agree," the countess said. "You could all come and stay with me at Castle Adlerstein. It's on a lake in Austria; it really is much more agreeable."

"It really does sound like a better idea," Babe agreed. "What do you think, Poopsie?" I tiptoed away and went back to bed. The plan seemed to be working splendidly!

Chapter 19

Castle Rannoch and a mountainside
August 19, 1932
Morning.

When I next awoke it was to Maggie bringing in the tea tray. "A glorious morning, your ladyship," she said. "I hope you'll be taking advantage of it."

Oh, golly, I thought. I had been coerced into taking the two princes climbing. Another wicked thought went through my head. The munro they wished to tackle could be ascended by no more than what we might describe as a brisk ramble. Of course there was a rather tricky ascent that involved the crag, if one went directly up from the lake. I could take them up that. They'd be terribly impressed. I just hoped I was still up to it and could remember the route.

When I appeared for breakfast, dressed for climbing in trews, shirt and Windbreaker, I met Siegfried, looking as if he was about to tackle Mount Everest.

"So we attempt the climb today, Lady Georgiana?" he asked, somewhat nervously. "We go for the summit?"

"Absolutely."

"I have all prepared. Ropes. Pitons."

"Ice axes?" I suggested with a grin.

He shook his head seriously. "I do not believe one needs ice axes in summer. I saw no ice yesterday."

Honestly the man had no sense of humor. I was tempted to say that we could easily manage without any equipment, but then, it rather amused me to think of Siegfried and Prince George going up our little crag, roped together.

"So we set off after breakfast, then?" I said.

"Unfortunately His Highness will not be joining us," Siegfried said. "He was summoned to Balmoral."

"Nothing's wrong, I hope?"

"His father wished to speak to him. Something about gambling debts, I believe."

So Prince George's sins were gradually coming to light, were they? Did I really want to be stuck alone on a mountain with Siegfried? "Should we not postpone our climb until he is able to join us?" I asked.

"He fears he may be sent back to London," Siegfried said. "And if he is able to join us once more, then I shall have learned the correct route and be able to lead. I have great experience, you know. I have tackled the Alps and the Dolomites. I know no fear."

"Jolly good," I said. "Then we may well attempt the part with the overhang."

He blanched, making his already pale face even paler. "But it seemed impossible."

"Not with a good rope and pitons," I said. "What is a thousand-foot drop if you are securely anchored? Until after breakfast, then."

I thought he looked a trifle green. I was beginning to enjoy myself for the first time in ages.

The Americans were also not looking at their best. Babe

looked particularly haggard. So did Mrs. Simpson. "How am I expected to get my beauty sleep if we're awoken in the middle of the night?" she demanded.

"I'm sorry," I said. "I realize you must need quite a bit of it these days."

I saw Mr. Simpson smirk. Again I felt sorry for the man. At least he had a sense of humor.

Lachan and Murdoch entered while we were in the middle of breakfast. I was tucking into the usual bacon, eggs and smoked haddock, while watching Babe and Mrs. Simpson having half a grapefruit and a slice of toast each.

"So are we all ready?" Lachan asked, helping himself to everything that was going.

"What for?"

"Did you no say you wanted to go on a haggis hunt?" Lachan asked.

"Not for me. Nothing fierce," the countess said quickly.

"Well, I think that might be fun," Babe said, eyeing Lachan's broad shoulders. "Let's do it, okay, Earl?"

"Whatever you want, baby."

"And where is that delightful young man Hugo?" Babe asked. "Maybe he'd like to join us."

"I think I saw him going out a while back," Mrs. Simpson said. "I expect he's gone back to his friends with the speedboat. Oh, and I gather from sources in the know that a shoot is being planned tomorrow at Balmoral, for any of you who enjoy such things. I may just go shopping in the nearest town, if there is a nearest town. I'm running low on nail polish."

"We have to stay and go shooting, Babe," Earl said. "You know I love shooting things. I've been looking forward to it. Wallis promised us shooting here every day and there has been none so far."

"My brother was not intending to step on a trap and nearly lose his foot," I said coldly. I was a trifle vexed by the way they discussed my family and my home as if we didn't exist.

"Of course not, poor sap," Earl said. "So should I take my gun on your little expedition today, young man?"

"Maybe not," Lachan said. "You might miss and that would enrage them."

I kept waiting for Lachan to burst out laughing, or for someone to let them in on the secret. But no one did and I wasn't going to. After all, it was rather fun and they had been rather annoying. I left them preparing for their quest and set off with Siegfried. The walk across the estate to the foot of Bein Breoil took some time, owing to the amount of equipment Siegfried was carrying and the fact that his new climbing boots pinched his toes.

As we walked I looked back at the road snaking over the pass and tried to imagine where one could roll a boulder down onto a car with any degree of success. It seemed impossible. Close to the estate, which was where they said they had been struck, the area beside the road was tree lined and reasonably flat. Surely any boulder would hit a tree first. Up at the top, where the pass narrowed, there would have been greater chance of success, but that wasn't apparently where the prince's car was struck. Interesting.

At last we reached the base of the crag. I had to admit that from down here it did look rather formidable, rising some two hundred feet of sheer granite.

"Right. Off we go then," I said. "Do you want me to lead first or will you?"

"Ladies first," Siegfried said. He was already sweating from carrying all that equipment.

I began to climb the rock face, my fingers and toes remembering the old tried-and-true route. When you knew where the handholds were, it wasn't too alarming. When I reached a suitable point for Siegfried to pass me, I drove in a piton and signaled for him to come up. He did, passing me with much heavy breathing and sweat on his brow. In this fashion we made it almost to the top and I showed him how to skirt around the overhang. At last we hauled ourselves up to the top of the crag and rested, sitting on a large boulder while we admired the view. A fresh wind blew in our faces and the loch below reflected the mountains. I breathed deeply, savoring everything about the scene, except for the person sitting beside me.

"So we achieved it with no problem, you see." Siegfried was looking very pleased with himself. I could see this story would be embellished and retold among the courts of Europe.

"Well done, Your Highness," I said.

"Please, call me Siegfried," he said, "and I shall call you Georgiana when we are alone."

I hoped that wouldn't be too often.

"You know, Georgiana," he said, "I have been thinking. It would not be such a bad idea if we were to get married."

I'm glad I had a firm seat on that boulder or I might have plunged to my death.

"But Your Hi—I mean, Siegfried—I believe you are as little attracted to me as I am to you," I said tactfully. This actually meant *I know you prefer boys,* and it was better than shouting "Not if you were the last man in the universe" for all of Scotland to hear.

"That has nothing to do with it," he said. "We of noble birth do not marry for love, we marry to cement alliances among the great houses of Europe. It is important that I choose the right wife. I may be king someday."

"If your brother and your father are assassinated, you mean?"

"Possibly."

"And what makes you think you won't follow suit?"

"I shall be a just and popular king, unlike my brother and my father. And you will make a suitable consort for me. I know that your family is in favor of this match and do not think you could do better."

The local gamekeeper would be better, I longed to say.

"I shall make few demands on you," he went on, waving a hand expansively. "Once you have produced me an heir, you will be free to take lovers, as long as you are discreet at all times."

"And you will also take lovers, and be equally discreet?"

"Naturally. That is how things are done."

"Not for me, Siegfried," I said. "I intend to marry for love. I may be naïve, but I believe that I will find true happiness with the right man for me someday."

He looked extremely put out. "But your family wishes this alliance."

"I'm sorry. My family doesn't contribute a penny toward my sustenance. They don't have a say in my happiness. I wish you well in finding a suitable princess."

"Very well." He got to his feet. "We shall now make the descent. After you, my lady."

"We can belay down past the overhang," I said. "Do you want me to go first, while you play out the rope for me?"

"If you wish." He was cold, remote and correct, obviously not used to being rejected. I adjusted my harness and walked out backward over the cliff. I had only gone down a few feet, past the worst part of the overhang, when I heard a sound I associated with sailing ships at sea. It was the creak and groan of a rope under stress. While my brain was still processing the thought that the rope was about to break, it did and I fell.

I made a grab at the rock face but my fingers were torn from their handholds as I plummeted down. I had an impression of rock wall flashing past me, and the words formed themselves in my brain, *I am about to die. Bother.* And for some reason I was remarkably annoyed at being about to die a virgin.

It was almost as if I was descending in slow motion. I steeled myself for the inevitable crunch when I crashed into the scree at the bottom of the rock face. Then suddenly I was jerked upward and tipped upside down. I swung dizzily in my harness with the sky beneath my feet and the ground twirling above me. I didn't know how I'd been saved from certain death, but I presumed the rope must have snagged itself on some outcropping. In which case it could give way again any second. I continued to twirl, upside down. I tried, ineffectually, to right myself, but I was scared of putting any sudden pressure on the rope.

So I hung there, swaying in the breeze, just praying that Siegfried had the sense to find the easy route down and go for help. If not, I wasn't sure how long I could hang here. I could already feel the blood rushing to my head and singing in my ears. I was going to pass out if I stayed in this position much longer. Wind whistled past me, swinging me around. Clouds were rushing in, already blotting out the higher peaks. Soon I'd be hidden from sight.

"Help," I yelled into nowhere. "Somebody come and help me."

The singing in my head had become a roaring. Spots were dancing in front of my eyes. Gradually the world slipped away.

Chapter 20

A mountainside near Castle Rannoch
August 19

When I opened my eyes two pale beings hovered over me, looking down at me with concern. For a moment I wondered whether this was heaven and that angels were actually blond. Then I noticed that one of them had fish lips and the other said, "She's coming round, thank God." I realized that one face belonged to Siegfried, the other to Hugo Beasley-Bottome.

"Where am I?" I asked. "Did I fall?"

"You, old fruit, are the luckiest girl in Scotland, I'd say," Hugo said. "I heard yelling and went to investigate, and there was the prince here, gesturing like a madman at the cliff. Then I noticed that you were dangling in midair. The bally rope was caught on a small tree that was jutting out from the rock. It was dashed impossible to get at you, you know."

"Then how did you get at me?" I tried to sit up. The world swung around alarmingly and I lay back again.

"Your cousin Lachan arrived to join us. He climbed up and attached a second rope, which was held by a piton, then with him bracing, we were able to break the branch that held you and lower you down. Dashed tricky maneuver, I can tell you."

"Thank you, very much," I said. "I don't know where you got the ropes from, Siegfried, but they must have been old. We should have tested them first."

"The rope was not old," Siegfried said. "Prince George brought it over himself from Balmoral. We laid it out to measure it and it was in fine form. Nothing wrong with it."

"Obviously something was wrong with it or it wouldn't have broken," I said.

Then I noticed Hugo's face. It had a strange, wary look to it. What was he doing up here in the first place? Or Lachan, for that matter? This was rather out of the way for a good haggis hunt, surely, and I thought I remembered someone saying that Hugo had gone down to be with his friends on the loch.

Lachan himself appeared at that moment. "Och, she's awake and talking. That is good news. Well, let's carry you back to the castle, wee Georgie, and get some brandy down you for shock. Your Highness, why don't you run on ahead and tell them we're coming so that they can have a bed with a hot water bottle ready."

"Very well," Siegfried said. "If you are sure the two of you can carry her between you."

"Between us?" Lachan laughed. "Why, she weighs no more than a feather." Then he swept me up into his arms.

"I'll bring the rest of their equipment, then," Hugo said.

Lachan strode down the steep path as if I weighed nothing at all.

I was beginning to recover. "So what happened to your

haggis hunt, then?" I asked. "Surely you didn't bring them up here to do their hunting?"

He grinned. "It was canceled. They made the mistake of telling one of the groundsmen about it and he laughed himself silly. Now they're right put out about our little joke."

"I thought it was rather a good joke, personally," I said.

"So did I, but your brother has given Murdoch and me a stern warning. No more silly tricks or we're on our way home."

"Have you played any other silly tricks, then?" I asked.

"What? Oh no. Nothing at all." I was sure from his face that he was lying. Had he confessed to Binky that he was responsible for setting the trap? Surely he wasn't the White Lady. Nobody could have mistaken anything as large, red and obviously male for a ghostly woman.

As we approached the castle, servants ran out to meet us. Siegfried must have embellished the story or told it with great drama because they were looking terrified.

"Oh, my lady, thank goodness you're safe," Hamilton said. "And thank you, Mr. Lachan, for saving her for us. Your room is ready, my lady, and I've taken the liberty of having some hot tea and brandy sent up."

"Thank you." I smiled, feeling for a moment safe and cared for. Lachan carried me up the stairs and placed me on my bed. "Well, you'll be all right now, I expect," he said. Fig appeared at that moment in a frightful fluster. "They say you nearly died, Georgiana. I thought no good could come of climbing."

"The climb was no problem," I said. "The rope snapped on the way down."

"Who is in charge of ropes here? I'll see he's fired immediately."

"Fig, the rope came from Balmoral with Prince George,"

I said. "And Siegfried said it looked just fine when they laid it out."

"Then I suppose a sharp rock must have cut through it." She pushed Maggie aside and placed the hot water bottle beside me. This was a good idea as I was now feeling decidedly shivery. The tea tray arrived and Fig poured a generous helping of brandy into my cup. I drank, gasping at the combination of alcohol and heat, then I lay back.

"Have a good rest now, and then we'll send up some lunch," she said. "And by the way, have you heard? The Americans came back in a frightful temper. It seems your dreadful cousin had spun them a yarn about hunting for haggis. Really those men are too much."

"That's rich, coming from someone who made the piper play at dawn," I said with a grin. "You're just as bad as they are."

"Well, I suppose if it helps to drive them away, I can't complain."

"I think it was jolly funny," I said. "You should have heard Lachan describing how ferocious the haggis were and how they went for your ankles."

"I suppose that is rather amusing." Fig's face actually cracked into a smile. "I wonder what they'll say when we have haggis for dinner tonight. Cook has it all prepared, you know."

"Excellent." I closed my eyes. Fig shushed Maggie out of the room and I lay there alone. All in all it had been a surreal morning, with Siegfried asking me to marry him and then the fall. It did cross my mind that the two could be related. Had he cut the rope in a fit of pique because I had turned him down? Foreigners were known to be so emotional and he did come from a part of the world where vengeance was a daily occurrence.

I must have drifted off to sleep because I awoke to hear the sound of a door creaking open. All Castle Rannoch doors creak, as do the floorboards. It's positively a requirement in a castle to have creaking doors. My eyes opened in time to see Hugo Beasley-Bottome creeping into the room.

"Hugo!" I exclaimed. "What are you doing here?"

He started, as if he had expected me to be asleep. "Sorry. I just thought—well, I thought that you and I might have a little chat."

"I'm not in a chatting mood at the moment," I said warily. "I've just woken up."

"I wanted to get you to myself," he said, "and now seems like a good time. There are always so many bally people around."

He came over toward my bed. I sat up hastily, drawing my covers around me in a good display of maidenly effrontery. "Mr. Beasley-Bottome, this is my bedroom and I certainly didn't invite you in."

At that a smile flashed across his face. "A chap has to take whatever opportunity he can in this life. That's what they taught us at school, don't y'know?"

"Please leave," I said.

"Hold on a jiffy, old bean. I said I only wanted a chat. I'm not intending to ravish you on the spot, although I must say the idea is tempting. . . ." He paused. "I don't quite know how to put this but I think you'd want to know . . ."

At that moment the door burst open and Lachan stood there, giving a good imitation of an avenging relative. "What do you think you're doing in here?" he demanded. "Out, this minute. Can't you see the wee lassie needs her rest and quiet?"

"I only wanted a few words with her," Hugo said.

"Do you want a few words with yon boy?" Lachan demanded.

"I really don't at the moment," I said.

"Then out." He made a grab for Hugo, who took the hint and headed for the door.

"And just in case there are any more interruptions, I think I'll set up camp outside your door tonight," he said.

"Lachan, you really don't have to guard my honor." I didn't know whether to laugh or not.

He went across to the door and closed it. "It's not that. I took a good look at yon rope. It didn't seem to have broken because it was worn. It looked more like a clean cut to me. Someone had cut almost through it and left the last strands to break."

"I see." I took a deep breath. "And how do I know that you weren't that person, playing one of your famous jokes?"

"Some joke, wee Georgie. You'd have fallen on your head from a great height and we'd currently be holding your wake." He leaned closer. "That's why I've been keeping an eye on yon Hugo person. How did he arrive so quickly on the scene, that's what I'd like to know. He was no climbing with you, was he?"

"No, I hadn't seen him all morning."

"Then what was he doing in such a convenient spot as to be offering help when you were stuck up there, unless he knew what was going to happen to you?"

"Oh, dear," I said. "I did feel awfully uneasy when he came creeping in a few minutes ago. I'm glad you turned up when you did."

He patted my leg under the blankets. "Don't you worry now. I'll be outside the door and it would take a strapping man to get past me."

"Thank you, Lachan," I said.

He went to go, then turned back. "Georgie, about my wee jokes—you know about the rock that landed on the Prince of Wales and Mrs. Simpson?"

"That was you?"

"Not me. Murdoch. And it was an accident, I can assure you. He decided he might as well get in some practice for the Braemar Games. It's a good spot here, away from the competition. He was up to throwing the hammer and he didn't have a hammer on the spot, so to speak, so he had improvised by tying some rope around a large rock. Well, somehow it came loose as he was twirling it around his head and it went flying off in the wrong direction. We heard the awful clunk and the yells, and when we saw it was the Simpson woman, we made ourselves scarce."

"Well, that's good news," I said, trying not to smile. "At least it wasn't deliberate. And you didn't accidentally put out the trap for Binky to step on, did you?"

"Good God, no. I'd never hurt a kinsman. I might be tempted to do it for a Campbell, maybe, but who'd want to hurt Binky? He can't have an enemy in the world. A bit soft, maybe, and not overly endowed with brains, but there's not a mean bone in him."

"That's true," I said.

He leaned over and gave me a kiss on the forehead, then patted my shoulder. "Sweet dreams, young lady," he said. "I thought you did a fine job today. No silly hysterics. Just what one would expect from a Rannoch."

He left me then, with several thoughts to consider. Was he seriously considering marrying me? He and Murdoch had described themselves as penniless, but Binky had referred to their farm as prosperous. But Lachan was the younger brother. He wouldn't inherit anything.

"This is ridiculous," I said out loud. Of course I wasn't considering marrying him. I could have had a prince, a possible heir to a throne. I could always have someone like Gussie if I wanted, but I didn't want. I knew who I wanted and he had nothing to offer me in the material sense. Ah, well, two men who were interested in me in one day. That wasn't bad. Things were looking up in some ways.

They were looking down in others, of course, because it was apparent that someone had tried to kill me today. Or rather not to kill me, but to kill one of us. I thought that Siegfried's brutish countrymen would probably go more directly for a bomb through the window. Then, of course, I realized what should have been obvious all along: the rope had come from Balmoral. It had been intended for Prince George. Once again someone was targeting an heir to the throne—and this time somebody sixth in line. It was about time I stopped lying here and started working, before it was too late and one of the accidents took its toll.

Chapter 21

Castle Rannoch
August 19

I must have dozed off for quite a while because when I awoke the room was bathed in pink twilight and there were sounds of commotion outside my door. Raised voices. A man shouting. I got up and opened the door cautiously. The first person I saw was Earl, standing at the top of the stairs. "She's nowhere to be found, I tell you," he was saying.

I came out onto the landing. "What's wrong?" I asked.

"It's Babe. She's disappeared," he said. "I can't find her anywhere."

"Maybe she went out for a walk before dinner," I suggested.

"We went out for a walk earlier," he said. "We came back and she said she wanted to take a bath before dinner. She'd never go out walking again after she'd taken a bath. I did other things. Wrote a letter. Tried to make a telephone call to London—without success, I might add. Then when I went back to the room, she wasn't there. I just don't understand it."

Fig had now come up the stairs to join us and together we went up the second flight to Earl and Babe's bedroom.

"There, you see," he said. Her dinner dress was laid out, ready to wear, on her bed. "She went to the bathroom in her robe. And her toilet bag is missing."

"Have you checked the bathroom?" I asked. "She could have fallen asleep in the bath, or even passed out."

"That was my first thought," Earl said. "But the bathroom is unoccupied."

We walked down the hallway to the nearest bathroom. It was, indeed, unoccupied and there was no sign that Babe had ever been there. No lingering steam on the mirror to indicate that a bath had been taken recently. (Of course, steam does not tend to linger long at Castle Rannoch, owing to the gale coming in through the open windows.)

"Is it possible she used another bathroom?" Fig suggested. "She might have found this one occupied and decided to look elsewhere."

We crossed the landing to the hallway on the other side where the Simpsons and the Von Sauers were currently staying. That bathroom was occupied, but the annoyed voice coming from it was that of Mrs. Simpson, who told us in no uncertain terms to go away.

"Would she have gone downstairs and used one of our bathrooms?" I asked. There was one on my landing and another on Fig and Binky's side.

"I don't think Babe would want to be seen going down the staircase in her robe," Earl said. "I didn't think of checking another floor, but I'm willing to give anything a try right now."

We went downstairs and examined my bathroom. Also empty. Lastly we went across to the grandest hallway, the one that contained the bedrooms of Fig and Binky, Prince

Siegfried and also that of Prince George. The bathroom door was closed. We tapped on it. No answer. Earl rapped on it loudly. "Babe, are you in there?" Still no answer. "Oh, God," he exclaimed. "What if she's drowned in the bathtub? We must break down the door."

"Nobody is breaking down a door," Fig said. "We'll get a key."

I was dispatched to summon Hamilton, who arrived with the pass keys. We tried several and at last the bathroom door opened. The window faced the back of the castle and this part of the house had already descended into darkness. But we could make out a white shape lying on the floor.

"Oh, my God!" Earl sprang forward, while Fig turned on the light.

The harsh glare of the bulb revealed Babe, lying sprawled next to the lavatory in a pool of water and blood, while around her lay shattered pieces of what had been the lavatory tank. One could see where it had come away from the wall, high above the loo, revealing a brighter patch of tartan wallpaper. Most embarrassingly, she had obviously been sitting on the throne when she was struck. She was wearing nothing but a short kind of negligee and her little white bottom stuck up piteously.

Pandemonium ensued. Hamilton was sent to telephone for our doctor and an ambulance. Earl was on his knees pleading for Babe not to die, having first covered her posterior with his jacket to prevent further embarrassment. The countess appeared at that moment, started to have hysterics and had to be led away by her son, moaning, "A house of horrors, I knew it. What did I tell you? Somebody get me out of here before doom befalls us all."

No sooner had she disappeared than Prince Siegfried arrived in a silk dressing gown with a black sleeping mask pushed up on his forehead, wanting to know what all the infernal row was about when he was trying to take forty winks. Fig and I were the only ones staying calm and sensible. Fig had always boasted about her Girl Guide training and I must say her first aid badge came in rather useful. She was down on her knees among the muck, feeling for a pulse. She looked up eventually and nodded.

"She's still alive. Get towels to mop up this mess and blankets to put around her. We shouldn't move her until a doctor examines her. She could have a fractured skull."

I attempted to move the pieces of shattered lavatory tank from her.

"It must have toppled onto her when she pulled the chain," I said.

"How extraordinary. I've never heard of that happening in my life," Fig said. "She must have pulled the chain jolly hard."

"You've no business having guests to stay in a house that is falling to pieces," Earl said angrily. "This place is a positive death trap. I said so to Babe only this morning."

"What an extraordinary day," Fig muttered as we moved out of the way to make room for the maids who had arrived with piles of towels and blankets, and had begun to mop up the floor. "First you fall off a mountain and nearly kill yourself, and now this. Anyone would think there was a curse on the castle or something. You've never heard of any curses on the Rannoch family, have you?"

"There was that witch who was thrown into the lake," I suggested. "But she's had six centuries to curse us so I expect she would have done it by now."

Fig sighed. "I don't suppose we'll hear the last of it. That man Earl will want to sue us or something. That's what they do in America, isn't it? We'll be bankrupted. Destitute. We'll have to go and live in one of the cottages. . . ."

"Don't you start getting hysterical," I said, putting a calming hand on her shoulder. "Remember, a Rannoch never loses his nerve."

"Blast the stupid Rannochs," she said. "This place has brought me nothing but grief. I should have married the nice young vicar at St. Stephen's in our village, but I wanted to be a duchess." She really was closer to hysterics than I had ever seen her.

Fortunately the doctor arrived at the same time as the ambulance, causing Fig to put on a brave face and resume her role as duchess. His face was grim as he examined her. "A nasty business," he said. "I don't see any signs of a fractured skull, but to have been knocked out this long would indicate a severe concussion at the very least. We must try and transport her to hospital without disturbing her. Lift her very carefully, men. I'll come with you."

They put her onto a stretcher and off they went. Earl went with them, as did the countess and Fritzi. The nearest hospital was in Perth and they announced that they'd take a hotel room nearby. Mrs. Simpson, on the other hand, did not go with them.

"Of course I want to offer support to dear Babe," she said, "but I see no point in sitting in dreary waiting rooms or hotels, waiting until she is well enough to receive visitors. In fact I rather think it wouldn't be wise for me to be spotted in a Scottish hotel room. It might give rise to gossip, you know."

So the prince won out over her dearest friend. Mr. Simpson looked fed up. I wondered how much longer she'd keep him around for respectability's sake. But they did go out to dine, as did Hugo Beasley-Bottome, so it was essentially only family plus Siegfried who were at dinner when the haggis was ceremonially piped in. Then, of course, we had to pretend that we enjoyed it. It wasn't awful or anything, just not, as Fig had put it, our cup of tea. But after all the trouble we'd forced poor Cook to go to, we simply couldn't send any back. So we struggled with it manfully, except for Siegfried, who pushed his portion away, declaring that he never ate anything when he couldn't identify what part of the animal it came from.

Only Murdoch and Lachan tucked into it with glee, with much chomping and smacking of lips. I glanced across at Lachan. Oh, dear, I could never marry a man who smacked his lips over haggis.

There was no suggestion of any kind of evening jollity tonight. I went up to bed almost immediately after coffee. I was feeling completely exhausted, I suspect by the shock of two alarming events in one day. I lay there, listening to the sigh of the wind while I tried to blot images from my mind—the world swinging crazily as I hung upside down, and then Babe, lying in the midst of all that blood and water with the lavatory cistern broken around her and her little white bottom exposed for all to see. Someone was at loose in our midst who had evil, if not murder, on his mind. I had been charged with trying to find out who it was and I hadn't done anything so far. I had better get a move on with my investigation. This had to be stopped.

Chapter 22

Castle Rannoch
August 20, 1932
Promising to be a lovely day.

I was woken by the sound of tapping on my door. It was already misty daylight. I must have slept through the piper, if indeed he had played again this morning. Maggie came in with my morning tea, followed by Hamilton, with a perplexed look on his face.

"I'm sorry to wake you, my lady, but . . ."

"What is it, Hamilton?"

"There is a person in the front hall, wishing to speak to you."

"What kind of person?"

"A person from the lower classes, my lady."

"And what does he want with me?"

"He says to tell you that he came 'as quick as he could, and Bob's your uncle, he's here.' But I don't think that Bob is your uncle, is he, my lady?"

I sat up in bed, laughing. "It's a Cockney expression, Hamilton. And it's not a person, it's my grandfather."

"Your—grandfather, my lady?" There was a distinct gulp.

"My mother's father, Hamilton."

"Am I to understand that he will be staying here, at the castle?" He must have been rattled. He forgot to add "my lady."

"Oh no. Not at all. He's going to stay in one of the empty cottages on the estate. The one next to Nanny looked quite nice, I thought."

I saw the relief sweep over his face. "Very suitable, my lady. And what should I do with him until you come down?"

"Put him in the morning room with a cup of tea and the paper," I said. "He is house-trained, you know."

"My lady, I wasn't implying . . ." he stammered.

"Tell him I'll be down immediately," I said and jumped out of bed. Hamilton backed out and I instructed Maggie to hand me the first items of clothing she could find. I was so excited, I wriggled impatiently as she did up my buttons. If Granddad was here, then everything would be all right. I could stop worrying because he'd know what to do. As I came down the stairs, a sticky problem presented itself. If my grandfather had taken the night train, he'd want breakfast, and I wasn't quite sure how to handle introducing him to the breakfast room. I couldn't risk letting him come into contact with Fig. Not that I didn't think he could give as good as he got, but Fig could be crushingly snobby and he didn't deserve that. Maybe if it was early enough, we could have the room to ourselves.

I positively ran down the stairs. Granddad was in the morning room, perched on the edge of a brocade and gilt chair, a cup of tea in his hand, looking uneasy. He stood up as he heard my approaching feet and a big smile spread across his face. "Well, look at you." He put down the teacup and opened his arms wide. "Don't you look a treat. Blimy, some gloomy great place you've got here, haven't you?"

"You've never been to Castle Rannoch before?"

"Never been invited, my love. And never had the desire to come this far north, if you want to know. We in the Smoke have the belief that civilization ends south of Birmingham. I only came because I got the feeling you wanted me here."

"I do," I said, hugging him fiercely. Fig would never have approved of such a wanton display of affection. She and her parents only ever shook hands. I wondered how little Podge was ever conceived, but then I supposed she had been instructed to close her eyes and think of England. "It was good of you to come so quickly," I went on. "I really didn't expect to see you for days."

"It's all right, my turning up now, isn't it? I mean, there is a place for me?"

"Of course. The cottage is unoccupied. I looked at it the other day."

"So let's take a look at this cottage, shall we?" Granddad asked. "This place is giving me the willies."

We were just crossing the great hall when Fig appeared, looking worried. "They're all off to Balmoral. A day to ourselves, thank heavens," she said, and then noticed my grandfather. "Oh, I didn't realize . . ."

"This is my grandfather, Fig," I said. "He's come up to Scotland for a while."

"Your grandfather? You mean your mother's father?"

"I don't think he's the old duke's ghost, the one who plays the bagpipes on the ramparts at midnight." I grinned. "Of course he's my mother's father."

Fig held out her hand and said, "How do you do?" in the frosty manner she employed with anyone not of her class.

Granddad took the hand and pumped it heartily, "Pleased to meet yer," he said.

"Are you just passing through the area?" Fig asked, still plum-in-mouth frosty.

"No, he's going to be staying for a while." I watched her face. "If that's all right," I added.

I could see Fig trying to picture my Cockney grandfather at table with a prince or two. She opened her mouth several times then shut it again.

"In one of the empty cottages," I said. "He'll be able to keep Nanny company."

Relief spread across her face. "One of the cottages. Of course. Of course." And she gave an almost hysterical laugh.

"I'm taking him there now," I said. "Please excuse us."

I led him out of the front door and down the steps.

"Blimey," he said. "That's your sister-in-law?"

I nodded.

"Looks like she's got a bad smell under her nose, don't she?" he said.

"She does rather."

"No wonder you wanted to get away."

We crossed the forecourt. I noticed one of the shooting brakes being loaded up with guns and bags in readiness for the shoot at Balmoral. Poor Earl—he had been looking forward to a shoot. Now the party from here would be reduced to Prince Siegfried, the cousins, and Hugo Beasley-Bottome. I wondered if the Simpsons were included in the invitation. Hardly.

"So what did your friend Mrs. Huggins say about leaving her to travel up here?"

"It worked out nicely because her daughter's taken a cottage down in Littlestone on the Kentish coast and she wants 'Ettie to go with them. 'You go and enjoy yourself, Albert,' she said to me. 'It will do you a world of good.' So here I am."

"I'm so glad." I beamed at him.

It was a misty morning and rooks were cawing madly from the big elms. The cottages loomed as indistinct shapes through the mist. We opened the one I had in mind and I set to work taking dust covers off furniture and then locating a broom to give the place a good sweep.

"Cor blimey, look at you wielding that broom." Grand-dad laughed. "Don't let that lot up at the castle see you doing that. They'll have a fit."

"It's what I do for a living these days," I said. "I'm actually getting rather good at it, don't you think?"

"Oh yes. Smashing," he said, coughing through my cloud of dust.

"Now, we need to make you up a bed. . . ." I found a linen closet and we made the bed between us. "And I'll have supplies sent down from the kitchen. I'd invite you to come up to the castle and eat with us, but I'm afraid . . ."

"Don't get your knickers in a twist, ducks," he said. "I wouldn't feel right among all those toffy noses. I shall be right as rain in this snug little place, if you don't mind coming down to visit occasionally."

"Of course I will," I said. "In fact I'm going to need your help."

"What's up?" he asked, looking at me with concern. "Something's wrong, I can tell."

I knew I was sworn to secrecy but I felt that I could tell my grandfather anything. So I did. I recounted the whole story from the encounter on the train to the various accidents that had happened since.

"I can only conclude that the rope was meant for Prince George," I said, "and that the cistern that came down on that poor woman was also designed for the prince, although Binky and Fig also use that bathroom."

"Are you sure you're not reading too much into this? Accidents do happen. Back when I was on the force, we used to say that bad luck came in threes. Maybe what you've told me was bad luck, no more: a rope that broke, an old lavatory that collapsed?"

"That rope was cut, Granddad. I'm sure of it. And what about the ghost that the countess saw? And the trap that caught Binky's foot? It's too much at once, especially after what Sir Jeremy told me. A whole string of accidents, all aimed at the royal family."

He nodded. "Supposing you're right, do you have anything to go on?"

"Nothing at all," I said.

"Back when I was working for the Met, my old inspector would have said the first question to ask is 'Who benefits?' "

"I can't think," I said. "Someone next in line of succession? But then nobody here fits that bill."

"Are you sure?" Granddad asked. "What about that Siegfried fellow you went climbing with?"

I laughed. "He's an heir to his own country's throne, if they don't assassinate everyone in the near future, and I don't think he's related to us at all. Besides, why would Siegfried lure me up onto a mountain and then have a rope break? There are plenty of ways to bump somebody off at Castle Rannoch without that long trek."

"So anyone else staying here who might see himself with a crown on his head someday?"

I laughed nervously. "Granddad, I'm thirty-fourth in line and I believe I know everybody ahead of me. So it would have to be somebody who wanted to bump off at least thirty-four people, which simply doesn't make sense."

"Maybe it's someone with a grudge against the royal family, then," he said.

"Like the communists, you mean? But Sir Jeremy said that they'd checked that possibility and it couldn't be an outsider."

"Then maybe someone who's staying in the area isn't what he claims to be. What about that whole nasty affair with your foreign princess? The communists managed to fool you all then, didn't they? And almost bumped off Their Majesties."

My thoughts went straight to Hugo. I remembered how he had miraculously appeared to rescue me the previous day and then how he'd tried to sneak into my bedroom when I was resting. Had he been coming to finish me off? I wondered.

"It seems to me that the first thing I should do today is to take a look at that line of succession," I said. "And to have a talk with Binky about one of our guests, called Hugo Beasley-Bottome."

"Blimey, what a name," Granddad said. "So you think he might be suspicious, do you?"

"Well, he was right there on the spot when I had to be rescued from that rope. What was he doing hanging about on a mountainside? And I know nothing about him. He just invited himself to stay at the castle and appeared out of nowhere."

"How did he manage to invite himself?"

"He was at school with Binky, apparently."

"Then ask your brother about him. And if that rope was tampered with, find out who had a chance to tamper with it. Where was it kept?"

"It came from Balmoral with Prince George, so Siegfried said."

"Now that's a thought," Granddad said. "Which one is Prince George?"

"He's the king's youngest son. Sixth in line."

"He's 'ere, is he?" Granddad asked.

"He was. He was called back to Balmoral."

"So either someone could be working to get rid of him or"—he paused and looked up at me, his bright little Cockney eyes twinkling—"or he set up the accidents himself to make it look as if they were aimed at him."

"Why would he do that?"

"I can't tell you that. But why wasn't he climbing if he'd brought the rope?"

"He was summoned back to Balmoral, apparently," I said, my voice trailing off at the end of this.

"Which is why he didn't use his lav either, I suppose."

I nodded, then I shook my head vehemently. "That's silly. He'd have no motive for playing these tricks on other people. For one thing, nobody here is ahead of him in the line of succession. And anyway, he said how glad he was that he wouldn't have to be king one day and how he didn't envy his oldest brother."

"All the same, I'd check into that rope if you feel you must do something. So is there anything I can do to help you?"

"Nothing at the moment. Why don't you get yourself settled and I'll introduce you to Nanny. She bakes wonderful scones. Then you might want to take a walk around the estate. See the lay of the land."

He put a hand on my shoulder. "Look, you take care of yourself, my love. I don't want you putting yourself in harm's way and if you ask me it's ruddy cheek of this Sir What's-His-Name to ask you to get involved."

"But I am involved, Graddad, whether I like it or not. I

was the one dangling on that rope yesterday and my brother has a crushed ankle. This person has to be stopped before he kills one of us."

Granddad made a tsk-tsk noise with his tongue. "Then you leave the stopping to the trained professionals—those blokes in the special branch. Why aren't they up here, doing their job?"

"I expect they are," I said. "Or at least one of them is. I was told that someone was in position at Balmoral and would introduce himself to me." My mind immediately jumped one stage ahead as I said this. Was it possible that Darcy was that person? Why else would he be up here?

"Well, the sooner you pop over to Balmoral and find this bloke, the better," he said. "I don't want you sticking your neck out again. This sounds to me like a spiteful, twisted kind of person—the sort of person who gets his pleasure out of other people's suffering. That trap, for example—just downright nasty."

"Don't worry about me. I'll be extra careful," I said, as breezily as I could manage, but as I walked back to the house I began to wonder. How could I be extra careful when danger could be lurking anywhere around me and I didn't know whom to trust?

Chapter 23

Castle Rannoch
August 20

When I returned to the castle, after having made sure Granddad was comfortable in the cottage, I noticed that the shooting brake had already left for the day's grouse shoot at Balmoral. I also remembered that I hadn't yet had breakfast. I found the breakfast room empty, so I tucked into a plate of bacon, kidneys and fried bread, plus a couple of slices of toast and Cooper's Oxford marmalade. It's amazing what country air does for the appetite.

Then I went into the library and sat down with paper and pencil. First I made a list of everyone who had been staying here, or in the area, then I checked what connection they might have to the British throne. I was half expecting to discover that Babe was a long-lost relative, but she wasn't. Gussie had distant connections, as did Darcy, through his mother. But I couldn't come up with anybody in the direct line in the top hundred or so.

Maybe we've got this wrong, I thought. Maybe this is

some kind of personal grudge. I knew that Prince George, for example, ran with quite a wild crowd. What if he was involved in drugs or some kind of underworld pursuit? Both of the accidents yesterday seemed to have been aimed at him. But then, there were the previous ones—the broken saddle girth on the Prince of Wales's polo pony, the wheel that came loose on his car . . .

I broke off and shook my head. If there really was one person causing these accidents then he certainly didn't mind taking frightful risks. How could an outsider have been able to tamper with the girth on the prince's pony or with the wheel of his car? The answer, of course, was what Sir Jeremy suspected—not an outsider. One of us. As improbable as it seemed, someone staying at Castle Rannoch must have tampered with that loo. I went upstairs and examined it. Unfortunately there was now nothing to see. The maids had done a good job of cleaning up, and apart from the lack of a tank, the room looked perfectly ordinary. In any case it wouldn't have been hard to have made the tank unstable enough so that a good yank on the chain would have brought it down.

I went along the hall to Binky's bedroom. Fig was sitting with him, watching him while he ate a boiled egg. He looked up as I came in.

"Dashed funny business, Georgie," he said. "Have you ever heard of a lavatory tank falling off the wall onto anybody?"

"Never," I said, "but then I don't think it was an accident that it fell. I think that maybe someone tampered with it."

"Why would anyone do that?"

"I have no idea. But why would you step on a trap? Why would the rope snap when I was climbing?"

"Are you trying to say that these were all deliberate?" Fig demanded. "How utterly beastly. Who would do such a thing?"

"I don't know," I said. "I'm as much in the dark as you are. None of it makes sense."

"You don't think those cousins of yours think that this kind of thing is funny, do you?" Fig demanded. "Remember the time they took that pig dressed up as a baby, into church, and tried to have it christened?"

"There's a difference between high spirits and mean-spiritedness," Binky said. "Any of these accidents could have killed someone. They may have killed someone. Have we heard any news on the American woman this morning?"

"Improving, thank God. She woke up before the ambulance reached the hospital, but they are keeping her there for observation."

"Well, that's good news, isn't it? Will they be coming back here?"

"I believe they have decided it is safer to stay in a hotel," Fig said with what could only be taken as a triumphant look. It did cross my mind to wonder whether she might have tampered with the lavatory tank in her desperation to get rid of unwanted guests.

"So our little house party is dwindling," Binky said. "Is the Simpson woman going to stay on?"

"As long as the Prince of Wales is within driving distance," I said.

Binky grinned. "And how about you, old bean? I hear you had quite an ordeal yesterday. Fully recovered?"

"Oh yes, thank you. It was rather frightening at the time. I thought I'd had it."

"I should speak to Harris about not checking those ropes." Harris was the head gillie. "After all, it's his job to make sure they are sound."

"But Prince George brought the rope with him from Balmoral," I said. "I'm going over there today, if I can have a car."

"Don't see why not, do you, Fig?"

She tried to come up with a good reason why I couldn't use her petrol, but in the end she had to nod. "No, by all means. Go and join the shoot. It will do you good. I'd go too if I weren't stuck here as hostess."

"And Binky, there's one other thing." I paused near the doorway. "This Hugo Beasley-Bottome. Tell me about him."

"Not much to tell," Binky said. "He was a new boy in my house at school when I was prefect. A skinny little runt at the time. Got bullied a lot so I stepped in. He was dashed grateful. But I haven't seen anything of him since I left school. I was surprised when he wrote and asked to come and stay, but one can't say no to a fellow old boy."

I went back to my room to change into something suitable for Balmoral. A skirt in the Rannoch tartan (rather disgusting mixture of red, yellow and brown) and white blouse. On my way to the garages I sought out Harris, our head gillie. He was an old man with a shock of white hair and skin like brown leather, and he was busy sorting out fishing tackle.

"Would you take a look at this," he said, holding up a reel of twisted line to me. "The mess they make of things. You'd think they'd never fished in their lives before."

"They probably haven't," I said. "I wanted to ask you about the rope that broke on the climb yesterday."

"Aye, I heard about that," he said, nodding seriously. "Verra nasty business, my lady."

"It was. Did you have the rope stored here overnight?"

"No rope ever went out from this place," he said. "I don't know who put together the equipment for yon climb, but it was not I."

I thanked him and went to find a car. Our chauffeur had

gone with the shooting brake so I helped myself to the estate car rather than the Bentley. I hadn't driven in months and I relished the freedom of sitting behind the wheel, driving along the familiar lanes with the windows down and the fresh breeze blowing in my face. There was no sign of activity at the dock today. It was still misty in places and I assumed that some of the group had been invited to take part in the shoot. Max, for one. When I came to a straighter piece of road at the far end of the loch, I put my foot down and felt the rush of excitement as the car picked up speed.

Obviously I was going a little too fast, but as I came around a sharp bend, I encountered a car going even faster. I was only conscious of a long, sleek shape hurtling directly at me. I swung the wheel. My car went up the bank, teetered, almost tipped over then righted itself again. I came to a stop with my heart pounding only to see the sports car speeding away in my rearview mirror.

"Bloody fool," I shouted after him as he disappeared into a patch of mist. Yes, I know a lady never uses the word "bloody" but this was a moment of extreme stress. Besides, only the Highland cattle were around to hear me and they'd never tell. Then the mist swirled and I got a good look at the driver as he sped away along the lochside. It was Paolo, driving alone.

Of course my thoughts now ran riot: had he come at me deliberately, or was he just driving too fast in his usual reckless manner? I couldn't come up with any good reason for Paolo wanting to kill me, but I found my thoughts straying to Ronny's maid, who had been run down by a motorcycle at Croydon Aerodrome. Was that also Paolo and had he not even bothered to stop then? And of course it did occur to me that Paolo was just the kind of risk-taker who could have carried out the various things that had happened to us. But why would a rich Italian count wish harm on the British royal family?

I wondered whether I should say anything to Belinda. She was my best friend and Paolo seemed in every way unsuitable—not only was he a reckless driver with an obsession for speed, but he was also engaged to someone else. I didn't want her to be hurt, but then, women in love don't want to hear anything bad about the object of their affection, do they? If I said anything I'd have to be careful.

I drove on, considerably more cautiously than before, until I came to the main gate of Balmoral. The gatekeeper came out of his funny little octagonal lodge, then recognized me and saluted as he opened the gate. I nodded graciously as I passed. The driveway took me through lush woodland, so much in contrast to the starkness of the bleak moorland around Castle Rannoch. Then the road emerged again and there was Balmoral Castle across its broad expanse of lawn. It looks like any other old and distinguished Scottish castle, with its dramatic towers and ivy covering, but of course, it's a complete fake, having been built in the 1850s for Queen Victoria. If I'd built something, I would have gone more for comfort and elegance and less for authentic castle feeling.

I drove around to the back of the castle and under the arch that led to the stables and various outbuildings. I parked inconspicuously and went to look for one of their gillies. Of course, I realized instantly that all the available men would be out acting as beaters for the shoot, so I took the opportunity to do some snooping around. I discovered various tack rooms and saw other ropes hanging in neat coils. From the ease with which I had gained entry, it became clear that almost anyone could have wandered in without being seen—if they had gained admittance to the estate, of course. But then if someone had come on foot over the hills, as opposed to the road, he could probably have found a way onto the estate, again without being spotted.

I checked some of the other ropes and they all seemed to be in perfect condition, and I remembered that Siegfried had said that he and Prince George had also laid out the rope to see how long it was, and hadn't seen any defects. Wouldn't they have noticed if someone had almost cut it through at one point? Did this then indicate that the damage had been done after the rope reached Castle Rannoch, the night before the climb, in fact?

I had no way of finding out. I gave up and went to pay my respects to Their Majesties, King George and Queen Mary. As I came out into the stable yard I heard the sound of children's voices, and there were the two little princesses, holding hands with a woman I supposed to be their governess. They looked up in surprise and then the older princess's face broke into an enchanting smile. "I remember you," she said. "You're our cousin Georgiana, aren't you?"

"I am. And you are Lilibet and this is Margaret." I smiled back at them.

"You have to say Princess Margaret," the three-year-old said, wrinkling her little nose, "because I'm a princess."

"In which case you have to call me Lady Georgiana," I replied, trying not to smile.

She looked perplexed at this. "Is a lady better than a princess?" she asked her governess.

"One hopes a princess will grow up to be a lady someday," the governess replied solemnly.

"Oh," Margaret said and fell silent.

"We've been to visit our ponies," Elizabeth said. "We take them treats." Suddenly her face lit up. "I know. We can go riding together. When I'm with the groom he won't let go of my bridle and we have to walk slowly, but now that you're here I can go out with you and we can gallop."

"I don't mind," I said. "If your parents agree."

"I'm sure they'll agree. You're our cousin. So when can we go?"

"Not today," I said. "I have to pay a visit to your royal grandmamma."

"Everyone's gone out shooting," Elizabeth said, "but I don't think Grandmamma went with them. She doesn't like all that noise. I feel sorry for the dogs, don't you? I bet they don't like the sound of the shooting. Dogs have very sensitive hearing, you know."

"I'm sure they get used to it," I said.

"You have to come and see our new corgi puppy. He's beautiful." The princess's eyes were shining.

"I will, I promise."

"And now we must go and wash our hands before lunch," the governess said, nodding to me. "And we mustn't hold up Lady Georgiana any longer."

The girls looked back wistfully as I parted from them. I watched their progress, wondering if they could be in any kind of danger and whether anyone was watching over them. Whom could I tell? Where would I find Sir Jeremy's man?

I found the castle bathed in sleepy silence. The chiming of a clock in a distant room was the only sound as I stood on the tartan-carpeted floor and wondered where to go next. Then I thought I heard the murmur of voices coming from a hallway to my left and I headed in that direction, past the watchful gaze of black marble sculptures—Balmoral being more ornate in its decoration than Castle Rannoch. The voices were coming from an open doorway to my left and I knocked before going in. Her Majesty was seated at a table in a big bay window, apparently writing letters. Several older women sat in a group around the empty fireplace, chatting. Their conversation broke off as I came in.

"Georgiana!" The queen sounded surprised. "I had no idea you had arrived. We weren't expecting you until next week." She sounded a trifle vexed. She was a person who did not like to be taken off guard.

"I came up to Castle Rannoch because of my brother's accident, ma'am," I said. "I couldn't leave my sister-in-law to entertain a house party alone." I went over to her and attempted the usual combination of kiss on the cheek and curtsy, as usual getting this wrong and bumping my nose against the royal cheek. "So I felt I should come over and pay my respects as soon as I settled in."

"I'm glad you did, my dear." She patted my hand. "You will stay for luncheon, I hope. It's not the most stimulating of gatherings, I'm afraid. Everybody's gone off to shoot except for us elderly females."

"Thank you, ma'am. I'd be delighted to stay."

The queen looked over at her ladies. "You know young Georgiana, don't you? Henry Rannoch's girl? Lady Peebles, Lady Marchmont, Lady Ainslie and Lady Verian."

Four serene and elderly faces smiled at me.

The queen patted the seat next to her. "And how is your poor brother faring? What an extraordinary thing to have happened. My son George told us all about it."

"He seems to be improving, thank you, ma'am."

"That is good news. Such a strange summer. The king hasn't been at all well. He's looking so much better since he's been up here in the fresh air. I just hope the shoot won't be too much for him."

A gong summoned us to luncheon. I followed the queen and her ladies into the dining room. As we walked down the hallway, I wondered how I could find out exactly who was staying at Balmoral. The servants would know, if I could slip off unobserved for a chat.

Luncheon was, as usual in royal circles, a rather heavy meal. The king was fond of good solid English food, so we had mulligatawny soup, followed by steak and kidney pudding, followed by a rather grand version of bread pudding with custard. Feeling somewhat replete, I went with the ladies back to the sitting room.

"I think we might drive up to see how the shoot is progressing, don't you?" the queen suggested. "I want to make sure that the king is not overtaxing himself."

A shooting brake was ordered. We bumped along a track through some leafy woodland and then up a steep hillside until the vehicle could go no farther through the rocks and heather. Then we got out and walked, following a narrow track through the bracken. It was still misty and the grouse moor ahead loomed like a ghostly shape as the breeze parted the mist then drove it in again.

"They can't have been too successful today," the queen said, turning back to us. "How do they expect to see birds through this mist? I don't hear any shooting going on, do you? I hope everything's all right." She strode ahead with Lady Ainslie while the rest of us followed.

"It's touching to see how concerned she is about the king, isn't it?" Lady Marchmont muttered, drawing closer to Lady Peebles. "Did you ever see a couple so attached to each other?"

"Especially since she was supposed to marry his brother," Lady Peebles replied. "I must say she changed her allegiance rather rapidly."

"Well, wouldn't you, given the choice?" Lady Marchmont retorted.

I was close enough to overhear this little exchange, and

turned back to them. "I remember hearing about that," I said. "The Duke of Clarence, wasn't it? What exactly happened? He died, didn't he?"

"Right before the wedding."

"How tragic."

"Oh no, my dear," Lady Peebles said. "It was a great blessing for everyone. A great blessing for England. He would have made an awful king—so lacking in moral fiber. He was a completely dissolute person, an embarrassment to the family."

Lady Marchmont nodded. "There was that scandal with the homosexual club, wasn't there?"

Lady Peebles shot her a glance, warning that such matters probably shouldn't be discussed in front of my delicate ears.

"She probably doesn't know anything about that kind of thing," Lady Marchmont said, dismissing me with a wave of her hand. "I know I didn't at her age. No idea such creatures existed. I remember someone saying that one of my suitors was a 'pansy boy' and I thought that meant he was keen on gardening."

I laughed with them.

"So was the Duke of Clarence really a homosexual?" I asked.

"I suspect he was AC/DC," Lady Marchmont said. "They say he couldn't keep his hands off the maids, and there were rumors of visits to prostitutes. . . ."

"I've even heard it suggested that he was Jack the Ripper," Lady Peebles said with a disparaging sniff, "although that's simply out of the question."

"But I suspect the rumors about prostitutes are true enough. And there were enough tales of drugs and drink. No, I think Her Majesty had a lucky escape. He would have led her a frightful dance. King George may be a boring old stick, but at least he's dependable. And he clearly adores her. And England is in good hands."

"How did the Duke of Clarence die?" I asked.

"Flu epidemic," Lady Peebles said shortly. "Almost as bad as the big one of 1918. I remember clearly because I was a young girl" (she pronounced it "gell") "at the time, and due to be presented at court that year, but my parents put it off until the next season because they didn't want to risk bringing the family up from the country. I was most disappointed. I couldn't understand what all the fuss was about with a simple influenza. Of course we now know that influenza isn't always that simple."

"I heard a rumor that he didn't die at all," Lady March-mont said in a low voice. "The story went around that he was being kept a prisoner in an insane asylum."

"What utter rot," Lady Peebles said hotly. "My father attended the funeral himself. And don't ever let Her Majesty hear you repeating that kind of street gossip."

She stopped talking as we heard the sound of dogs barking up ahead.

"Ah, there they are." The queen turned back to us with a nod of satisfaction. She quickened her pace. For an older woman she could certainly stride out wonderfully. "I expect they've seen us," she added because someone was coming toward us. He was running very fast and the way he almost barreled into us made it clear that he hadn't seen us until then nor was he expecting to meet anyone on the path.

"Oh, Your Majesty," he gasped, his face red with exertion and embarrassment, "I had no idea. I wasn't expecting . . ."

"It's all right, Jack," she said. "Why such a hurry?"

"They've sent me down to fetch a doctor and the police," he said, the words still coming out between gasps. "There's been a horrible accident. Someone's been shot."

Chapter 24

Lady Peebles took charge.

"We must take Her Majesty back to the castle immediately," she said.

"I'm not likely to faint at the sight of a little blood, Blanche," Her Majesty said, "but what happened? Who is it?"

"I couldn't tell you that, Your Majesty. One of the young gentlemen."

"Is he badly hurt?"

"Looks nasty from what I saw, Your Majesty."

"Should we not transport him back to the house in the motorcar?" Her Majesty suggested. "It's close by."

"I don't think he can be moved, ma'am," the servant said. "They'd have taken him to the shooting brakes, wouldn't they? But they told me to go for the doctor, and the police."

"Then you must ride back in the motorcar with us," the

queen said. "I suppose we'd only be in the way if we stayed and we don't want to find that our motor is blocking the way for an ambulance, do we?" She nodded to her ladies. Lady Peebles went to take her arm, then thought better of it.

I slipped away from them and continued up the track, into the mist. I felt an absurd sense of panic. A young gentleman had been shot. I didn't know whether Darcy was part of that shoot or not, but I found myself praying "Please not Darcy, please not Darcy" as I broke into a run, stumbling over tussocks of heather, rocks and rabbit holes. Figures loomed ahead through the mist but there was an eerie silence. I could hear a lark singing somewhere above the gloom. Then the mist parted and I came upon them. They were standing still, almost posed as a tableau: the king, still holding his gun, at the middle of the scene; three of his sons, the Prince of Wales, the Duke of York and Prince George; plus his daughter-in-law, the Duchess of York, standing around him in a protective knot; with the lesser players off to one side. Further off were the servants, holding the bags of game, the spare guns and the dogs, who strained at their leads as they saw me coming and began barking again. There was a look of bewildered shock on all the faces. And out beyond the tableau I could make out something lying on the ground with two people on their knees beside it.

"Who's that coming now?" The king's voice carried through the clear air.

"Looks like young Georgie," someone said, probably the Prince of Wales by the voice.

"Georgie?"

"Binky's sister, from Castle Rannoch."

I reached them, a little out of breath from having run uphill.

"Hello, sir." I nodded to the king. "Her Majesty was coming to see how you were doing, but now she's gone back in the motorcar with your man to fetch a doctor."

"I'm afraid it's a little too late for a doctor," the king said, in a clipped voice that was fighting to show no emotion. "Poor fellow's had it."

"Who is it?" My heart was thumping so loudly I could hardly breathe.

"Some young chap staying with you, I gather," the Prince of Wales said. "Beastley something. I wouldn't look if I were you. Not a pretty sight."

My gaze moved past the group to the smaller tableau on the ground. As I moved toward it I spotted my mother. She had been clinging to Max's arm, but now she broke away and ran up to me. "Isn't it too, too horrible?" she said. "That poor boy. So handsome too. What a ghastly thing to have happened. I feel quite weak and nobody thought to bring a flask of brandy. I just hope they take us back to the house soon. I might faint any moment."

"Mummy, you're as strong as an ox," I said. "I'm sure you'll hold out splendidly."

"Such an unfeeling daughter," she said with a dramatic sigh. "Max, you will catch me if I faint, won't you?"

"What must I do, *Liebchen*?" he asked, the word "faint" being beyond his English vocabulary. Probably also the word "catch."

I moved past her to see for myself. Hugo Beasley-Bottome was lying, staring up at the sky with a look of utter surprise on his face. There was a considerable amount of blood splashed around him. Kneeling beside him were Darcy and an older man with a neat little gray mustache. Darcy stood up quickly as he saw me.

"What are you doing here?" he asked.

"I came over to visit the queen," I said. "What happened?"

The older man stood up a little stiffly, as if he'd been kneeling too long. He was tall and of a military bearing. "I said we should not have gone out in this kind of weather," he said. "Too risky with the mist coming and going. Young fool must have wandered ahead and got into the line of fire. That's what happens when you introduce newcomers who don't know the damned rules. Did you know the fellow?"

"He was staying at Castle Rannoch," I said, staring down at him with pity and revulsion, "but I'd never met him before."

"I'd never come across him until a few weeks ago either. He showed up at the house a couple of times," the man said. "Believe he was rather keen on my daughter." He came across to me. "I'm Major Padgett, by the way. We have met before. I've known your family for years. We're neighbors."

"Yes, of course. Georgiana Rannoch. How do you do?"

"And you know this young man?" He indicated Darcy.

"Yes, I do." Darcy's eyes met mine. "Hello, Darcy."

"I was friendly with his father at one time," Major Padgett said. "Owned a dashed fine stable of racehorses."

"Not anymore," Darcy said. "Joined the ranks of the paupers, I'm afraid."

"Haven't we all?" Padgett said, and there was bitterness in his voice. "Haven't we all? Forced to live on the proverbial crust these days. Bad times, what?"

"Look, I don't think Georgie should be up here," Darcy said. "Not a suitable place for a woman. Why don't I take her back to the castle?"

I was about to protest that I could stand the sight of a dead body as well as anybody else, but I saw Darcy's look. He was trying to tell me something.

"Good idea," Major Padgett said. "Take all the women back in the first of the motorcars, but we chaps should probably stick around until the local constable gets here. I don't know what he'll be able to do—decent fellow, but not the brightest—but one must do the right thing and there has been a death that needs to be officially ruled accidental."

It was just beginning to sink in that there had finally been a death. Several near misses over the course of a couple of days and now someone had actually died. It could, of course, have been an accident. With this kind of weather conditions someone could have been shot accidentally if he'd wandered off from the main group, lost his bearings in the mist and moved into the line of fire. But it was just one accident too many. And why Hugo, was completely beyond me. Not one of our set. Not someone I had even met before.

"All right," I said. "I don't suppose I can be of use up here anyway. I'll do more good making sure that tea is ready by the time the rest of you get back."

Darcy took my arm and led me away. "There's something funny going on here," he muttered to me. "Hugo Beasley-Bottome wasn't out ahead of the group. I saw him standing over to one side, next to the Prince of Wales."

I must have turned white and opened my mouth in surprise. "Well, that explains it, then, doesn't it?" I whispered. "Someone was aiming at the prince and missed and got Hugo by mistake. Or they thought that Hugo was the prince. They both have blond hair and are similarly dressed."

Darcy looked at me strangely. "You don't seem unduly surprised."

"I think one was expecting it to happen eventually." I stopped walking and turned to look at him. "I take it you are my contact here."

"Contact? Sweetheart, you know I'm all too willing to

make any kind of contact with you at any time, but I really don't know what you're talking about."

"Then if you're not, who is?" I blurted out. I'd probably have made a rotten spy. I tend to say the wrong thing under duress.

"Do you mind clarifying before I decide you have gone potty?"

"Do you mean to tell me that you weren't sent here by Sir Jeremy?"

He looked at me warily. "I came up here because I thought you were going to be up here, if you want to know. And I had a chance for some free board and lodging with Paolo and friends. And you know I never turn down a free meal. Or the offer of a bed." He gave me a wicked grin. "And the only Sir Jeremy I know is head of some boring department of the Home Office." He was reading my face. "That's the one? You think I might be a pencil pusher for a civil servant?" He reached out and touched me lightly on the arm. The effect on me was unnerving, even in these circumstances. "Look here, Georgie, what's all this about? Did you know that someone was trying to kill the Prince of Wales?"

"I'm sorry, I can't tell you," I said. "I'm sworn to secrecy."

"You don't trust me?" He withdrew his hand from my arm. "I took a bullet for the king and queen, and you still don't trust me?"

"Of course I trust you," I said. "Only, Sir Jeremy told me that nobody was to know and that I'd find a contact working undercover at Balmoral."

"You thought that contact might be me?"

I nodded.

"Sorry to disappoint you," he said. "And this Sir Jeremy

asked you to protect the Prince of Wales from a mad assassin, did he? Exactly what training do you have in that department?"

"No, he asked me to keep my eyes and ears open. And it's not just the Prince of Wales, Darcy. He suspects that someone is trying to kill the heirs to the throne. And now I've seen for myself, I have to agree with him."

"But why ask you?"

"Because he thinks it has to be one of us, not an outsider. And I can observe from the inside, so to speak."

"Interesting. So what have you observed so far?"

"Until now it's all been apparent accidents, nothing you could say was deliberate. There was Binky's foot caught in a trap. The lavatory cistern that crashed down on Babe . . ."

"I heard about that from her husband. Frightfully miffed, he was."

"Well, wouldn't you be if your wife was nearly killed by a flying lavatory tank?"

"Not the prettiest way to die. But I gather she survived to flush another day."

"It's not funny, Darcy," I said, going to slap his hand and then thinking better of it. "It fits the pattern of these accidents."

"So what other accidents have there been?"

"There was the rope that broke when I was climbing with Prince Siegfried—"

"What?" Darcy demanded.

I related the details of the incident. "And you think the rope was deliberately sabotaged?" Darcy demanded. He was no longer flippant. His face was grim.

"I haven't had a chance to look at it since the accident and I don't know if I could tell if a rope had been deliberately cut, but Siegfried said the rope had come over from Balmoral with Prince George and they'd laid it out to measure it and it was in fine condition."

"So do you think someone was trying to get rid of you or Prince Siegfried? I know which I'd choose," he added, making me smile.

"I was wondering whether it was Prince George that was the target. After all, he brought the rope, and that lavatory tank that fell on Babe—it was in the bathroom he used."

"I see." Darcy and I walked side by side in silence. "So I wonder who this contact of yours really is," he said at last. "And obviously your Sir Jeremy is not quite the boring cove I took him for."

"So tell me who exactly took part in this shoot."

"The king and three of his sons. The Duchess of York. Your mother and her fat German friend. Prince Siegfried. Major Padgett and a couple of older men who I believe are His Majesty's equerries. Then there were the outsiders: Gussie, myself, Hugo, your two hairy cousins—oh, and the American, Earl, turned up with a young Austrian count."

"That would be Fritzi," I said. "I'm surprised Earl is here. You'd have thought he'd be sitting at Babe's bedside."

"He said he couldn't turn down the chance to shoot with the king. He'll be able to dine on that story forever back in America."

"Yes, I suppose he will." My mind was already working overtime. Earl so keen to be part of the shoot, with Babe lying in hospital. That didn't sound like the devoted husband. Was it possible something quite different was going on here? What if Earl had rigged up that cistern to fall on his wife's head, and Hugo had seen him? I didn't think that Hugo would be beyond a bit of blackmail. Hugo's death might have nothing whatever to do with the royal line of succession.

The first of a line of shooting brakes appeared below us at the edge of the moor. Darcy put his hand on my arm and turned me to face him. "Look, Georgie. I don't like the sound of this at all. I don't want you involved in it in any way. I hope you weren't the intended target when that rope broke, but we can't rule out the possibility that you were. You are also part of the line of succession."

"Thirty-fourth, Darcy. If someone wanted to be king, he'd have to kill off an awful lot of people ahead of me. Somebody would catch him before he got to number one."

Darcy was still frowning. "I wonder what motive anyone would have. Surely nobody could believe that he'd wind up as king if he killed off everyone between him and the throne! Maybe it's a particular grudge against the Windsor family or royalty in general? Somebody the king could have pardoned and didn't?"

"That's a thought," I said, "but it rules out one element: it had to be somebody who was part of our set. An outsider would have been spotted creeping through Castle Rannoch, and how could an outsider have got to today's shoot? There's a wall around the estate to start with, isn't there, and he would certainly have been spotted."

"Not necessarily," Darcy said. "As for finding a way onto the estate, that's not hard. And there's plenty of woodland cover below the grouse moor and with today's mist I believe that someone could have crept close enough to shoot somebody."

"Did you see where he was shot?" I asked.

"In the back and neck. I got there a little late but that's what Padgett said."

"I wonder if you can kill somebody with a grouse gun," I said. "Surely those little pellets couldn't kill a person, could they?"

"If one of them hit the right spot, it could. If it struck an artery in the neck, for example. There was a lot of blood around."

"So could you tell if it was pellets or a single bullet hole?"

Darcy shook his head. "When we saw that he was already dead we left him where he was. Didn't want to tamper with evidence until the police got here."

"So we should know pretty soon whether it was one of the party with his grouse gun, or an outsider with a different type of weapon."

"Are you thinking of joining the police force?" he asked, looking amused for a moment. "A nice, well-bred girl like you is not supposed to discuss weapons without feeling faint."

"That's rubbish and you know it," I said. "Think of all the nice, well-bred girls who volunteered as nurses in the Great War and saw the most unimaginable horrors without fainting."

"That's true enough, I suppose," he said, "but I'd be much happier if you didn't stick your nose into this any further and you stayed safely at home. At least now there will be a police investigation, we hope. Something might come out that we hadn't suspected: perhaps one of the beaters with a good motive?"

"If it was a beater then Hugo would have been shot in the chest, not the back," I pointed out.

"You know what I'm getting at—someone who works his way into royal service with the goal of harming the family."

"Sir Jeremy said they had done extensive background checks and come up empty. He said it had to be one of us."

Darcy shook his head. "We were standing in little groups, but pretty much in a line. And we had a line of beaters out in front of us. And gillies behind us with the dogs. And when you think about it, who the deuce among us would want to kill? The only people I know nothing about are the American and the Austrian count."

"Would you have noticed if anyone had dropped back?"

Darcy shook his head. "Can't say I would. When you're intent on waiting for the next grouse to be flushed you don't look around."

We had reached the cars. Darcy took my hands in his. "You go on back to the house. I should stay with the shooting party until the police arrive. And Georgie, don't go off on your own. Stay with the queen and the ladies, understand? The police will be coming now. This is in their hands."

We stood there for a moment, holding hands, just looking at each other.

"I owe you an apology," I said. "I felt sure you were the one who tipped off Sir William to my stupid blunder."

He actually blushed. "Ah well, I'm afraid that was me."

"See. I knew it." I tried to snatch my hands away. He held on tightly.

"Listen, Georgie, the only reason I called him was to tell him there had been a horrible mistake and if the press got wind of anything, he was to tell them not to print. I was protecting you, nothing more."

"I see. Then you weren't part of their nefarious scheme to trick me into coming to Scotland and do their dirty work for me?"

"I promise you I wasn't."

We looked at each other again. "And did you really come to Scotland just to be near me?"

He grinned. "I knew you were due at Balmoral soon, so I thought I'd take my chances."

I couldn't help thinking how wonderful he looked standing there with the breeze ruffling his untidy dark curls. I longed to run my hands through them. I longed to—I wrenched my thoughts back to the current problem.

"You'd better get going," he said. "I shouldn't leave them up there alone. They'll mess everything up. Take care, won't you?" He leaned forward to kiss me.

"Oh, good, there they are." A woman's voice rang out. We looked up to see the Duchess of York hurrying down the hillside with my mother in tow. "Don't leave without us," she called.

We waited patiently until they reached us. "You're about to go back to the house, are you?" the duchess continued. "Jolly good. Your poor mama was feeling quite faint and I felt that I should get back to my daughters. This is the sort of thing they should hear directly from me, not from palace gossip. Elizabeth is very sensitive, you know. I don't want them upset."

I nodded. "I saw them a little while ago, ma'am. Elizabeth wants me to go riding with her."

"Oh, she'd love that, if you have the time. She gets so frustrated at having to go slowly beside Margaret and the groom, and she really is turning into a splendid little horsewoman."

"I'll come over tomorrow, if you like. It may be better if she's away from the castle if the police are going to be there again."

The duchess looked surprised. "The police? Why would they be at the castle?"

"There has been a death," I said.

"Yes, I know, but an accidental shooting. It's unfortunate and very sad for the poor young man but hardly a matter for the police."

I was going to remark that grouse are usually shot in the

air so unless Hugo had the power of levitation he was unlikely to be in the line of fire, but then I saw Darcy's warning glance and kept quiet. The chauffeur had come around and helped the duchess into the backseat. My mother hopped in beside her. I looked back at Darcy as I climbed in.

"Take care of yourself," he said.

Chapter 25

Balmoral, then the loch beside Castle Rannoch
August 20

We were a subdued little group who took tea in the sitting
room at Balmoral later that afternoon. The men had arrived
back, grumbling about the day's shoot being ruined and
who had invited a boy like that who had no idea of the rules
of shooting etiquette. I noticed that Darcy was no longer
among them. Neither was Major Padgett, nor were Earl and
Fritzi. I looked around the assembled company: the king
and queen, their older companions, their sons, my cousins,
Siegfried, Gussie, my mother and Max. Surely nobody here
could have shot Hugo, and certainly none of the above was
my contact from the special branch.

I noticed the tragedy hadn't put them off their tea.
There was the usual delightful assortment of teatime favorites on the low tables—hot buttered crumpets, warm
scones with cream and jam, freshly baked shortbread, slices
of Dundee cake, a Victoria sponge. Maids went among us,
refilling teacups. The men were tucking in with relish.

Much as I adored such things and had been deprived of them recently, I couldn't bring myself to eat more than a couple of bites. I hoped Darcy made the local constabulary see the possibility that this was murder and not an accident and that extra precautions should be taken around the royal family.

I waited around for a while to see if Darcy would join us or if there were any developments with the police. I rather feared that the local constabulary would be so in awe of the participants in this drama that they would be quick to write it off as an accidental death. And maybe it was. I hoped that Darcy would at least suggest to the police that they bring in an inspector from Aberdeen. Suddenly I wanted to be away from the stifling atmosphere of that sitting room. I took my leave and drove back to Castle Rannoch—more slowly this time. I didn't want to risk running into Paolo, the racing maniac, again. As I turned onto the stretch of road that ran beside the loch I saw there was activity at the landing stage and I pulled off to see what was happening. The blue speedboat was in the water, a few yards offshore, with several people working on it. Belinda was sitting with Conchita on the dock, the latter sporting a rather daring halter top and shorts. Belinda was also wearing shorts and their bare toes dangled in the water. It was a delightfully innocent scene. I got out and went over to join them.

"Having fun?" I asked.

"Oh, oodles of fun, buckets of fun," Belinda said, rolling her eyes. "Conchita and I were just agreeing we can't remember when we had a more scintillating day."

"Is there anything more boring than men who talk about nothing but machines?" Conchita agreed. "First Darcy and Augustus go off and leave us, in order to shoot poor little birds, and then Paolo and the American and Ronny do nothing but talk about motors and propellers and equally boring things. We were so glad when the weather improved and at least Belinda and I could sunbathe, but the boys forgot to bring any deck chairs."

"An altogether annoying day," Belinda said. "Were you part of the shoot at Balmoral?"

"I was over there, paying my respects to the queen, but I didn't shoot with them. And I'm rather glad I didn't join them because there was a horrible tragedy. You remember Hugo Beasley-Bottome? He was shot and killed."

"Madre de Dios," Conchita said, and crossed herself.

"How utterly awful," Belinda said. "Frankly I thought he was a frightful bore and a little too greasy, but he didn't deserve to die. Who shot him?"

"They don't know. The theory is that he wandered ahead in the mist and into the line of fire."

"Horrible." Belinda shuddered. "What a dope he was. You'd think someone would have basic common sense about staying with the group, wouldn't you?"

I nodded. Belinda looked at Conchita. "I don't suppose Ronny's heard yet," she said.

"She'll probably be relieved," Conchita replied callously. "She didn't like that he make cow eyes at her all the time. And he was too young for her. Almost cradle snatching, she said."

"Where is Ronny?" I asked.

Belinda nodded. "In the boat. Where else. Honestly, she enjoys tinkering with motors like a man. And she's trying to persuade Paolo to let her have a go at driving the wretched thing."

"She'd probably be very good at it," I said. "We've watched her land planes."

"I'm sure she'd be fabulous, but you know Paolo. He's not about to share his new toy, even if he's not paying for it."

Conchita stood up, stretching luxuriantly like a cat. "I have had enough of this. I go back to the house to take a nap. I thought racing motorboats would be exciting, but it is very boring. And no interesting men around."

"There's that little American in the boat," Belinda said with a smirk.

"Him? He would not know what to do with a real woman if he found her in his bed. Darcy—he would know, but I do not think I interest him."

"There's always Gussie," I said, cheered by the knowledge that Darcy had not taken advantage of Conchita's being ready, willing and very able. "He's rich and available."

"Then you have him," Conchita snapped. "Englishmen make the most hopeless lovers. They make love as if they are playing rugby, with horrible grunting noises. And they do not even consider that a woman likes to enjoy it too." She ran her hands over her swimsuit in a very suggestive gesture, then turned her back on us and started to walk away down the lakeside.

"She's sulking because Darcy turned her down," Belinda said. "I hope you're not going to let him slip through your fingers this time, Georgie. He really is keen on you, you know. He has to be. Not many men would turn down such an open invitation from someone like Conchita—especially since she is so filthy rich."

"I don't want to let him slip through my fingers, believe me," I said. I took Conchita's place on the dock beside her. "So are you still madly in love with Paolo?"

She shrugged and kicked her feet up and down in the water. "I don't think I was ever madly in love. Madly in lust, maybe. And I have to confess the sex is heavenly, and I love the excitement of all that speed."

I hesitated, wondering if I should share my suspicions. After all, he had been driving away from Balmoral in an awful hurry. "You should be careful about all that speed," I said at last. "He nearly ran me off the road this morning."

"I know. He doesn't think anybody has the right to be on the road but him. Completely selfish, like most men. And he has these odd moments of Catholic guilt—mumbles about needing to go to confession and worries about spending hundreds of years in purgatory. They are a funny lot, aren't they?"

"So the bloom has gone off the rose, has it?" I smiled.

"To tell you the truth, I don't quite like playing second fiddle to a boat. I mean, darling, since we've been up here he has hardly noticed I'm alive. Except for at night, of course, but then he's been working so hard all day that he doesn't have the energy to do it more than once. And he's talking about needing to go back to his fiancée for her birthday."

"I'm glad," I said.

"Glad he's going back to his fiancée?"

"Glad you haven't fallen for him in a big way. I wouldn't want to see you get hurt."

"Don't worry about me." She patted my knee. "I'm a survivor, Georgie. I'm like a cat. I always land on my feet like your mama."

"I don't want you to end up like my mama."

She shrugged. "It's not such a bad life she's had. At least she's never been bored, and boredom is what I dread more than anything. I'm terrified if I got married that I'd be stuck on some dreary country estate and my main excitement of the day would be picking roses and hearing the children recite their party pieces at teatime."

"You obviously need to marry someone rich," I said, "then you can have houses all over the place and flit from one to the other."

"And keep a lover in each place." Her eyes positively twinkled. Then she frowned, staring past me at the road. "I didn't know the local policeman had a car," she said. "I thought they were only issued bikes."

"He does only have a bike," I said, turning to follow her gaze. "I expect that's the plainclothes boys from Aberdeen coming to examine the scene of the shooting at Balmoral."

"In which case, why are they driving away from Balmoral?" she asked.

"Good point. Perhaps they are heading toward Castle Rannoch to talk to me. I should let them know I'm here."

But as I stood up, the police car had already come off the tarmacadam and was crunching over the gravel toward the dock. Two men got out, both of them plainclothes detectives, wearing macks and trilby hats in the time-honored tradition. I didn't recognize either of them—not that I've had much to do with local police. I was about to say, "Can I help you?" when one of them called out, "We're looking for Count Paolo di Martini. Either of you girls know if he's around here?"

My hackles rose a trifle at being addressed as "you girls."

"You'll find him out in that blue boat," I said coldly.

"What do you want him for?" Belinda asked, but they walked past her as if she didn't exist. Out at the end of the dock they shouted Paolo's name and gestured that he should come to shore.

"Go away," Paolo called. "Can't you see that I'm busy?"

"Detective Inspector Manson, Metropolitan Police," one of them shouted, and held up his warrant card. "We'd like to speak to you immediately, if you don't mind, sir."

"I do mind," Paolo said.

"Then let me rephrase it. Signor di Martini, we would like you to help us with our inquiries."

"Go to hell," Paolo said.

"In which case you leave me no alternative. Paolo di Martini, you are under arrest."

"What? What are you talking about?"

I don't know how long the shouting might have gone on if Ronny hadn't got the motor started and brought the boat to the dock.

"What nonsense is this?" Paolo demanded as he scrambled ashore.

"Paolo di Martini, I arrest you in the name of the law for the manslaughter of Mavis Pugh."

Paolo looked almost amused. "Who in God's name is Mavis Pugh? I have never heard of her."

Ronny gave a little cry and leaped ashore after him. "It was you, Paolo. You ran her down. You horrid, callous beast. How could you do such a thing?" She flung herself at him as if she was about to strike him.

Paolo put up his arms to defend himself. "But I do not know this person." He looked bewildered and scared now. "What is this? I am innocent. Belinda, tell them I am innocent. You say I have killed someone? Is not possible."

"You own a motorcycle, do you not? A motorcycle that we found in your hangar at Croydon Aerodrome?"

"Yes, but . . ."

"On that motorcycle we found conclusive evidence linking you to the hit-and-run death of a young woman. We found traces of her hair and fiber from her jacket on your tires and frame. Now I should warn you that you have the right to remain silent, and anything you say can be used as evidence against you. So if you'll just come with us without a fuss." He put a big hand on Paolo's arm.

"No. There is a mistake. I never run down a person. Never in my life."

"If you're indeed innocent I'm sure it will all be sorted out quite easily, sir." He steered Paolo toward the waiting car and opened the back door for him. "In you go, sir."

"Belinda, don't let them take me away!" Paolo shot Belinda a frightened look as the car door closed on him.

Belinda looked utterly stunned. "Oh, God, Georgie. This is awful. I should do something. You know about things like this. What can I do?"

"Belinda, you've seen the way he drives. Don't you think it's possible that he's guilty? Remember he almost ran me down at your mews."

"But he didn't run you down, did he? That's the point. He drives fast but he has a racing driver's reflexes. And I'm sure he'd never hit somebody and then drive off without stopping. He's not like that. He's a gentleman." I could see she was fighting back tears. It was the first time I had ever seen Belinda not composed and in control of herself.

"Come up to the castle and have some tea," I said gently. She shook her head.

"No, I have to get back to the house so I can be there in case he telephones for me."

"Come on, I'll take you back to where you're staying," Ronny said. "I have my car here. I'm sure Digby can put the covers on the boat, can't you, old thing?" She smiled at the young American, who was standing beside her, staring openmouthed with shock.

"Do you want me to come with you?" I asked.

Before she could answer we heard the sound of running

footsteps and a figure could be seen racing up the road toward us. As it neared it revealed itself to be a figure not cut
out for such activity: round, short, stubby little legs. It was
Godfrey Beverley.

"My dears, such excitement," he said. "Was that really
a police motorcar? I thought I could spot policemen a mile
away. They call it plainclothes but they all wear identical
macks, don't they? And that was never that handsome Italian count they were dragging away, was it? I presume it was
to do with the shooting accident."

"Shooting, what shooting?" Ronny asked sharply.

"My dears, haven't you heard? Someone was accidentally
shot at Balmoral today. I was up there, tramping around a
little myself, and now the place is absolutely crawling with
police."

"Who was shot?" Ronny snapped.

"Some young man, I gather. Nobody I had heard of before. Rumor has it that he was staying with you at Castle
Rannoch, Lady Georgiana. Hugo something?"

"Oh no." Ronny put her hand to her mouth. "Not Hugo.
How awful. I was so horrid to him and he was so potty about
me. Now I feel like a rat."

"And they've arrested the count for it, have they?" Godfrey's eyes were positively bulging. "And I was on the spot.
My dears, what a coup."

"They haven't arrested the count for it," I said coldly. "They
want him to help them with something quite different. A
little matter in London. They weren't even local police."

"Oh, I see. Well, no matter."

Ronny put an arm around Belinda. "Let's go, shall we? I
can't bear it here another second."

"And I must get back to the castle," I said. "Please excuse
me."

Godfrey was staring down the road in the direction of Balmoral as Ronny and Belinda walked up to Ronny's weathered old Morris Cowley. "Now that was strange," he said.

"What was?"

"Two guns," he said. "Why would one need two guns?"

Chapter 26

A cottage and then a lochside
August 20

As soon as I arrived back at the castle I put the estate car away and was going up the front steps when I decided instead to find Granddad. I needed someone solid and unflappable at this moment. The last few days had all been too much excitement. Perhaps Granddad and I could even have a simple dinner together at the cottage, away from the hustle and bustle and the Simpsons and the cousins and Fig. I almost broke into a run as the cottages came into sight on the other side of the walled kitchen garden.

Granddad was sitting outside with a cup of tea beside him. He stood up as I came toward him. "This is the life, ain't it? Nice fresh air, good cup of tea. I can just feel these old lungs getting better already."

"I'm glad," I said.

"The pot's still warm," he said. "Fancy a cuppa yourself, love?"

"Yes, I would, actually."

He looked at me critically. "You're looking decidedly peaky. Don't tell me something went wrong today?"

"Horribly wrong." I recounted the whole thing. "So it seems to me that someone was aiming at the Prince of Wales," I said. "They were standing quite close to each other and they would have looked awfully similar from behind. Because nobody would have wanted to kill Hugo. He's nothing to do with the royal family."

"And you are sure this really wasn't an accident?" He looked up from pouring hot tea into a coarse earthenware cup decorated in blue and white stripes.

"How could anyone mistake Hugo for a grouse? It was misty, but surely anyone could have made out the shape of a person through the mist. And after everything else that has happened, I can only conclude the shooting was quite deliberate. Darcy thinks so too."

"Oh, so he's here, is he?" Granddad gave me one of his cheeky Cockney smiles. "Well, that should make you perk up."

"It would if I weren't so horribly afraid. I was supposed to keep my eyes and ears open, and so far I've done nothing except almost get killed. And if the special branch sent up a man of their own, then he's lying really low." I took a long drink of tea. It was sweeter, stronger and milkier than I usually have it but it felt most reassuring.

"Maybe he's among the servants and just hasn't found a way to talk to you yet," Granddad said. "And anyway, I presume the police have been called in?"

I nodded.

"Well, unless they are complete fools up here in Scotland, they'll be able to tell if foul play has taken place. And it's now out of your hands, thank God. Since it's Balmoral, they'll no doubt send up some bigwig in the police force, so you could always have a word with him—let him know what's been going on. Then they'll conduct their inquiry and you stay out of it."

"Yes," I said. "That will be wonderful."

"How about a freshly baked scone, ducks?" Granddad asked.

"Wonderful. Did they send some down from the kitchen?"

"No. They sent down enough stuff to feed an army but the scones came from my next-door neighbor, your old nanny."

"Did they? How sweet of her."

"Apparently she's a really good cook, and what's more, she loves to cook. In fact she's making me a meat pie tonight. I can see I'm going to be fatter than a pig if I don't get out and walk." Then he made a face. "I suppose you're thinking that you brought me up here to help you, but frankly I don't see what help I could be."

"You could talk to servants," I said. "You could get pally with the gun bearers."

He chuckled sadly. "I stick out like a sore thumb up here, my love. No Scottish gun bearer is going to get pally with a bloke from the Smoke."

I realized this was probably true, but he added, "Besides, like I told you, you're off the hook. It's now in the hands of the police, and about time too."

Then his face lit up. "Tell yer what. Why don't you join us for a bite of supper?"

"I wasn't invited," I said.

"The more the merrier."

"Perhaps Nanny has set her cap at you and won't welcome the intrusion."

"Listen, ducks." He grinned. "Mrs. 'Uggins next door set her cap at me long ago and I ain't got snared yet, 'ave I? You come along and join us. Your old nanny will be thrilled to pieces. You mark my words."

Of course he was right. Nanny positively beamed throughout the meal. I had sent word back to the castle that I wouldn't be joining the family for dinner, then I'd changed out of my trousers into a simple silk dress. At least I thought it was a simple silk dress until I saw their faces.

"Blimey, this ain't Buckingham Palace, you know," Granddad said, looking at Nanny and laughing.

"We don't usually dress for dinner in the cottages, but we're very flattered that you've done so," Nanny said. "At least I know I brought you up with good manners."

"I only changed out of dirty old trousers," I said. "And whatever you are cooking smells heavenly."

I returned to the castle just as the last of the daylight was fading, feeling replete and content. I don't think I had ever been in a room with two people who loved me before. As soon as I stepped into the front hall, Hamilton appeared. "Oh, my lady, you've just had a visitor. The Honorable Darcy O'Mara."

"Where is he?" I looked around expecting him to emerge from the shadows.

"He left again. We told him that you were dining out and he said that he couldn't stay."

"How long ago was this?" I asked.

"About half an hour, my lady."

I thanked him as patiently as I could, kicking myself for not mentioning that I was dining at the cottage with Nanny. Then I ran back out into the night. I realized I had little hope of catching him, but I roused the chauffeur and had him bring out the estate car for me. Then I drove into the night.

"This is ridiculous," I said to myself. "I shouldn't be chasing a man. Besides, he'll be back at the house across the loch by now."

Then, just as I reached the loch, I spotted someone going down to the jetty. I parked the car and jumped out.

"Darcy?" I called.

My voice echoed back from the hills, unnaturally loud in the evening stillness. He started at the sound of his name, then came toward me, a big smile on his face.

"They said you'd gone out. Were they just keeping me away because I didn't look suitable? I had to mention that I was the son of a peer to stop your butler from looking down his nose at me."

I laughed. "Yes, he can be awfully snooty at times. I was having supper with my old nanny and my grandfather in one of the cottages."

We stood there, looking at each other.

"What are you doing on the dock?" I asked.

"I have no car and I couldn't seem to borrow one tonight. So I rowed across and then walked."

"That's a long walk."

"I just wanted to make sure you were all right."

"I'm very well, thank you."

"That's good. Look, Georgie, I want you to be careful because I may have to go away for a while."

"Oh." My voice obviously conveyed my disappointment.

"I don't think the local police are going to investigate Hugo's death," he said. "Major Padgett has persuaded them to treat it as an accidental shooting, so that the royal party is not upset any further. His thought is that they can't risk embarrassing a member of the royal family, in case one of them was accidentally responsible for the fatal shot. The police agreed that nothing could be gained by trying to find out who pulled the trigger."

"I see. So we're back to square one."

"So I'm going to have a word with those who might be persuaded to take this further, including your Sir Jeremy." He saw me about to speak, "Oh, don't worry, I won't divulge that you spilled the beans to me."

"I'm glad you're doing that. Someone has to. So what has happened to Hugo's body? Won't there be a medical examination to determine how he died?"

"There will. But if it just shows that an unlucky pellet struck an artery, then it will only affirm that the shooting was a horrible accident, won't it?"

"Yes, I suppose it will."

"Anyway, let's hope someone will risk rocking the boat and start a proper investigation." He reached out and touched my cheek. "And in the meantime, please don't do anything to put yourself in harm's way. No climbing or shooting or any unsafe pursuit, do you hear?"

"Very good, sir," I said.

He laughed and ran his hand down my cheek. "I have to go. I've a taxi coming to take me to the station. I'll be back as soon as I can."

I nodded. His touch on my cheek made me feel as if I was going to cry. Then he pulled me toward him and kissed me, full and hard on the mouth.

"That's a first installment," he said, breaking away rapidly. "More to come later."

Then he ran down the dock and lowered himself into a rowing boat. I heard the splash of oars as he pulled away.

Chapter 27

Castle Rannoch
August 21, 1932

The piper must have been told that he need no longer pipe in the day because it was fully daylight when I awoke to a tap on my bedroom door. I expected it to be Maggie with the tea tray and looked up, bleary eyed. Instead of Maggie's sturdy figure in a white apron, I focused on a frock coat and sat up. It was Hamilton.

"I'm sorry to wake you, my lady, but there is a gentleman to see you."

"A gentleman?" I remembered that he had referred to Granddad as "a person." So this was someone from the upper class then.

"Yes, my lady. He presented his card. Sir Jeremy Danville from London. He said it was urgent."

"Thank you, Hamilton. Please put him in the morning room and tell him that I'll be down as soon as I can."

"Very good, my lady." He gave a slight bow and went to back away, then turned to me again. "Strange men turning up at the crack of dawn. Will this be an ongoing occurrence, do you think, my lady?"

"Let's hope not," I said, laughing.

I washed, dressed and went downstairs. Sir Jeremy looked as if he was suffering from the effects of taking the night train. There were bags under his eyes and his hair wasn't quite as perfectly groomed as the last time I had seen him. He stood up smartly as I came in.

"Lady Georgiana. I'm so sorry to disturb you at this early hour, but I took the night train as soon as I heard the news."

"I'm so glad you're here," I said. "Would you like some breakfast or should we go somewhere where we can talk privately?"

"A cup of coffee would be most welcome, but I think we should talk as soon as possible. Time may be of the essence."

I ordered a pot of coffee and some toast to be sent to Binky's study then ushered Sir Jeremy inside.

"You heard about the unfortunate shooting death, of course."

"I arrived on the scene just after it had happened," I said. "Well, now we have conclusive proof of your suspicions, don't we? Somebody was obviously trying to kill the Prince of Wales and mistook Hugo Beasley-Bottome for him from behind."

"Is that what you think?" Sir Jeremy asked, looking at me strangely.

"What else should I think?"

"Did BB get a chance to speak with you? Did he share any suspicions? Because it's my feeling that someone shot him deliberately because he had found out something important."

"Hugo, something important?"

"So he didn't have a chance to share his suspicions with you? I thought it would be easier if he were staying at Castle Rannoch."

"Oh no," I said as light dawned. "Are you trying to tell me that Hugo was the contact you placed up here?"

"Of course. I assumed he would have had a chance to speak with you by now."

"Oh, dear," I said. "He did try, several times, but I thought, you know, he was just being fresh. He came across as a young man with an eye for the ladies. I thought he was just trying to get me alone for—entirely different reasons." I could feel my face turning red.

Sir Jeremy sighed. "As you say, 'oh, dear.' He did tend to play up the young wastrel image, didn't he? He thought it was the perfect cover. 'Everyone thinks I'm a harmless, spoiled idiot,' he used to say."

"And you think that he had made an important discovery so someone had to silence him?" I felt a shiver running through my body. If someone had killed Hugo then he would have no compunction about killing me, if he thought Hugo had told me anything. Did he know I had been sent here to spy? Then of course it came to me that the broken rope on the climb might not have been intended for Prince George or someone else at all. It might have been intended for me. And if it hadn't snagged on that little tree on the outcropping, I'd have been dead by now.

There was a knock at the door and one of the maids came in with a tray of coffee and freshly baked toasted buns. "Cook says she'd just got them out of the oven so she thought you'd like them better than toast," she said, placing the tray on a side table. "She remembered you were always fond of her buns."

"Thank you." I felt tears threatening to come. It was the ridiculous contrast of normality—a home where I should feel safe and the knowledge that nothing was safe anymore.

I poured coffee and Sir Jeremy sighed with pleasure as he took his first bite of the toasted bun. "One misses so much living in a service apartment in London," he said. "My man is adequate in the cooking department but if I want more than a boiled egg I have to go to my club."

"To get back to Hugo," I said. "Do you have any idea what he might have discovered? Had he shared any suspicions at all?"

He shook his head. "Nothing. He'd been up and down between London and Scotland several times this summer but gave me no indication he was onto anything at all."

"That's too bad," I said. "As I say, I arrived on the scene not long after he had been shot. I saw the members of that shoot. There was nobody present who could possibly have shot Hugo. Apart from an American and an Austrian count, I know everybody."

Sir Jeremy wiped his mouth fastidiously. "In my long career one thing I have learned is that murderers are remarkably good at concealing their true personalities. I can tell you of several brutal serial murderers who were described as good family men, even by their wives. However, I have been supplied with the list of those present and we will be trying to match guns and fingerprints. I fear it will be a thankless task, however."

"Surely you can't match bird shot to any particular shotgun," I said.

"Quite right," he said. "Only BB wasn't actually killed by bird shot."

"He wasn't?"

"No. The killer was crafty, Lady Georgiana. He fired

a single shot, from a rifle, we suspect, to bring down his quarry, then he fired his shotgun at close range to finish him off and make it seem as if it was this that struck an artery and killed BB."

"Goodness," I said. "That's interesting. So that's what Godfrey Beverley meant."

"Godfrey Beverley? The gossip chappy?"

"Yes, he's staying in the area. He mentioned something about why anyone would need two guns. Do you think he might have seen something important?"

"I'll check him out. Do you know where he's staying?"

"At a nearby inn. That's all I know. It shouldn't be too hard. There aren't many inns around here."

"I'll put men onto it, then."

"And all you have to do is look for a rifle that's been fired recently."

"As you say, 'all we have to do,' " he echoed dryly. "I doubt that the killer will just leave the rifle out for inspection, and it won't be easy to gain permission to search the rooms of certain royal personages."

I stared at him, coffee cup poised in midair. "Surely you can't think that a member of the royal family could have done this?"

"I have to consider everybody on the scene as a possible suspect," he said. "Regardless of birth."

"Golly," I said, before I remembered that it made me sound like a schoolgirl. Note to self: Work on developing more sophisticated means of exclamation.

Sir Jeremy put down his own cup and stood up. "What I would like to do now, if you don't mind, my lady, is to take a look at BB's room."

"Certainly," I said. "If you'll come this way. I'm not sure which one it was but one of the servants can tell us."

I led him up the central staircase. He nodded in satisfaction at the swords, shields, banners and stags' heads on the walls. "None of this namby-pamby stuff," he commented.

"No, we Rannochs have been killing people very successfully for generations," I said.

He gave me a quizzical half smile. "So am I to consider that a relative of yours might be an ideal suspect?"

"Nothing to gain," I said. "Binky's thirty-second in line. I don't think he's up to bumping off thirty-one people. Besides, he's laid up with a mangled ankle." And I related the details.

Sir Jeremy frowned. "And you think this could be related to our investigation?"

"I'm almost sure of it," I said. "I don't know if you've met my brother, but he's a harmless, likeable chap. I'm sure he has no enemies. The only thing that differentiates him from the man in the street is that he happens to be a duke and cousin to the king."

"But not close enough to the throne to make any difference," Sir Jeremy said. "So someone who has a grudge against those with any amount of royal blood—is that what we should be looking for?"

"Possibly," I said.

I led him to the end of a long hallway and opened the door. As in all rooms at Castle Rannoch, the wind was swirling from an open window. It was a brisk morning and clouds were racing across the sky. Either Hugo was a tidy person or the maid had been in. His dressing gown lay across his eiderdown; his slippers were at the foot of his bed. His silver-backed brushes and shaving things were on the chest of drawers. But there was no hint as to the personality of the man who occupied the room. Sir Jeremy opened drawers, then closed them again.

"Nothing," he said. Then he bent and looked under the bed. "Aha." He pulled out a briefcase and tipped the contents onto the bed. There was a copy of *Horse and Hound*, train tickets and a small notebook. Sir Jeremy opened it expectantly, then he groaned. "Look at this," he said.

Several pages that had clearly been written on had been ripped from the book. The remaining pages were blank.

"Someone got here first," he said.

I stared at him. "You don't think someone came into this room and tore pages from his notebook?"

"That's exactly what I think."

"But that's impossible. There's nobody in the castle at the moment except for the Simpsons, Prince Siegfried and my two cousins, and it wouldn't be them."

"Prince Siegfried? Of Romania?"

I nodded.

"A friend of the family?"

"I rather think the queen is matchmaking," I said. "She wants me to marry him."

"But you're not keen?"

"Absolutely not."

"And why should Prince Siegfried not be on our list of suspects?"

"He's wet and harmless, I'm sure," I said. But even as I said it I remembered the climbing accident, Siegfried was on the spot. But why tamper with a rope he was using himself?

Sir Jeremy walked over to the window and looked out. "We're a long way up," he said, "but it wouldn't be impossible for someone to reach this room from the outside. He could climb up the ivy with very little risk of being seen."

I stood behind him and looked out. "A long climb," I said, "and a risky one."

"We've seen this as a person who takes risks," he said. "It took an enormous amount of gall to wait for the perfect moment to shoot someone, then calmly walk up to him and deliver the second shot."

"Yes," I said, and shivered again.

We continued to search the room but there was nothing more of interest, apart from a postcard Hugo had written to his mother. *Having a fine time in Scotland. See you soon, I hope.*

I put it back on the dressing table.

Chapter 28

The laird's lug and later Balmoral
August 21

Sir Jeremy took his leave soon after, saying that he had an appointment with the Aberdeenshire police at Balmoral. He'd be taking a room at the inn in Braemar, to be on hand, and I could always leave a message for him there.

"But this is in the hands of the police now," he added as I escorted him down to the front door. "They'll take fingerprints and with any luck the right guns will turn up. And we're putting extra men to guard the members of the royal family."

I watched him drive away, feeling empty and frightened. I wished that Darcy hadn't gone. My grandfather was in a cottage nearby but this case was out of his league. He couldn't barge into Balmoral and find a member of my social set who was trying to kill members of the royal family.

Then I stopped to think about this. Had I witnessed, actually witnessed personally, anyone trying to kill members of the royal family? The tumbling lavatory, the broken rope were not necessarily meant for Prince George. Hugo had possibly been shot quite deliberately because of what he had found out. So who had done something he needed to keep concealed? Of course my thoughts went straight to Paolo. He loved anything risky. He was currently under arrest for running down a helpless servant girl. I remembered how fast he was driving away from Balmoral yesterday. Had he shot Hugo and then gone to Castle Rannoch to retrieve Hugo's notes before showing up at the boat, as cool as a cucumber?

I went out of the front door and started to walk across the park. A herd of fallow deer stood in dappled shadows. At the sound of my footsteps they looked up and darted away. I watched them bounding away and wondered how it would be if one always had to live on the lookout for predators. I identified with them at this moment. My thoughts moved on, replaying everything that had happened since I came to Scotland. I cringed with embarrassment as I remembered Hugo trying to talk to me. He had tried to get me into the laird's lug—the one place where we had no chance of being overheard.

I froze on the spot. The laird's lug—was it possible that he had left something there for me to find? I ran back to the house and through the great hall, then pushed aside a tapestry in the darkened hallway beyond. The small door in the wall opened and I felt my way up the steps into the small round chamber. It was only when the door closed behind me, plunging me into complete darkness, that I realized that of course there was no electric light. I was seized by a sudden and irrational fear that the killer would be waiting for me and I half stumbled, half slithered back down the stairs. I couldn't find the doorknob for a moment and was about to hammer on the door when my fingers closed around it. I pushed out past the tapestry, nearly giving one of the maids a heart attack.

"Oh, my lady, you gave me such a fright," she gasped. "I had no idea there was a door there. Oh, my goodness." And she had to lean against the wall with her hand over her heart.

"Go and have a cup of tea, Jinty," I said. "I'm sorry. I didn't mean to startle you."

Off she went and I went to find a candle and matches. Luckily they were not hard to locate in a place where frequent power cuts were the norm during bad weather. I also brought with me a doorstop and propped the door open. The candlelight flickered from the stone walls as I went into the chamber. Of course it was quite empty. It most resembled a prison cell, with a stone bench running around the wall and the ceiling tapering to a vault just above my head. Set into the wall were narrow slits that allowed past lairds to listen in to conversations in the rooms on the other side—presumably to see if anyone was plotting to assassinate him.

I felt silly about my panic and was about to leave when I noticed the map, lying on the bench in the far corner. I picked it up. It was a road map of central Scotland, put out by the RAC. Someone had drawn a circle extending about twenty miles out around the Balmoral area and written the words: *CastleCraig? Gleneagles? Dofc?* The last looked as if he had left a word unfinished.

I stood staring at it in the flickering candlelight. Had this map lain in the laird's lug for ages, left by someone who wanted to do a bit of rambling through the glens, or had Hugo left it for me to find? The latter seemed a bit far-fetched until I looked down at the floor and noticed that it hadn't been swept for some time and that there were signs of fresh footprints from a shoe bigger than mine. A man had been in here recently.

Leaving, I shut the door behind me and smoothed the

tapestry into place, and encountered Hamilton coming out of the servants' quarters. I asked him about the names.

"Castle Craig? Gleneagles? Dof-something? No, I can't say I've heard of any of those places."

"So you don't think they are around here?"

"They are not any towns with which I'm familiar, my lady," he repeated.

I wasn't sure what to do next. Pass on the information to Sir Jeremy, I supposed. I also wondered what Fig would say if I requested the use of a car again. All that petrol to and from Balmoral would be beginning to add up. As I came into the great hall, I heard the sound of voices coming from the breakfast room.

"And I rather think they've gone out riding." It was Fig's voice, sounding annoyed.

But her words triggered a memory: I had promised Princess Elizabeth that I would take her out riding today. I had a perfect excuse to return to Balmoral and to pass on my information to Sir Jeremy. I went upstairs to change into my jodhpurs and hacking jacket, then I grabbed the remaining bun from the plate in Binky's study and went out to find a motorcar.

"I am most happy to drive you, my lady," our chauffeur said in a peeved voice when I asked for the keys.

"I really think you should be available in case Their Graces require you," I said diplomatically. "Besides, it's a rare treat for me to be able to drive myself."

"I understand, my lady." He handed me the keys and I climbed into the estate car. The moment I turned out of the carriage court I remembered that I hadn't visited my grandfather yet. I should at least pop in to see him before I left. He'd be happy to know I was doing something harmless like going out riding with a princess. I pulled off the drive and left the estate car under the shade of a horse chestnut tree, then crossed the kitchen garden to the cottage.

I was just passing the runner beans when I had a brilliant idea: I broke into a run and arrived at Granddad's cottage out of breath.

"Where's the fire?" he asked.

"What fire?"

"You came bursting in here like all the 'ounds of 'ell were after you," he said. "Don't tell me something else 'as 'appened."

"No, but I've just had a wonderful idea. I'm about to motor over to Balmoral. I wondered if you'd like to come along, as my chauffeur."

He looked at me then burst out laughing. "As your chauffeur? I wouldn't be no ruddy good at that, ducks. I can't drive. I never learned. Never had no need either, what with living in the Smoke."

"Come anyway. I can drive. Lots of my sort of people drive themselves and bring their chauffeur along to watch the motor when they leave it. I'll find you a peaked cap, and bob's your uncle, as you would say."

He looked at me, head to one side like a Cockney sparrow, then laughed again. "You're a card, I'll say that for you. Now, can you see a bloke like me at Balmoral, hobnobbing with royalty and gentry?"

"You'd only be hobnobbing with their servants and that might be a great help to me. You might be able to worm some information out of them about the shooting yesterday. Servants love to gossip. And how often would you have a chance to visit a royal palace?"

His smile had faded. "You really want me to come along, don't you?"

"Yes, I'd like it very much. I feel more secure with you around."

He frowned. "You don't anticipate any more funny business, do you? Because if so, I don't want you going near that place."

"I'm going out riding with Princess Elizabeth. I'm sure we'll be quite safe," I said.

"All right, then. What are we waiting for? Where's me titfer?"

"Your what?"

"Tit for tat. Hat. Rhyming slang. Ain't I taught you nothing yet?"

Five minutes later we were breezing down the side of the loch. There was no sign of activity at the jetty. For one thing it was clearly too windy to attempt any trials of the speedboat; besides, its driver was under arrest and presumably facing charges in London. Poor Belinda, I thought. Then I changed my mind. From our last conversation it sounded as if she was growing tired of him. Besides, Belinda always landed on her feet. She'd be off to new pastures without a second glance back.

I left the loch behind and concentrated as the road climbed and wound through the mountains. The gatekeeper at Balmoral looked weary as he opened the gate for me. "So much coming and going, your ladyship," he said with a dignified bow. "It's been like Waverley Station at the rush hour. The police are here again. There's men tramping all over the place." And indeed I noticed a man standing not far from the driveway, watching us. Sir Jeremy and Darcy had already produced results, I thought with a sigh of relief. At least some investigation was being done.

At the castle I left Granddad guarding the estate car in the back stable yard, then was shown up to the princesses' nursery where the two girls were busy playing with toy horses. Elizabeth leaped up with delight. "You've come!"

she exclaimed, eyes glowing. "I was hoping and hoping that you would." She turned to her governess. "Now may I go riding, Crawfie?"

The Duchess of York was consulted and it was agreed that it would be fine for the princess to go out with me, providing we didn't venture too far afield. Elizabeth changed into her riding togs and we left the nursery to Margaret's wailed protests that she was a good rider too. Ponies were saddled up and off we went. It was a glorious day for riding and we set out at a brisk trot.

"Could we go a bit faster?" Elizabeth asked after a while. "Trotting is so boring, isn't it?"

"All right. But don't fall off, or I'll be in trouble."

"I never fall off," she said scornfully and urged her pony into a fast canter. I let her ride ahead of me. She really was a splendid little rider. Up a broad path we went, through the woods and then out onto the moor.

"Hey, Lilibet, slow down," I called. "We shouldn't go too far from the house, remember."

She brought her pony to a halt and waited for me.

"Isn't it heavenly up here?" Elizabeth said, looking around at the vast sweep of hills and glens. "I love the way we can be free to be ordinary at Balmoral, don't you?"

"I'm usually ordinary," I said, "but I do understand."

We walked on.

"Mummy even takes us down to the village shop and I can spend my pocket money," Elizabeth went on. "I wish we could stay up here all year long."

"Your daddy has important work to do for the country," I said.

"I'm glad Uncle David will be king," she said. "Daddy would hate it. So would I. When I grow up, I want to marry a farmer and have lots of animals—horses and dogs and cows and chickens." She looked at me. "Who do you want to marry?"

"Oh, I don't know."

"You're blushing," she said. "I bet you do know who you'd like to marry. Is he handsome?"

"Very."

"Are you going to tell me his name? I promise I can keep a secret. Then I'll tell you the name of a handsome boy I know."

She broke off as we heard a strange humming, whooshing sound. Something whizzed past us. At first I thought it was a bee. Then, when the second one came, followed by a metallic ping as something hit an outcropping of rock, I realized what it was.

"Someone is shooting at us," I said. "Ride as fast as you can."

"But surely—" she began.

"Go on. Ride. Go!" I slapped her pony's rear and it took off like a rocket. I let her get a head start before I followed. Her pony was going as fast as it could but it was small and our progress seemed painfully slow. At any moment I kept expecting to feel a bullet hit me in the back. Then the path dipped into a stand of trees and swung around some rocks. Only then did I realize that we were probably out of range and slowed to a trot.

"Are you sure someone was shooting at us?" Elizabeth asked, wide-eyed.

"Pretty sure. The speed those things went past, they had to be bullets. And I heard a sort of ping when one struck a rock."

"But who would want to shoot at us?"

"I've no idea. But somebody was shot yesterday."

"I know. Mummy told me. She said he was silly to have

wandered off, and the other shooters couldn't see him in the mist, but it's not misty today, is it, and we're not near the grouse moor."

"There are supposed to be policemen all over the estate, looking after us," I said. "Let's hope we run into some of them soon, because we can't risk going back the way we came."

"There's a house over there." Elizabeth pointed to a large gray stone building nestled in a dip in the landscape and half hidden by large pine trees.

"Good idea. Let's go and they can presumably telephone the castle."

We urged on our horses again and dismounted outside a white gate.

"Do you know who lives here?" I asked.

Elizabeth shook her head. "Someone who works for Grandpapa, I suppose."

We tied the horses to the front fence.

"We should loosen the girth straps if we're going to be here long," Elizabeth said. "We don't want my pony to be uncomfortable."

"I'm sure he'll be fine. And we shouldn't be here long."

We left the horses and walked up a short gravel path to the front door. I was about to rap on it when I saw the name. Gleneagles.

Chapter 29

Gleneagles
August 21

The door was opened by a tall thin woman wearing a rather shapeless green silk dress. Her iron gray hair was drawn back into a bun, making her narrow face look even longer. She looked at me warily.

"Yes? Can I help you?"

Then she looked past me and saw the princess. "Your Royal Highness!" she exclaimed, and bobbed a curtsy. She frowned at me, trying to remember, then smiled. "And it's Lady Georgiana, isn't it? I haven't seen you for a long while. How very kind of you to pay us a visit."

"I'm afraid we weren't intending to visit anybody," I said. "We were out riding and came here because someone was shooting at us."

"Shooting at you? You mean with a gun? Are you sure? You didn't wander into the path of a shoot like that poor man yesterday?"

"No," I said. "We were nowhere near a shoot and I have to conclude that someone was actually aiming at us."

"Goodness gracious," she gasped. "Please come inside." She peered out past us as if expecting to see a hooded figure with guns standing there. She shut the door hurriedly behind us. "Won't you come through to the sitting room?"

"I should telephone the castle first and let them know what has happened," I said. "You do have a telephone, don't you?"

"Usually yes." She frowned. "But the line came down when an oak fell in a big storm and I've been waiting for the men to reconnect us. And I'm afraid my husband and daughter have taken both of our vehicles. But you're quite safe here. My husband should be back soon and he can drive you back to the castle."

She ushered us through to a spacious but rather dark sitting room. The furniture was good quality but with a faded air to it. "Please take a seat. I'll have the girl make you some tea, or you'd probably prefer milk, wouldn't you, Your Royal Highness?"

"Thank you very much. Milk would be lovely." Even in moments of stress, Elizabeth didn't forget her manners.

The woman went back into the hallway again, calling out to a servant. I leaned close to Elizabeth. "Who is that? Do you know?"

She nodded. "I think her husband is in charge of the estate for Grandpapa."

"Major Padgett, do you mean?"

"That's right. He's nice, isn't he? He helped me with my riding last summer."

We stopped talking as Mrs. Padgett came back in.

"Tea will be ready in a moment," she said. "What a horrible ordeal. I trust that neither of you was hurt?"

"No. Luckily Princess Elizabeth is a good horsewoman. We rode out of range quickly."

"Extraordinary. Quite extraordinary." She shook her head. "On the estate too. Who could possibly get onto the estate without being noticed?"

"I suppose it's not hard if one is determined," I said.

"Do you think it could be foreign anarchists? One reads of such things in other countries but surely Britain is safe." She stared at me. I noticed she had mournful brown eyes, like a cocker spaniel's, but not as bright.

"I would hope so," I said.

Tea was brought in, plus a glass of milk for Elizabeth. Mrs. Padgett poured and handed around a plate of oatcakes. "Our cook is a dab hand with the local cooking," she said. "Her oatcakes are famous."

I tried to eat but in truth I was still too upset. I kept hearing the strange whoosh of that bullet passing close to me and then imagining it thudding into Elizabeth's back. The thought of it made me quite sick.

I looked around the room, trying to make light conversation, and my gaze fell on a collection of silver-framed photographs on the little writing desk in the corner. I recognized a much younger Major Padgett, with resplendent mustache and a chest full of medals, standing beside Queen Victoria. Another one with King Edward VII. Yet another on a polo pony. He had been a dashing man in his time. Then there were pictures of Ronny: standing beside her plane, holding up a trophy, as a young girl in her swimming suit, laughing amid the waves.

"Is Ronny your only child?" I asked.

"Yes," she said. "She came to us rather late in life. We couldn't have children, you see. And then we were offered her. It seemed like a miracle at the time."

"She's certainly gone on to wonderful feats," I said.

A smile flashed across the sad, tired face. "Yes, hasn't she? And we've been so happy to see so much of her this summer. Usually she finds Scotland too boring, but this year she's been coming and going all summer. I realize it is the speed-boat trials and not her parents that entice her, but it's very nice all the same. We are rather cut off here for most of the year." And her expression reverted to sadness again.

"Hester, old thing, any chance of a cup of tea?" came a booming voice down the hallway, and Major Padgett came in. He started visibly as he noticed us. "Good gracious," he said. "Your Royal Highness. Lady Georgiana. What on earth are you doing here?"

"They were shot at," Mrs. Padgett said. "They took refuge here and of course we still have no telephone so I couldn't let anyone at the castle know."

"Shot at? Are you sure?" He frowned. "But there is no shooting going on today. In fact we've had the place full of blasted policemen, tramping over everything and asking damned fool questions. Well, I hope my wife has kept you entertained?"

I noticed a look that I couldn't interpret pass between them.

"Very well, thank you."

"Then we'd better get you back to the castle, hadn't we?" he said. "Your parents will start to worry about you if you don't show up soon, Your Highness."

"We have our ponies," Elizabeth said firmly. "We can't leave them here."

"Princess Elizabeth can ride in your motorcar with you, and I'll follow with the horses," I said.

"Splendid." He smiled at me. He was still a handsome man when he smiled.

We arrived back at the castle without incident. Sir Jeremy was not in evidence but Major Padgett brought me to Chief Inspector Campbell, who listened with a disbelieving scowl. "Are you sure this wasn't just an overactive imagination?" he said. "After hearing about yesterday's little incident, maybe?"

"Quite sure," I replied coldly. "If you'd care to send out some men, I'll accompany you and show you where the bullet struck the rock. Then you'd know this wasn't girlish hysteria. And you could retrieve the bullet and see if it matched the gun used in yesterday's murder."

"Good God," he said, looking at me as if I was a sweet puppy that had suddenly revealed itself to be a dangerous wolf. "Very well. I'll arrange for men and a car."

We retraced our steps and I was delighted when I was able to locate the rock, point out the scar where the bullet bounced off, and finally see them find the bullet. They were suitably somber as we drove back. So was the chief inspector. Deferential, almost. And he remembered to call me "my lady" this time.

Sometimes it's nice to be right.

Nobody seemed to know where I might find Sir Jeremy, which was annoying. He had told me I could leave messages for him at the inn in Braemar where he was staying, so I decided I'd have to do this. As I was crossing the hallway the gong sounded for luncheon. I was definitely hungry by this time, but I couldn't face polite conversation with the queen and her ladies, so I slipped out of the front door. There was nothing else that could be accomplished at Balmoral. I was just on my way to find my grandfather and the car when I encountered Lady Peebles, coming up to the front door with a basket on her arm.

"Hello, my dear," she said. "Was that the luncheon gong I heard already?"

"Yes, it was."

"Dear me. How time flies." She brushed back a wayward strand of gray hair. "What a shocking business yesterday, wasn't it? I hope you've recovered."

"Thank you. I'm very well."

"That poor boy," she said. "Not one of us, of course. What was he doing here, anyway? Who invited him, do you know?"

"He came as part of the house party from Castle Rannoch," I said, "but I had never met him before. A school friend of Binky's, I understand."

"Then that's not so bad, is it?" She smiled easily. "I mean, it's easier to take if it is not someone with whom one is intimately acquainted."

"Of course," I said. I looked down at her basket. "You've been picking flowers."

"Yes. Aren't they lovely roses? The queen is so fond of the white ones, so I enjoy bringing her some when they're just opening up. And where are you off to?"

"I've been out riding with Princess Elizabeth," I said. "Now I'm going home again."

She smiled. "She needs the company of some younger people like yourself. It's not good to be stuck with us old dinosaurs all the time. She deserves a normal childhood, I feel."

We were about to go our separate ways when a thought struck me. "Lady Peebles. Tell me about Major Padgett," I said.

"Major Padgett? What do you want to know about him?"

"How he comes to be in his current position, I suppose."

"What is there to tell? Been in royal service most of his life. Army man, of course. Distinguished military career before he went into the old queen's household. Pally with King Edward when he was the Prince of Wales."

"And what happened to him?"

"I don't exactly know. I was not at court myself at the time. In fact I was preparing to be presented. But I gather there was some kind of scandal. All very hush-hush. I heard from someone that he'd had a nervous breakdown. Anyway, he was sent up here to recuperate and here he's stayed. I must say he runs the estate most efficiently, but perhaps he's the kind of man who can't take any strain."

I left her then and went to find Granddad. He was sitting on a wall in the shade and got up when he saw me, hastily putting his peaked cap back on his bald pate.

"Ah, there you are, love—I mean, yer ladyship. All finished, then?"

"Yes, we can head for home."

"That's good. This place gives me the willies."

"You said Castle Rannoch gave you the willies."

"So it does. I ain't used to this kind of thing. Even the servants here are a toffy-nosed bunch. One of them asked me why her ladyship had brought a chauffeur up from London when there were perfectly good men wanting employment up here."

"I suppose he has a point," I said. "So what did you tell him?"

"I said her ladyship was being specially kind and giving me a chance for some fresh air, because I've had a bad chest. Which is true," he added.

"So did you learn anything?"

"They were all talking about it," he said. "Rumors flying like crazy in the tack room where we went for a cup of tea. Most people thought it was an accident, but someone thought the young man was a Russian spy or a German spy and that someone working for our government had finished him off. No suggestion as to who might have done the shooting. But one thing was clear: he wasn't out in front of the group. Several of the beaters were there and they swore they always kept an eye out for shooters who wandered into potential danger."

We left the estate and drove along the River Dee toward Braemar. I decided to keep quiet about today's shooting incident. There was no sense in worrying my grandfather unduly. But I found that I couldn't put it out of my mind. I kept hearing the whooshing noise of those bullets flying past me. Who would want to shoot at us?

I went over the scene in the Padgetts' dreary living room and my head started buzzing with strange thoughts. Someone with a grudge against the royal family? Someone who was not entirely mentally stable? Someone with unlimited access to the royal lifestyle? Didn't all these add up to Major Padgett, who had seen a promising career and royal favor shrink to a dreary house tucked away in the back of beyond?

Chapter 30

Castle Craig, Braemar
August 21

As I drove I worked out what I should say in a note to Sir Jeremy. I was, after all, making a preposterous accusation. But it seemed the only concrete lead so far. I remembered Mrs. Padgett's anxious, guarded face. Had she had to shield a husband with mental problems all these years? Did she suspect that he had anything to do with the shooting? If she did, she was a good actress, I decided. She had looked genuinely startled. So had the major himself. Tread carefully, therefore.

The road ran along the side of the river through a dramatic valley framed by soaring hills. In places the valley narrowed and the river flowed swiftly, dancing merrily over stones on its way to the coast. In other places it was more sedate, with meadows on either side. Fly fishermen in waders stood in the shallows flicking their lines in and out of the water. After a pleasant drive the old granite tower of the Braemar church was visible through the trees and we came into the village. There was nobody at the inn except for a daft-seeming young girl who giggled as she spoke in such broad Scottish that I had trouble understanding her. Something "she'd no ken and she'd whist but she was oot the noo." Although who "she" was and where she had gone were beyond my comprehension. I presumed this girl was not the normal receptionist or it would have been extremely bad for trade.

Given the circumstances I wrote a simple note. *I need to speak to you urgently. Georgiana Rannoch.*

I was just leaving when a large woman came in, panting with exertion. "Och, I'm sorry, my dear," she said. "I was out delivering a meal to old Jamie. He canna cook for himself these days and yon girl is too daft to be trusted not to spill it—aren't you, you daft ha'porth? What can I do for you?"

I told her I had left a note for Sir Jeremy and please make sure he got it immediately. As soon as I opened my mouth she turned pale and bobbed a curtsy. "Och, I didna recognize you at first, my lady. How is your dear brother, the duke? Keeping well, I hope."

"Yes, thank you." I didn't really wish to go into the details of the trap. I left her and was walking back to the car but those words continued bouncing around my head. "Your dear brother, the duke."

And I found myself thinking of a recent time when that same phrase had been used, in a letter to me from Mavis Pugh. *Older brother, the Duke of . . .* What had she wanted with my brother? What had she wanted to tell me, or ask me? And of course now a nagging doubt crept into my mind. Had she found out something important and was she killed because of it?

Then I remembered that Lady Peebles had also uttered a similar phrasing as we walked up the path toward the grouse moor. *She was engaged to the king's older brother, the Duke of Clarence . . .*

The Duke of Clarence, I thought. The eldest son who was so unsuitable, so morally unsound, and who had conveniently died, leaving the throne to the more reliable younger son. And I remembered how Lady Peebles had jumped on Lady Marchmont for mentioning the stupid rumor that he hadn't actually died, but that he was shut away somewhere. Absurd, of course. Someone in the country would have had to know about this and something would have leaked out by now. It was forty years ago, after all. The Duke of Clarence would now be an old man, almost seventy.

"Right," I said. "We've done all we can do. Let's go home." I began the long, winding drive that would take us over the pass and then down to Castle Rannoch. About a mile outside Braemar we passed a tall wrought-iron gate on our left. I had half noticed it before, but not given it a second thought. My mind associated it with some kind of hospital. Now I slowed and noticed there was a plate on the brick wall beside the gate. It said *Castle Craig Sanitarium.*

I brought the car to a halt and jumped out. "I'll be right back," I called.

Beyond the gate a driveway disappeared into trees. I caught just a glimpse of a building beyond. I tried to open the gate, but it was locked.

"You'll no get in there," a voice behind me said, and I turned to see an old man with a grinning sheepdog beside him.

"Is it under quarantine because it's for TB patients?"

He shook his head, a slow smile spreading across his lips. "That's what they'd like you to think, but it's for those who are wrong in the head."

"An insane asylum, you mean?"

"They don't like to call it that. Nervous breakdowns—that's what they say these days, don't they? It's where rich folk put the relatives who've gone a wee bit funny. You know, think they are Napoleon or something." He chuckled. "What did you want in there anyway?"

"I was just curious."

"You need an appointment before they'll let you in," he said. "Terrible strict on security they are, ever since one of their patients escaped and killed his mother with an ax. You must have read about it."

"Oh, I see. Thank you."

He nodded and went on his way. I walked slowly back to the car. I was thinking of the three names written on that map. I'd now found two of them. And the third: Dofc . . . "Oh no," I said out loud. Could those letters possibly stand for the Duke of Clarence? And that rumor that he hadn't died at all, but had been locked away somewhere so that his more suitable younger brother could take the throne. I remembered how quickly and firmly Lady Peebles had squashed this thought. Did she know something? Was it possible that he was here and that someone was trying to kill heirs to the throne on his behalf? It seemed almost too preposterous for words. . . .

"What's up now?" Granddad asked as I returned to the car.

"Granddad," I said cautiously, "how good are you at acting?"

"Acting? We left that to your mother. A proper little show-off she was from the word go."

"I was wondering if you could possibly play my loony old uncle for a few minutes? You don't have to do much, or say much, because I don't want them to hear your London accent. But you could look vacant and smile a lot, couldn't you?"

"What's this in aid of, then?"

"This place is a posh insane asylum," I said. "I need a reason to go and visit and you'd be the prefect reason."

" 'Ere, you ain't thinking of leaving me in there, are you?"

I patted his knee. "Of course not. But I need to find out if a certain person is locked away in there, so I need an excuse to go inside."

"I suppose I can manage it," he said. "Yer grandma always said I must be twins because one person couldn't be so daft." He smiled, wistfully.

"Super. We'll drive back into the village to find the nearest telephone box."

Soon I was standing outside the Cock 'o the North pub, asking the operator to connect me with Castle Craig. A refined voice that sounded as if it belonged on Princes Street in Edinburgh came on the line.

"Castle Craig Sanitarium."

All I had to do was to pull rank. "Good afternoon, this is Lady Georgiana Rannoch," I said, switching into full royal mode. "I would like to come and speak to your matron about my great-uncle. He has been acting, well, a little strangely lately and we in the family feel that—he needs a place where he would be looked after."

"I quite understand, my lady," she said. "And we would be just the place you are looking for. When would you like to come and visit us?"

"The thing is that I have Uncle in the car at this moment, so I wondered if I could bring him to see you in a few minutes. He goes back to his own house in the far north tomorrow and frankly he shouldn't be going there alone."

"This is most irregular." She sounded flustered now. "Matron never lets anybody visit without an appointment."

"I rather hoped you'd make an exception," I said, "seeing that this property is on land originally purchased from the Rannoch estate, and that we are neighbors of long standing." It was completely untrue that Rannoch land extended this far east, but she wasn't to know that.

"One moment, please. Let me go and talk to Matron," she said. "Please hold the line."

There was a long silence, then I heard the sound of footsteps and the voice said, a trifle breathlessly, "Matron says she'd be willing to make an exception in your case."

"Splendid," I said. "You may expect us in a few minutes."

"Do you mind telling me what this is all about?" Granddad asked as we drove back to the sanitarium. "Exactly why do we need to get inside a loony bin?"

"Because its name was written on a map that was left for me, and the person who wrote it was subsequently murdered," I said.

"You think it's one of the inmates who is running around causing mischief?"

I thought about this. If by some ridiculous chance the Duke of Clarence was shut away there, a virtual prisoner, then it wouldn't be likely that he'd have the ability to influence actions in the outside world. His captors would see that he had no contact with anybody.

I shook my head. Too ridiculous for words. "I'm not quite sure why we're going there," I said, "but I just know it has to be important. We'll keep our eyes open—especially for an old man, about your age."

"What kind of old man?"

I shook my head. "I have no idea. One who looks like King George?"

By the time we reached the gate it was open and a man in a dark uniform with brass buttons was standing beside it.

He saluted me as I drove through. I noticed in my rearview mirror that he was locking the gate behind me. A shiver of apprehension shot through me. Was I recklessly driving into a lion's den? The driveway led through parklike grounds until it reached an elegant redbrick house, built in the shape of an E. A woman in a crisply starched white uniform was standing on the steps in the middle part of the E.

"This is a pleasant surprise, my lady," she said in her cultured voice. "Do come inside. And this must be your dear uncle."

"That's right. This is Mr. Angus MacTavish Hume. Uncle Angus, we're going to have a short visit at this nice place."

"Hospital?" He said the word in a stage whisper.

I laughed, gaily. "No, it's not a hospital. It's like a hotel. You'll see."

The woman in white ushered us in to a black-and-white-tiled entrance hall and offered us a seat on a leather sofa. "If you'd be good enough to wait here, I'll let Matron know that you have arrived."

Her heels tapped away on the tiled floor. As soon as she turned the corner I leaped up. "Keep guard for me," I whispered and I started to try the doors on either side of the hall. The first was a closet; the second opened into an office. There were filing cabinets against the walls but I didn't think I'd have time to go through them, not knowing what I was looking for. I didn't for one minute think there would be a file labeled *Duke of Clarence. Top secret.* If he was here, it would be under an assumed name.

But on the desk was a large visitors book, open at today's date. No visitors so far today. I turned back to the day before, and the one before that. Not many people came to visit their loony relatives, I noted. Then I saw a name I recognized: V. Padgett. And under the patient's name: Maisie McPhee.

"Someone's comin'," Granddad hissed through the door. I sprinted back to the sofa, just as a hatchet-faced older woman in a blue uniform appeared. "I understand you have brought your uncle to see over our institution, my lady," she said in disapproving tones. "This is highly irregular. We like to do things by appointment here."

"I understand, but it seemed so opportune that we were passing when I had Uncle with me in the car. Naturally he has to be comfortable with any arrangements made for him." I glanced at him and he gave his best imitation of an inane smile. I helped him to his feet.

"How exactly did you hear about us?" she asked.

I gave her a rather patronizing smile. "We are almost neighbors," I said. "I've lived here since I was born. One knows what happens on estates that border our own."

"I see." Did I detect a slight hardening of her expression? "Our fees are not paltry," she said, "but of course that should be of no concern to someone like yourself."

"My uncle is not without his own funds," I said, taking his hand in mine. "But we have to make sure this place is right for him."

Granddad grinned inanely, as instructed.

"He has certain definite requirements," I went on. "He likes morning sunlight, you see, and a good view, and plenty of lawns for strolling, and some good conversation with his fellow guests. So I wonder if we could be shown around and see some rooms?"

"We didn't know you were coming." She sounded slightly flustered. "We're not prepared . . ."

"Oh, come now"—I was now giving a good imitation of my austere great-grandmother, Queen Victoria—"if your place is so substandard that it has to be prepared to be seen by an outside visitor, then it's hardly a suitable spot for my great-uncle."

"My lady, we adhere to the highest standards," she said frostily. "It's just that I don't know which rooms are available for viewing. Some of our residents are easily startled by outsiders. Some can even be violent and I wouldn't like you to witness anything unpleasant."

"I think it is important that I see the place as it really is, don't you? If I'm to trust you with my dear uncle, I have to know what I'm doing."

"I see." A ghost of a smile touched her lips but not her eyes. "Well, I suppose I can give you some idea of what we have to offer. As it happens we do have a couple of vacancies at present. If you'd please follow me."

As she walked ahead I grabbed Granddad. "See if you can find a Maisie McPhee," I whispered. He shot me an inquiring look.

Matron looked back. "Come along. This way," she said briskly. She led us down a long, well-lit hallway. The doors on either side had small windows in them and nameplates on them. I tried to glance in each.

"So do you have many men of my uncle's age?" I asked. "He is a very sociable chap. He'd like to be able to play chess and talk to other old codgers."

She gave me a warning look, glancing back at Granddad, who was deliberately trailing. "Most of our residents are no longer able to play chess and chat. Are you sure your relative wouldn't be happier in a residential facility for the elderly?"

"But he wanders," I whispered. "He tries to escape all the time. The staff found him standing by the road, trying to hitchhike, wearing only his combinations."

"Ah. I see." She turned into a light, open area with armchairs and low tables. There was a piano in the corner and a radio on a side table. "Our more—uh, sociable residents usually meet in the common room."

A few of the chairs were occupied. One old man was wearing what looked like a nightcap and had a tumbler of what seemed to be whiskey on the table beside him. He looked up as we came in.

"Lunchtime yet?" he asked.

"You've just had lunch, Mr. Soames. It was grilled plaice, remember?"

A hollow-eyed woman looked up. "I want lunch too," she said. "They try to starve us here, you know. No food for weeks."

"Rubbish, Lady Wharton. You do tell awful stories." Matron attempted a laugh.

"Could we have a tour of the kitchen and dining room?" I asked. "Uncle is very particular about his food."

"Our food is of the highest quality, my lady," Matron said, "and the kitchen staff will just be washing up after luncheon, but I can show you the dining room." She led us through the common room and into a pleasant room set with small tables. It had windows on either side, opening onto a view of the hills, and the ceiling was half timbered.

"You see. Pleasant views. Just what your uncle ordered," she said with a smile to him.

"So how many other elderly men do you have in residence at the moment?" I asked.

Did I detect a slight hesitation? "Let me see. Colonel Farquar, Mr. Soames . . . I believe there are ten of them. And we have fifteen ladies in residence. Ladies always seem to live longer than men for some reason, don't they?" Another attempt at a smile.

"And if I could just peek at the kitchen," I said. "Is it

through here?" I went through the doorway without waiting for permission. Startled kitchen staff looked up as I came in. It was all perfectly all right—spotless, in fact—and the smells were not unpleasant. In fact if I really had a senile uncle, it would not have been a bad place for him.

"My lady, I really don't think—" Matron actually grabbed my arm. "We shouldn't disturb them now. Carry on, everyone."

She almost dragged me out of the kitchen, then looked around. "Where has your uncle gone?"

Granddad had done a bolt. Good for him!

"Oh no," I said. "You see what I mean? He's always trying to run away. He can't have gone far."

Matron was already running, her heels tapping on the bare floor. "James, Frederick, there's an old man loose in the building," she called and two young men set off in pursuit.

"Don't let him get out. We'll never find him in all that shrubbery," I called after them. One changed course and ran for the front door. I followed the other one up the stairs. We ran along one hallway, then out to the side of the E. I slowed and tried to read nameplates on the doors, and to glance inside each room. Then I heard shouts and sounds of a scuffle. I sprinted around the corner, to see two young men in white coats wrestling Granddad into submission. They appeared to be using what I deemed to be considerable force.

"Let go of him!" I shouted.

Matron appeared, breathing hard, behind us. "He's not one of ours yet, Sims," she called. The young men dropped Granddad's arms. He stood there giving a good imitation of being terrified. I went up to him. "You are naughty, Uncle," I said, taking his hand. "You promised not to run away, remember? Come along."

Matron caught up with us, breathing heavily. "That was

silly, Mr. Hume," she said. "You don't need to run away. You are among friends. You'll be well taken care of here." She drew me to one side. "I see that he is a handful," she whispered. "If you'd like to leave him with us now, perhaps?"

"No, I think he'd like to go home and have a chance to say good-bye to his staff and set his affairs in order first," I said hastily, drawing him closer to me. "And we haven't yet had a chance to see a vacant room?"

"Oh yes. We were interrupted, weren't we? I believe the one in Sunshine wing is the closest, and you said it was important for your uncle to receive morning sunlight. James, would you run ahead and make sure the room is ready to receive visitors?"

The young man ran ahead while we walked slowly back to the spine of the E and then along its length to the other wing. As we walked along this wing I spotted the nameplate *M. McPhee.* I tried to peer in through the window but all I could see was a lump in a bed.

"Ah, here we are," Matron said, and opened the door to an empty room. It was spartan, to say the least. "We encourage our guests to bring their own furniture. It makes the transition from home easier for them."

"Very nice," I said. "Quite suitable, in fact. I think he'll resist the idea at first, but he'd be quite happy here." I turned to smile at him again. Matron was standing behind him this time, blocking any chance of escape. "I will talk this over with my brother, the duke, and we will contact you as soon as possible with our decision."

"We look forward to your uncle joining us, my lady," she said with a groveling smile now.

As we came back along the hall I appeared to notice the nameplate for the first time. "Good heavens. That wouldn't be Maisie McPhee, would it?" I asked.

"Yes. Did you know her?"

"If it's the same one, she used to work for us years ago, when I was a small child," I said.

"I don't believe it could be the same person," the matron said.

"I'd recognize her right away," I said, "and perhaps she'd still remember me. She was very kind. Very nice."

I had my hand on the doorknob, attempting to open the door.

"I don't think she'd know you, my lady," the matron said, hastily removing my hand from the door. "She doesn't know anybody any longer."

The noise outside her door had roused Maisie McPhee. She sat up in bed and stared anxiously. I was surprised to see a young-looking, unlined face, light blue eyes and hair that had once been red, but was now faded and streaked with white.

"It's all right, dear," Matron called through the closed door. "You're quite safe here. Go back to sleep."

"But she's so young to be here," I said. "What a shame."

Matron nodded. "Advanced syphilis, I'm afraid," she said in a low whisper. "Nothing can be done." She took my arm and led us away.

Chapter 31

The road home from Braemar
August 21

I heaved a big sigh of relief as we drove out of those gates and turned onto the road again. Granddad beside me gave a similar sigh. "Blimey, ducks, what I do for you. I thought I'd had me chips then. I thought they were going to drag me away and lock me up on the spot. Talk about giving you the willies. That place certainly did."

"Yes, it did, didn't it? Although it was all very nice and clean and bright. You were brilliant, by the way. Absolutely perfect. Now I can see where Mummy got her acting ability from."

"Go on." He almost blushed. "I just had to stand there and look stupid."

"But you ran away and gave us a chance to see more of the building. We'd probably never have gone upstairs if you hadn't done that. And I'd never have seen Maisie McPhee."

"Who's she when she's at home, anyway?"

"I don't know," I said. "But Veronica Padgett goes to visit

her regularly, and she doesn't strike me as the philanthropic type who would visit an old servant."

"What makes you think she's an old servant? I thought they were all posh types in there."

"Maisie McPhee is the sort of name servants around here would have," I said. "But why would they pay to put an old servant in a place like Castle Craig?"

Then suddenly it hit me. "Unless—she's Ronny's real mother. Mrs. Padgett said Ronny was adopted. What if one of their servants got into trouble and they did the kind thing and adopted the baby?" After all, she had remarkably similar coloring to Ronny's. But why would they have continued to support her all these years, and end up by keeping her at a very expensive institution—unless Major Padgett was the father, of course.

Everything started to fit into place. Major Padgett who had had what was described as a scandal or a breakdown and been shipped off to a cottage on the estate. What if it had come out that he had contracted syphilis, then fathered a child of a maid? Queen Victoria could stand no kind of immorality. Had she done the kind thing and kept him in her service but effectively banished him? And syphilis often led to insanity, didn't it? Was Major Padgett really insane?

"You're awfully quiet," Granddad said.

"Just thinking things through and they are beginning to make sense," I said. "I hope Sir Jeremy turns up soon. I suppose I'd better put everything in a letter and leave it for him at the Braemar inn if he doesn't come by tonight."

As we had been talking the clouds had come in, blotting out the mountains and covering the road ahead in wet mist. I gripped the steering wheel tightly as the road snaked down a series of hairpin bends.

"I'm starving," I said after a while. "I missed lunch."

"Don't talk about food now, please," Granddad said.

I glanced at him. He did look rather green. "I'm sorry, I didn't know you got sick in motorcars," I said.

"I didn't know until now, did I? I ain't ridden in too many cars in my life, you know, and never on roads like this, and never with someone driving the way you drive."

"I drive jolly well," I said.

"I'm not disputing it, ducks, but you drive ruddy fast, and all these bends too."

"Sorry." I smiled and slowed to a crawl around the next bend. "Not too much further now, I promise. See. There's a glimpse of the loch down below."

We came around another bend and there was the loch, stretching black and gloomy before us. The clouds were darker now and it looked as if it might rain any second. As we approached the jetty, Granddad said, " 'Ere, what's going on over there?"

A small crowd had gathered and I saw that the blue speedboat was in the water again, in the process of being tied up at the dock. I pulled off the road and we got out, pushing our way through the crowd.

"What's happening?" I asked. "Is everyone watching the speedboat?"

"No, my lady. Someone's just seen the monster," a young boy said. I recognized him as the son of one of our estate workers.

"Seen the monster? What rubbish. Who saw it?"

"Ellie Cameron," he said, pointing to a slightly older girl, now standing gripping the arm of a friend.

"What's this about a monster, Ellie?" I asked.

She dropped a hasty curtsy. "I saw it, I really did, my lady. I was watching yon boat and then these strange waves started and I thought it was just, you know, the wake and the wind to begin with, but then I saw this monstrous head come out above the wave, and I screamed."

"A monstrous head?" I smiled. "I think you've a good imagination, Ellie."

"Och no, your ladyship. I know what I saw. A great big whitish thing it was, in the middle of the lake."

"Well, there's nothing there now," I said. "See, it's quite calm."

The boat crew were climbing onto the dock, when suddenly someone shouted, "Look there! What's that?"

Bubbles were rising from the black water. Then something broke the surface—something large and white. Someone screamed. Then someone else shouted, "It's a body!"

The boat's crew scrambled down into the boat again and were in the process of starting the engine when someone shouted, "Don't worry. I'll get it. Stay where you are."

I knew that voice. It was Darcy, the last person I expected to see here. I spotted him just in time to watch him strip off his jacket and dive from the dock, swimming out to the body with masterful strokes. We watched as he grabbed hold of a leg and then towed it in to shore.

"Stand back, please," he said, breathing heavily as he reached the shallows and stood up. "And somebody go and get the police."

Several boys ran off while the rest of the crowd watched in fascinated silence to see what would happen next. It was a strange picture: Darcy standing in the shallows dripping wet, his shirt and trousers clinging to him like a second skin, looking so very much alive, while behind him, bobbing in the waves, was the bloated body of Godfrey Beverley, clad only in his undergarments.

At that moment Darcy spotted me. "Georgie." I watched

his eyes light up, much to my satisfaction. "Do you have a car here? Could you go home and telephone the police?"

"It's all right, mister," one of the boys said. "Freddie Mac-Lain is already off away on his bicycle to the public telephone box."

"Do you want help with . . ." I couldn't finish the sentence properly, staring with fascination at the bloated, bobbing thing in the water.

"Only in keeping everyone away," he said. "I'm going to drag him up on dry land and then we'll try not to disturb him until the police are here."

"You think it might be foul play?"

"What else could it be?" he muttered, grunting with exertion as he dragged Godfrey's body ashore.

"He was always creeping around at the water's edge, trying to listen to other people's conversation," I said. "He could have slipped, fallen and knocked his head on a rock."

"Possibly. But why was he spying on other people?"

"He's Godfrey Beverley, the gossip columnist. Trying to find the next scoop."

"Then I say he found it and paid for it with his life," Darcy said grimly. "If there had been no other death around here, then I'd be prepared to call it an accident, but after what we are learning . . ."

He broke off as the boating party made their way down the jetty toward us and we heard a clear voice exclaiming, "Oh no. I simply can't go past that thing! I can't even look. Somebody come and give me a hand."

It was, of course, my mother, looking ridiculous stage-nautical in a navy and white sailor suit and matching hat. Several male hands obliged to help her down from the jetty. She started tottering over the stony beach in high-heeled platform-soled shoes until she saw me.

"Darling," she called, rushing to my arms, "isn't it too, too terrible? It is Godfrey, isn't it? That poor little man. I still can't believe it."

"You loathed him," I reminded her.

"Yes, but I certainly didn't push him into the water and drown him," she said. "Much as I'd like to have done. He really does look more disgusting in death than in life, doesn't he? Like a malformed balloon. Do you think he'd pop if one stuck a pin in him?"

"Mummy, don't be awful," I said.

"I'm just trying to make light of the situation because it's so horrible," she said. "God, I feel quite faint. I need a brandy. I do wish Max would leave that stupid boat alone and hurry up."

"Come on, old girl. Come and sit in the car," Granddad said, appearing suddenly from the motorcar.

"Good lord, Father—what on earth are you doing here?"

"What's this with the 'Father' nonsense? I always used to be plain old Dad and that's good enough for me. Always did give yourself airs and graces, didn't you?"

"Don't forget I used to be a duchess, Father," Mummy said, glancing around in case this conversation was being overheard. "And you didn't answer my question."

"Keeping an eye on your daughter, which is more than you've ever done."

"Now don't start that again," she said. "Some of us were just not cut out for motherhood. I did my best and she's turned out all right, hasn't she?"

"She's turned out a treat, but that's beside the point. Anyway, let's not argue now. Come and sit in the car. You look like you've had a nasty turn."

"Yes, I think perhaps I should sit down until Max gets here." She allowed herself to be led to my estate car and collapsed with great drama into the front seat. I turned my attention back to the dock to see if Max was anywhere in view and was amazed to see Paolo was coming toward me, with Belinda clutching his arm.

"Oh, Georgie," Belinda cried, letting go of Paolo's arm and rushing up to me. "What a horrid thing to have happened. I was looking out of the back of the boat and it just sort of bobbed to the surface and I couldn't think what it was to start with."

I put a comforting hand on her shoulder. "It is rather beastly, isn't it?"

She nodded. "So lucky Paolo didn't strike the body when he was going really fast. He'd have killed himself for sure."

"But what is Paolo doing back here?" I asked. "The last I saw of him he was being bundled into a police car."

"They had to let him go," she said, with a triumphant toss of the head. "He proved to them that he was actually dining with people on the other side of London when the poor girl was run down. Of course I knew he couldn't possibly have done anything like that."

Paolo took her arm. "Come, *cara*. I do not wish to be here when the police arrive. I have had enough of English police."

"These are Scottish police," I said.

He shrugged. "English, Scottish, all the same. All very stupid and cannot see past the end of their noses. I kept telling them they make a mistake and somebody steals my motorbike, but they do not listen."

"I'll see you later, Georgie," Belinda said, as Paolo dragged her away.

Max arrived with Digby Flute, and my mother extricated herself from the car to fly to his side. "Max, darling. It's been such a horrible shock. Take me away from here," she said, giving a fabulous rendition of a tragic heroine about to expire.

"Do not worry, *Liebchen*. We go," he said.

The crowd had dwindled. A few of the boys still lingered, watching wide-eyed. Darcy was bending over the body, covering it with his jacket.

"Someone's done a good job of giving him a nasty bash on the back of his head," he said, straightening up. "I suppose it was okay to let all the witnesses go. We know where they are staying if the police need statements."

I nodded. I was starving and I really wanted to go home, but I didn't want to leave Darcy alone to this unpleasant task. I just didn't want to leave Darcy.

"I thought you said you had to go away," I said.

"I changed my mind."

"I'm glad."

"Anything else happen that I should know about?"

"Nothing, apart from someone shooting at me when we were out riding this morning."

"Georgie—I thought I told you to stay put and be careful."

"I was with Princess Elizabeth on the Balmoral estate. And there were policemen on the property."

"Whoever is doing this is getting desperate," he said.

"Yes, well, I have some idea now about who that person might be," I said. "I tried to find Sir Jeremy but I couldn't locate him."

"You say you have an idea who is doing all this?"

"Only an idea," I said, "but I believe it might be Major Padgett."

"Padgett, who works on the royal estate? Ronny's father?"

I nodded. "It does seem strange, doesn't it, but he fits the picture and he had the opportunity."

"But he's been with the royal family for years," Darcy said. "Why would he want to harm anybody?"

"I thought that he might be, you know, insane? There was some scandal about him and someone said he'd had a nervous breakdown, which was why he was sent up to Scotland. And he was there on the shoot, wasn't he? And he did try to persuade the police not to investigate further."

"Yes, but—" He broke off, then nodded. "All right. I'll pass along the information if I get a chance."

"Oh, and Darcy," I said, "can you find out about someone called Maisie McPhee?"

"What about her? Accomplice?"

"No. She's in an insane asylum, but she's linked somehow, I'm sure. She's probably in her late forties. Can you find out if she had a child about thirty years ago? Can you find out if she married?"

"That's a tall order," he said, "but someone will know how to check through the records in Edinburgh, I suppose."

"You should get home. You're shivering," I said.

"I'll have to stay until the police get here," he said.

"Looks like there's a bobby on a bike coming this way now," Granddad called from the car. It was Constable Herries, red faced and peddling furiously. It turned out he had already summoned an ambulance and was going to stand guard until it arrived.

"Have you notified your superiors?" Darcy asked.

"No sir, we don't usually bother them about a drowning," Constable Herries said. I saw Darcy frown. "The boy told me that the body just bobbed up in the middle of the loch."

"It did. We both observed it," I said. "Mr. O'Mara swam out and dragged him into shore."

"Poor fellow. I wonder how long ago he fell in and drowned?"

"I saw him alive yesterday," I said.

Constable Herries frowned. "That's unusual, that is. Usually they lie on the bottom until their stomach contents start fermenting and that takes days."

"I don't think he drowned," Darcy said. "There didn't appear to be water in his lungs."

"What do you mean, sir?"

"I think somebody killed him and then dumped him into the lake."

"Murder, you mean?"

"That would be my guess."

"Dear me." Constable Herries pushed back his helmet and scratched his head. "Someone should be told about this."

"Don't worry, Constable. We'll telephone from Castle Rannoch and report it," I said.

"If you're sure, my lady."

"I am." I turned back to Darcy. His dark curls were plastered to his face and he was still dripping. "And I should probably take Mr. O'Mara home and let him change into dry clothes, if you don't mind."

"Of course, my lady. You do what you think is best."

I turned to Darcy. "You'd better come up to the house and get out of those wet clothes. We can supply blankets and have someone dry your clothes for you," I said.

"Thank you for the offer," he said. "I think that's the first time you've actually invited me to take off my clothes, but I'm afraid I should go straight back to where I'm staying and then get to work if you want me to notify people about your suspicions."

"Thank you," I said. "I'm very grateful."

"Just doing my job, ma'am." He touched his head in mock salute.

"Jump in the car, I'll run you home."

"I'd make the seats wet."

"We'll risk it," I said. "How else were you going to get there?"

"Well, I didn't fancy rowing in this wind," he admitted and walked toward the car, leaving a trail of drips behind him.

Granddad opened the door and Darcy climbed into the backseat. Then Granddad took the passenger seat beside me.

"You bring your chauffeur and then you drive?" Darcy sounded amused.

"This isn't my chauffeur, it's my grandfather." I laughed. "I'm sorry, I forgot you two hadn't met before."

"Holy Mother of God. You're full of surprises, aren't you?" He held out his hand. "How do you do, sir. Darcy O'Mara. A pleasure to meet you."

"Likewise, I'm sure. I take it this is your young man," Granddad said.

"Granddad—" I began, my cheeks turning red, but Darcy interrupted. "You take it correctly," he said.

Chapter 32

Castle Rannoch
August 21 and 22, 1932

I don't even remember driving home. I only came down off my cloud when I walked into Castle Rannoch to be met by an irate Fig.

"Where on earth have you been?" she demanded. "We've not seen hide nor hair of you for ages. You simply don't turn up for meals and I'm left to entertain and make conversation on my own."

"I'm sorry," I said. "I've been at Balmoral again. Princess Elizabeth wanted me to go riding with her."

"Well, in that case, I suppose you couldn't turn it down, could you?" she muttered, looking annoyed. It always made her cross that I was related to the royal family by birth while she was only related by marriage.

"Am I too late for tea? I'm starving," I said.

"I took tea with Podge in the nursery today," she said. "With all these people here I've been neglecting him fearfully. And there was nobody in for tea, except Binky. Siegfried's out somewhere. The Simpsons have finally gone, by the way."

"Have they really? Hooray."

"As you say, hooray. I thought we'd never get rid of them, especially when they elected to stay on after the other Americans went. But I think your cousins finally proved too much to endure. They are a trifle primitive, aren't they?"

"What happened?"

"We were in the middle of the meat course last night when Murdoch described how he'd dismembered a deer he'd shot. It would be venison, of course. Quite put them off their meal, I could see that."

I grinned. "Well, you finally have your way. They've all gone."

"Except for those awful cousins of yours. The amount they eat and drink. I've asked Binky to give them the boot, but you know how soft he is. We'll be reduced to tea and toast for the rest of the year." She eyed me critically. "What is wrong with you?"

"Nothing. Why?"

"You've had a silly grin on your face all the time I've been talking."

We passed an uneventful evening. I was tense and uneasy all through dinner, at which Fig, myself and the two cousins were positioned along the full length of the huge banquet table, making conversation almost impossible without shouting. I was waiting for Sir Jeremy to telephone or appear in person at any moment, but he hadn't contacted me by the time I was ready for bed. This probably meant that he had not returned to the inn yet, or that the idiot girl was manning the shop and had forgotten to give him the message. Either that or her accent was so broad that he hadn't understood what she was saying. I wasn't sure what to do about this. Apart from telephoning the inn again, to see if he'd come back, I had no way of getting in touch with him and I worried that something else might happen at Balmoral the longer Major Padgett was on the loose. I just hoped that Darcy had managed to contact the appropriate people and that all would be well. Anyway, there was nothing more I could or should do now. I would be acting foolishly to attempt to go back to Balmoral again. Instead I'd attempt to enjoy myself. I'd take Granddad for some of my favorite walks. I might even teach him to fish.

The next morning I slept late and awoke to glorious sun streaming in through my open window. I breakfasted well and was on my way to visit Granddad when I heard a voice calling across the parkland: "Hector. Come out this minute, wherever you are. This is no longer funny."

And Podge's nanny came into view, looking around anxiously.

"What's the matter?" I asked.

"That naughty boy, he's hiding from me," she said. "I let him out of his pram because he does so love to run across the grass and now I can't find him." She sounded close to tears.

"Don't worry, he can't have gone far," I said, but my insides clenched themselves into a tight knot. I kept telling myself this was a simple case of a naughty three-year-old, but my mind was whispering other, darker possibilities.

"Get Graham to round up the gardeners and gillies to help you look," I said, indicating one of our groundsmen, who was working in the kitchen garden. "Tell him I said so."

"Yes, my lady."

"And I'll start looking too. Where exactly did you lose him?"

"Not far from here. He was playing with his ball on that lawn, running around quite happily. I went to sit on the bench and when I turned back, he was gone. Of course I thought he was just playing a silly trick on Nanny, then I called him and he didn't answer. Oh, what can have happened to him, my lady?"

"Don't worry. We'll find him. You didn't hear the sound of a motor, did you?"

"What do you mean, my lady?"

No sense in alarming her unduly. "Not important. Go and get Graham now. Go on." I pushed her in the direction of the kitchen garden and I started to hurry toward the spot she had indicated. If he really had run off, or was hiding, he couldn't have gone too far. He only had little legs. And if his nanny hadn't heard or noticed a motorcar then it wasn't likely that someone had driven away with him.

I searched through the shrubbery, calling his name, telling him that Auntie Georgie wanted to play with him, then that his papa wanted to see him—Papa being the most important person in his life. Nothing stirred among the bushes. Perhaps I am overreacting, I told myself. Perhaps he went back to the house to fetch a toy. Perhaps he's safely in his nursery at this very moment. But I couldn't shake off the feeling of dread.

I had just reached the driveway when I heard someone calling my name and saw my grandfather waving. "What's the big hurry, ducks?" he said. "Are you training to run a race?"

"No, Granddad. It's little Podge, my nephew. He's missing and I'm worried that—" I let the rest of the sentence drift off into silence.

"Are you sure he hasn't just wandered off? Kiddies do that, you know."

"I know. But we've called and called and he's not anywhere."

He put an arm around me. "Don't worry, ducks. He'll turn up. You get on with your searching and I'll help. But he wouldn't have got this far from the house on his own, would he?"

"I wouldn't have thought so, but . . . wait! What's that down there?" I had spotted the glint of something red, lying on the light gravel not far from the gates. I ran toward it and bent to pick it up. "It's one of Podge's toy soldiers," I shouted. "Go and tell them."

I started to run as fast as I could until I reached the castle gate. I looked up and down the road. I heard no sound of a retreating motorcar. There was silence apart from the sigh of the wind in the pine trees and the gentle splash of waves on the shore of the loch. I stood, hesitant, at the side of the road, not knowing what to do next. I had no way of knowing in which direction he might have gone if he had, in fact, come out of the gate by himself. Someone should alert the police, of course. I hoped Granddad would do just that.

At that moment I heard the sound of an approaching vehicle. It was a small motorcar, a Morris, by the look of it. I stepped out into the road, waved it down as it approached and wrenched open the passenger door. "You haven't seen a small boy, by any chance, have you?" I asked. Then I realized that I recognized the driver. "Oh, Ronny, it's you."

"Oh, hello, Georgie," she said pleasantly. "A small boy? About how old? There were a couple of boys fishing about a mile back."

"He's only three. My nephew, Podge. He's run off. His nurse is beside herself."

"He can't have run far if he's only three. He's probably hiding somewhere." She grinned. "I used to hide when I was that age. I used to scare the daylights out of my parents. Once I got up in the attic and couldn't get down."

I held up the toy soldier. "I found this on the driveway, not far from the gate, so he must have come this way."

"In that case, hop in," she said. "I can help you look if you like."

"Thanks awfully." I climbed in and we started off slowly, scanning the lochside and hedgerow as we drove, windows open and constantly calling his name. It suddenly struck me how ironic this situation was, if her father was indeed the kidnapper and she was helping me to chase him down.

We had gone about half a mile when something caught my eye. "Wait. What's that over there?"

Ronny jammed on the brakes. I jumped out before the motorcar came to a complete stop and ran across to an old boathouse, perched on the edge of the loch. Outside the boathouse I had spotted another glimpse of red. It was a second toy soldier. Ronny had come to join me. I held it up for her.

"Do you think he's gone in there?" she asked. She started to open the rotting door with great caution. "He must be an adventurous little chap."

"Maybe someone's taken him in there," I said, my voice literally shaking with terror by now.

"The door wasn't properly shut," she said, pulling it wide open now. "It's awfully dark in here." She glanced back at me. "Podge? Is that his name?" she asked, then called, "Podge, are you in here?" Then she turned back. "I think I might have a torch in the car."

I stepped inside, dreading what I might be about to find. The only light came from the reflection on the water that lapped a long way below me. A walkway ran along three sides. Up here it was shrouded in gloom and smelled overpoweringly damp and mildewy. I started to poke around amid old sacks and rotting cartons, my heart thumping every time I touched something soft or wet. I was conscious of Ronny standing behind me.

"He doesn't seem to be in here," I said, looking up at her.

"No," she replied. "He's not."

"You've found him?"

"Let's just say I know where he is."

"Where is he?"

"Safe. For the moment."

"What do you mean?" I stared at her, trying to take this in. "Your father took him?"

"My father? My father is dead."

"Major Padgett is dead?"

"He's not my real father, but then you know that, don't you? Hugo must have told you. Why else did you visit Castle Craig yesterday? You know all about my real parents."

"Maisie McPhee is your real mother, I presume," I said.

"Well done. My real mother. She's gone insane. She doesn't even know me, but I still go to see her. I feel I owe it to her."

She looked at me and started to laugh. "You really are terribly naïve and trusting, aren't you? I planted the soldiers along the way and you, my dear, took the bait so easily . . . and now I've reeled you in."

That's when I realized that what she was holding was not a torch at all. It was a pistol.

"You kidnapped him? It was you?"

"Yes," she said in a matter-of-fact voice.

"Why? Why do that to a small boy who has done you no harm?"

"Security, my sweet. I might need a bargaining chip to

get me safely out of the country. And you"—she paused as if examining me—"you were becoming a blasted nuisance. Hugo told you everything, didn't he?"

I was still trying to take this in. "It was you who shot at me yesterday? Who killed Hugo?"

She laughed again. "Poor old Hugo. Too smart for his own good. And too soft too. He had it figured out but then he made the mistake of telling me. He wanted me to do the honorable thing and turn myself in. How silly can you be?"

"I was too slow," I said. "I should have realized. I knew there was something worrying me. You gave yourself away when we spoke together after Hugo had died. Godfrey Beverley told you that someone had been shot. He didn't say he was dead, but you spoke of him in the past tense."

"As you say, you were too slow."

"And Godfrey Beverley," I said, as pieces fell into place in my head. "He was looking directly at you when he asked why anyone would need two guns."

"Stupid little man," she said. "Always poking his nose where it wasn't wanted. I realized he must have seen me."

"And your maid? You borrowed the motorbike and ran her over?"

"She snooped. She had to go."

I stared at her, noting the easy way she dismissed these murders.

"What have you done with Podge?" I demanded.

"He's quite safe. You don't have to worry about him."

"Of course I worry about him. Take me to him."

"He's on my Gypsy Moth, right here on the lake. Climb down into the boat and you can row us out to him." She indicated a small rowing boat tied at the bottom of the steps and motioned with the pistol that I should go down them.

I was trying to control my racing thoughts, wondering

what chance I stood if I dove into the water and went for help. There was nothing nearer than Castle Rannoch and by that time she could have killed Podge or taken off with him. I wondered if I could reach the plane first if I dove in and swam to it. I was a strong swimmer and she would have to climb down the ladder then untie the rowing boat, which would give me a good head start. It was worth a try and it was better than doing nothing. She was obviously going to kill me and probably Podge too. What did I have to lose?

I took a deep breath and launched myself into the black water. I heard the shot echoing around the boathouse. At any second I expected to feel the sting of a bullet but I hit the surface and went under. I gasped at the cold and had to stop myself from coming up to take an immediate breath. Instead I kicked out underwater, praying I was heading in the right direction. I kept swimming underwater until I could see brighter daylight ahead of me. I held my breath until my lungs were on fire and I came up, gasping for air. No sign of the rowing boat yet. I struck out for the plane with powerful strokes, swimming faster than I had ever done before. I hadn't worked out what I'd do when I reached the aeroplane. She still had the pistol and I was still a sitting target, but I'd work that part out when I came to it.

The aeroplane bobbed on its floats tied to a buoy, within easy swimming distance now. I reached it, hauled myself onto the fin and stood up, holding on to the lower of the double wings. It felt flimsy and insecure. I hadn't realized before that aeroplanes were made of wood and fabric and wires, like large kites. The rowing boat was now clear of the boathouse and she was rowing hard toward me. This was good news, in that she couldn't shoot and row at the same time. If I could grab Podge and get him into the water with me, we might just be able to evade Ronny in her rowing boat.

As I stood up and looked into the aeroplane, I could see it had two open cockpits, one behind the other. I looked into the backseat first. No sign of Podge. There were a couple of what looked like rucksacks, half pushed under the seat, but they were too small to hold a child.

I maneuvered my way along the fin to the forward seat and couldn't see him there, either. I swung my leg over and climbed inside, reaching around on the floor to see if there might be a secret compartment where he could be hidden. But there was nothing.

I didn't have any time to decide what to do next. The plane started shaking, indicating that Ronny had reached it and was climbing on board. I'd better start swimming again. I swung one leg over the side.

"I wouldn't do that if I were you," Ronny said. She was standing only a foot or so away and the pistol was now pointed at my head.

"He's not here," I said lamely.

"No. He's not."

"But you said . . ."

"Georgie, you really must stop believing what people tell you. It's such a pathetic trait."

"Where is he?" I was really angry now, even though I knew she had the gun and she was probably going to shoot me. "What have you done with him?"

"I told you he was safe, and he is, for the time being. He's tied up in the boot of my car. He was there, behind you, all the time." She laughed as if this was a good joke as she moved nimbly along the float and untied the craft from its buoy.

"Then why take the trouble to bring me out here? You could have shot me in the boathouse and tossed my body into the water."

"I could have, but I decided that you'd do just as well as a hostage. You swam here under your own steam and I don't have to go to the trouble of carrying your nephew from the motorcar and risk being seen. Please sit down. I promised to take you up, didn't I? Well, now you're getting your chance."

I noticed, really for the first time, that she was wearing a leather flight jacket. She had come prepared. I was already soaking wet. It was quite likely I was going to freeze to death before she shot me or tipped me out.

"Sit," she commanded again, indicating the front seat. I had no choice. I sat.

She rummaged in one of the bags in the backseat and threw something at me. "Here." It was a pair of goggles. "Now strap yourself in."

"Why are you doing this?" I demanded. "What have we ever done to you?"

"Robbed me of my birthright," she said. "You know who my father was, don't you? He was the heir to the throne. The Duke of Clarence."

"The Duke of Clarence? He was your father? But he died long before you were born."

"He didn't die. It was a monstrous conspiracy," she said. "They kidnapped him and had him shut away up here. He never recovered his health and died when I was a baby, so I've been told. So when you look at it that way, I'm the rightful heir to the throne."

"Even if this is true, I'm sure he didn't marry your mother, so you're not the rightful heir to anything."

"He did marry her," she said angrily. "He did. She told me."

"No one would ever believe you," I said.

"No. That's why this was the only way to get back at the

stupid royal family. And I must say I've enjoyed it. I never intended to kill anyone, you know. Just frighten them. Just make them feel they were never safe. And I succeeded."

"But why? Why waste your energy on that when you have so much to live for? You're a famous woman. You've set records. You'll go down in the history books."

"It's never enough," she said simply. "There is never enough to fill the void."

She climbed into the rear seat. "Hold tight!" she shouted. The machine roared to life. The whole contraption started to shake.

Then without warning it started to move, faster and faster, bouncing over the water until suddenly it was airborne. Loch and mountains fell away beneath us. There was Castle Rannoch, nestled among the trees. There was the boathouse and the car parked beside it, looking like a child's toy. Scotland stretched beneath us—the bleak expanse of Rannoch Moor and beyond it the glittering of the sea and the Western Isles.

"Where are we going?" I turned to shout. It suddenly occurred to me that she was attempting to fly to America and that we'd never make it and come down somewhere in the middle of the Atlantic. I was shivering badly now, both from the cold wind and from the fear. She was sitting behind me so I couldn't see what she was doing. Not that I could take any action anyway. I was strapped into a seat, up in the air.

Then I felt the plane shake. I swiveled in my seat to look at her and saw, to my dismay, that she was standing up.

"What are you doing?" I yelled.

"I've always wanted to fly," she shouted back. "Now seems like a good time to try it." Then she laughed again. "Oh, don't worry about me. I have a parachute on my back.

You're the one who needs to worry. You'll be up here alone.
It's perfect really. Much simpler than a hostage. Either you'll
go down into the Atlantic or you'll eventually crash. If you
do, the plane is full of fuel. It will explode and you'll be
burned beyond recognition. Everyone will think it's me.
Poor Ronny Padgett. So sad. Give her a state funeral. And I
will be making a new life in America! Land of opportunity,
they say."

I was trying to unbuckle my harness to stop her, but I
wasn't quick enough. She launched herself over the side. I
watched her falling, spread-eagled, toward the earth.

Chapter 33

For a long moment I just sat there, too stunned to do anything.

"I am alone in an aeroplane, thousands of feet up in the air," I said out loud, and added, since there was nobody within miles to hear me, "Bugger." (I thought the occasion warranted a swearword. I only wished I knew some stronger ones. I'd have used them all. Loudly.)

Frankly I was finding it hard to breathe and it wasn't just the wind in my face. Even if I knew how to fly an aeroplane, there were no instruments in my compartment. And I didn't know how to fly an aeroplane anyway. Let's face it—I had never even been in one before. But I wasn't just going to sit there and accept my fate. "Do something," I commanded myself.

For the moment we were flying smoothly forward, out toward the Atlantic Ocean. I forced my freezing, trembling fingers to unbuckle the harness, then I turned and knelt on the seat. The wind was so strong I could hardly move. I grasped the struts that held up the overhead wing and pulled myself into a kneeling position on the space between the two seats. There was a windshield, making forward progress difficult. I had to inch one leg around, holding on to that windshield for dear life. The plane reacted to my weight as I slithered hastily into the backseat.

"So far, so good," I said to encourage myself. Then I took stock of the cockpit. I stared at the instrument panel in front of me, hoping for a glimmer of inspiration. Needles were moving on dials but I had no idea what any of them meant. There was also a metal handle coming out of the floor between my legs. I moved it tentatively to one side and the machine started to bank. Hastily I restored it to its previous position. So I could turn the machine if I wanted but what use would that be? I presumed that pushing the stick forward might therefore make it go down, but I had no idea how I would slow it down enough to land on water. We were heading due west. Soon we would be out over the Atlantic and then destruction was inevitable. Come to think of it, it was inevitable anyway. I've always been an optimistic sort of person and I do have the blood of all those impossibly brave Rannochs coursing through my veins, but I was finding it awfully hard to be brave.

I wondered if I dared experiment in trying to turn the aeroplane before it was actually over the Atlantic. Then I wondered what chance of survival I would have if I brought the plane very low over the water and then jumped out. That made me wonder if the other rucksack contained a second parachute. I opened it and it contained a change of clothing and a bar of Cadbury's chocolate. I started to eat it. I was halfway through when I became aware of a noise—a loud droning sound. I turned around and found that I was being followed by another aeroplane. Hope sprung up. They had come to rescue me! Then of course I realized that they thought this was Ronny's machine and they had no idea I was in it.

I waited until the other machine was very close, then I stood up, waving my arms.

"It's me. Help!" I shouted. Not very informative, but the best I could do in the circumstances.

The other aeroplane signaled to me, a thumbs-up, which I took to be a good thing. I could see two flyers in helmets and goggles staring at me before their machine rose and began to fly over me. It was hovering over me like a giant dragonfly, its shape blotting out the sun, then something snaked down beside me, almost whacked me on the head then swung out again. I realized that it was a rope ladder. Surely they weren't expecting me to grab it and climb up? On second thought this was a better choice than crashing into the ocean.

As I was leaning out, trying to catch it as it bobbed and danced in the wind, I realized that someone was climbing down it. Soon this person had hold of the upper wing and was standing on the wooden fuselage right in front of me.

"Can you climb up the ladder, do you think?" he shouted.

"I don't know." I looked up at the other plane. "My hands are freezing."

At that moment the decision was taken from me. A large cloud loomed in front of us.

"Too late," the man snapped and released the ladder. "Quick. Move up front. I need to fly this thing." I didn't really have time to think as we were swallowed up in cloud. "Careful now," he said, as I stood up and he stepped down into the cockpit beside me. He held on to me firmly as I reversed my previous maneuver, inching around the windshield and into the front seat.

"Good girl," he shouted. "Strap yourself in."

We came out of cloud into bright sunshine. There was no sign of the other plane.

"I don't want to do that again in a hurry," my visitor shouted. Finally I recognized the voice. I turned to look at him. It was Darcy.

"What are you doing up here?" I yelled back to him.

"How about 'Thank you for coming to rescue me'?"

"Do you know how to fly one of these things?"

"No, but I've got the instruction book here. You can read it to me." He reached into his jacket and then looked at my face and laughed. "Actually I have flown a plane before. I'll get us down safely."

Suddenly I felt my stomach drop as the plane swung to the right. We were circling, dropping lower and lower. There was a large sea loch ahead of us. We were skimming over bright water. Then we were bumping crazily until we came to a stop a few yards short of a rocky outcropping.

Darcy unbuttoned his helmet and took off his goggles. "Phew, that was close," he said, standing up. "I've never landed on water before."

"This is a stupid time to tell me that," I snapped and promptly burst into tears.

"Georgie." He reached forward and dragged me into his arms while the aeroplane rocked dangerously. "It's all right. We made it. You're safe now."

"I know," I said. I tried to stop crying, but I couldn't. I knelt on the seat with my cheek against his leather jacket and sobbed. "I feel such a fool," I said at last. "And I've made your leather jacket all wet."

"That's okay. Cows get wet from time to time, don't they?" He smiled and stroked my hair, which by now resembled a haystack. "But the rest of you is already wet. How did that happen?"

"I swam to the aeroplane. She tricked me. I thought that Podge was in it, but he wasn't."

"You've had quite a morning so far." He was still smiling. "At least you can't say it was dull."

"I thought you'd gone away again."

"Well, fortunately I got in touch with your Sir Jeremy and it turned out we had a few friends in common, so the need to go somewhere was avoided."

"How did you find me?" I asked, at last.

"Pure luck. We were sitting outside the house and we actually watched the plane take off. Next moment I received a telephone call to say that the rifle that killed Hugo Beasley-Bottome had been found at the Padgetts' house and that your nephew was missing. Then someone said they'd seen two people in the plane, so we assumed the worst. Luckily Paolo had come back from London in his own float-plane this time, so we were up in the air shortly after you. And Paolo's machine is a lot faster, so we caught you quite quickly. I take it Ronny *was* in the plane at some point? You didn't actually take off by yourself?"

"Of course she was in the plane."

"What happened to her?"

"She jumped out," I said. "She said she was wearing a parachute but I didn't see it opening. I think she just fell."

"A suitable ending for her." Darcy nodded gravely. "I would have hated to see someone like that be hanged or put into an insane asylum."

"Her mother is in one," I said. I was about to say that she had contracted syphilis, but I couldn't discuss such an unmentionable subject with Darcy.

"Maisie McPhee, right? Sir Jeremy's men looked her up at the New Register House in Edinburgh, you'll be pleased to know. She did have a child—unnamed baby girl about the right age for Ronny."

"And the father?"

"Someone named Eddy Axton, although it looks as if the birth certificate has been tampered with."

"Eddy Axton. That sounds very ordinary. And she didn't marry him or have any other children?"

"No."

"Poor Ronny, all those grand illusions for nothing."

"As you say, poor Ronny." He ran his hand down my cheek. "You are freezing. We should get you home as quickly as possible."

"Yes, we must get back to Rannoch immediately," I said, remembering, "I know where my nephew is hidden. We have to save him." I looked around us. Nothing but hills and moorland, lapping water and seagulls circling overhead. "Why on earth did you choose to land here? We're miles from anywhere."

"I have no idea where we are, but I wasn't taking any chances with a plane I'd never flown before. I chose the first open area of water I saw, where I wasn't likely to bump into a mountain."

"Well, come on. Let's not waste any more time. We have to get to shore and telephone the police."

"Your wish is my command, my lady. Now I suppose you'd like me to swim to shore."

"It's shallow. You can wade," I said. Then as he went to climb out of the aeroplane, I touched his hand. "Darcy. Thank you for coming to my rescue. You were very brave, and you landed it jolly well too, considering."

He laughed and lowered himself into the water.

"It's absolutely freezing," he shouted up to me. "The things I have to do for you!"

Chapter 34

Soon Darcy had found a telephone, rounded up a local policeman and borrowed a car. As we were driving back to Castle Rannoch, I sat beside him, snuggling up to him for warmth, for once in a glow of happiness. As we came over the pass to Castle Rannoch, we spotted Paolo and the American standing on the jetty, jumping up and down, waving their arms and pointing.

"What's going on there?" Darcy asked. He had the driver stop the car and we both got out. "What's happening?" Darcy shouted, running toward Paolo.

"She's taken my boat, without my permission," Paolo shouted back.

"Who?"

"Ronny, of course."

"Ronny? But I thought she was dead. She jumped out of a plane," I said.

"She must have had a parachute then," Paolo said, "because suddenly I heard my boat engine start and she was in it."

"Where is she now?" Darcy asked.

"Look, there, at the far end of the loch. You know what she's going to do, don't you? She's going to make a run at the speed record, but the boat isn't ready yet. Damned fool. She'll ruin everything."

"She hasn't got Podge with her, has she?" I shouted. "We must stop her."

Before I could get the words out, a blue shape came hurtling down the loch, motor screaming. Faster and faster it went until it shot past us as a blue blur. Then someone yelled, "Look out!"

And someone else screamed, "It's the monster!"

The wind was ruffling the water, driving it into a great wave that curled up along the middle of the lake, looking for anything like the coils of a giant serpent. The boat hit the wave full-on. It became airborne. For what seemed like an eternity it soared, flying over the surface of the water, then it rose straight up, flipped, bounced and broke apart, with pieces flying in all directions. The wave subsided. There was silence. Small pieces of blue floated on the oily surface of the lake.

I found I was running along the shoreline, yelling, "Podge. Not Podge."

Darcy caught up with me. "Georgie. Come on, I'll take you home. There's nothing you can do here."

"But he might still be alive."

"If he was in that boat, he won't be. But you told them where to find him. I'm sure he's safe."

I found I was holding my breath all the way up the drive to Castle Rannoch. As the car came to a halt outside the front steps, the door opened and Fig came running out to meet me, with Binky behind her, hobbling on crutches.

"Georgiana, thank God you're safe," she said.

"Never mind about me. What about Podge?"

"In his bed, sleeping," she said.

"They found him in time, then?"

"Thanks to your wonderful grandfather. He saw you driving off in a car and he was sensible enough to note the license plate number. The police found the car right away and discovered my little boy in the boot. Imagine doing that to a child. That woman is a monster. I hope they catch her."

"She's dead," I said.

∽

"She always was reckless." Major Padgett looked across at his wife, who sat silent and grieving in their cold, dreary drawing room. "Even when she was a small child she took risks and didn't respect boundaries. Too much like her father, I'm afraid."

"She claimed her father was the Duke of Clarence," I said.

"Did she tell you that?"

I nodded. "But her birth certificate gives her father's name as Eddy Axton. Not royal at all."

"Eddy Avon," he said. "I tried to alter it."

"Why? Who is Eddy Avon?"

"The Duke of Clarence was also known as the Earl of Avonlea and among the family he was always known as Eddy." Major Padgett sighed. "I knew it would come out eventually. How can such a monstrous secret remain hidden? It has eaten into me all these years."

"Then it really was true that he was kidnapped and kept alive? He didn't die of influenza?"

He sighed. "I'm afraid so."

"You were one of the people who kidnapped him? Who

held him prisoner in a mental institution?" I looked at him with undisguised revulsion.

"I was, God forgive me." He stared down at his highly polished shoes. "I was removed from a promising military career to act as equerry to His Royal Highness the Duke of Clarence, the heir to the throne. Everything I learned about him distressed me and disgusted me. His depraved sexual behavior with both men and women, his use of drugs, his errors of judgment . . . I hoped that he would never come to the throne. He would have been the ruin of the monarchy. When his doctor confided to me that he had contracted syphilis from a prostitute, I thought I should die of shame.

"Then a miracle happened: a most virulent strain of influenza swept the country. It felled the prince. He was at death's door, lying in a coma. There were certain powerful personages at court who saw this as a chance to make sure he never recovered. They wanted me to finish him off, but I would not be party to deliberate killing.

"However, a second miracle occurred. On that very day a young footman succumbed to the disease. He was not unlike the prince in stature and coloring. A small group of conspirators managed to replace the comatose prince with the dead footman. The royal family was kept at a distance because of the risk of contracting the disease. The footman was buried with royal pomp, while the footman's coffin contained several large rocks."

He looked up at us with hopeless eyes. "The Duke of Clarence was whisked away to the country estate of one of the conspirators. Against all odds he recovered, at least partially. The high fever had damaged his brain and his heart and also sped up the progression of syphilis. He remained bedridden, sometimes violent and not always coherent. A doctor told us he was not expected to live long, so it was decided to secret him far, far away, up here in Scotland."

"Did members of the royal family know about this?" Darcy asked.

Padgett shook his head. "Of course not. And they must never know. Nobody must ever know. Has it already gone beyond this room?"

"Sir Jeremy Danville knows what I suspected," I said.

"But he is head of the special branch," Darcy said quickly. "They do not divulge secrets. And you can rely on Georgie and me."

Major Padgett nodded. "It has been such a burden, all these years. I was assigned the task of being his keeper, you see. I can't tell you how I despised that task—how I felt the whole thing was morally wrong."

"Why did you accept if it was so repugnant to you?" Darcy asked.

"I am a military man," Padgett said. "I obey orders, put my country before myself and my word is my badge of honor. I was present at the first meeting of the conspirators when a vow of silence was made. I do not break vows whatever the consequences, but I have regretted it every day since. It meant the end of my career. It banished my poor wife to a life of loneliness and social withdrawal."

"I didn't mind, dear," she said from across the room. "I married you for better or worse, you know. Watching you sink into despair has been hardest. And we did have Ronnie for a short while."

"So he recovered enough to father a daughter?" I asked.

Major Padgett nodded. "Even in his incapacitated state he couldn't keep his hands off the maids. We watched him closely, but young Maisie McPhee was his night nurse and he didn't always sleep. My wife had always wanted a child so we decided to adopt this one and make sure it was raised in a good home. And the Duke of Clarence's heart finally gave out soon after Veronica was born. We raised her as our own. It was like two guinea hens trying to raise an eagle chick."

"You told her about her real parents then?" I asked.

"Of course not. Only a handful of prominent men were party to that secret. We thought it only right to tell Veronica she was adopted when she was old enough. As I said, she always sought danger and the forbidden. She went into my office, which was off-limits to her. She snooped through my private files and she found regular payments to Maisie McPhee. She went to visit that woman, who was already slipping into insanity. Apparently Maisie spun our daughter a grandiose tale about her royal parentage and claimed they had actually married, which wasn't true. Veronica black-mailed and coerced me into confirming who her father was.

"After that she started having grand ideas about being a member of the royal family. We tried to make her see sense. We were glad when she took up flying and started to make a name for herself as an aviatrix. But obviously it wasn't enough for her."

"She told me before she jumped from the aeroplane that nothing was enough to fill the void."

"God rest her soul," Mrs. Padgett said. Darcy crossed himself.

∞

Daylight was fading when Darcy and I finally drove down the winding road to Castle Rannoch. The sky was glowing pink and gold. A flight of wild duck circled the loch. It felt as if the world was finally at peace.

"Darcy," I said after a long silence, "why haven't you given up on me? What do you see in me? I'm not your sort of girl at all. I'm penniless, for one thing. I'm not glamorous. I'm not sexy. I'm not beautiful."

"True enough," he said with that horrible Irish candor. "I have to confess, to start with it was the challenge. You were so impossibly haughty and virginal, and it was intriguing to see if I could bed a granddaughter of Queen Victoria."

"Great-granddaughter," I corrected.

"Great-granddaughter, then. And after a while I started thinking, 'You know, I think one could have a good roll in the hay with her, once she'd been warmed up a bit.'"

He looked at me and I blushed.

"And now?" I said.

I suppose I was hoping he'd tell me that he loved me.

"I never like to give up on a challenge," he said breezily, "especially when the goal is in sight."

Not the answer I was looking for. We drove on for a while in silence.

"Is that the only reason?" I said. "I'm a challenge to you? And when you've finally achieved your goal, you'll lose interest instantly?"

"Not exactly," he said. "The problem is, Georgie, that I can't seem to get you out of my head. I know I should be going after a rich heiress who will keep me in the style to which I'd like to be accustomed. But I keep coming back to you. I don't know why."

He reached across and covered my hand with his own. "But here I am," he said. "And here you are. Let's just take it from here and see where it goes, shall we?"

"Yes, let's." I turned my face up to him to be kissed. Then I yelled, "Look out!" as several sheep wandered across the road.

Historical Note

Ronny Padgett is modeled on famous aviatrix Amy Johnson who broke many records in the 1930s, including flying solo to Australia in her Gypsy Moth. She was killed in WWII.

Prince Albert Victor, Duke of Clarence and Avondale, 1864–1892, has long been a subject of rumor and speculation. He was the oldest son of King Edward VII and thus heir to the throne. Although there is little firm evidence, his reputation was one of dissolute behavior. He is reputed to have frequented both male and female prostitutes, to have been whisked away from a raid on a homosexual brothel, and even to have been Jack the Ripper. So when he died of influenza at the age of twenty-eight, leaving the path to the throne open for his solid and reliable younger brother, who later became George V, rumors flew that his death had been aided or even that he had been kidnapped and was kept prisoner in an insane asylum.

None of these rumors has ever been substantiated, but they certainly make for a good story!

His future bride, Princess May of Teck, later married his brother George and the royal couple were reported to be extremely happy.

The activity on the Scottish loch—both the speed boat and the monster are quite correct for the time. Attempts were being made on the water speed record, some with fatal results, and the Loch Ness Monster was about to capture headlines and enthrall readers throughout the world.

Rhys Bowen

Naughty in Nice

· A Royal Spyness Mystery ·

Royalty has its privileges, even when you're thirty-fourth in line to the throne, as Lady Georgiana Rannoch discovers on the glamorous—and dangerous—French Riviera . . .

Why should my bothersome brother, Binky, and his decidedly disagreeable wife, Fig, be the only ones to enjoy the fun and sun of the French Riviera? Though they are disinclined to invite me along, Her Majesty the Queen once again comes to my rescue. She is sending me off to Nice with a secret assignment that's nothing to sneeze at: recover her priceless stolen snuffbox from the disreputable Sir Toby Groper.

As much of an honor as it is to be trusted by Her Majesty, an even greater honor is bestowed upon me in Nice—none other than Coco Chanel herself asks me to model her latest fashion. I'll even be wearing the queen's necklace. Unfortunately, things go disastrously wrong on the catwalk, and in the ensuing chaos, the necklace vanishes.

Now the queen is missing two priceless items! And before I can snatch the snuffbox, someone's life is snuffed out in a very dastardly way. With a murderer and a jewel thief on the loose—and my dearest Darcy seen in the company of another woman—how's a girl to find any time to go to the casino?

FROM NATIONAL BESTSELLING AUTHOR

Rhys Bowen

Royal Blood

Penniless and thirty-fourth in line to the throne, Lady Georgiana Rannoch finds herself in a truly draining state of affairs. To escape her hateful brother, Georgie accepts an invitation from the Queen to represent the royals at a wedding in Transylvania. But at the macabre-looking castle, Georgie finds the bride with blood running down her chin, and a wedding guest is poisoned. Now it's up to Georgie to save the nuptial festivities before the couple's vows become: to love and to cherish, till *undeath* do them part . . .

M824T01